I0615615

# Bria's Focus
# Captured

# Bria's Focus Captured
## (special second edition)

Written by
**Latoya Lake**

Copyright © 2019 by LaToya Lake.

All rights reserved. No part of this book may be reproduced, scanned, or distributed in any printed or electronic form without permission. The characters and events portrayed in this book are fictitious or exaggerated. Any similarity to real persons, living or dead, is coincidental and not intended by the author.

Photographer: Lario Duzanson
Cover models: Latiesha Lynch and Edsel Moñzon

First Edition: June 2019
Second Edition: June 2022
Printed in the United States of America
Published by BlackGold Publishing

# Dear Reader,

*"When you are afraid to let go of something because it is familiar, you can potentially miss out on something that could be amazing…"*

That said, to the one who holds my heart…
It's time I took it back!
Xoxo, Bria

# Please Enjoy
# "Bria's Focus Captured"
# Part II of the Trilogy

# Table of Contents

# Acknowledgement

**my friends and family- It's been a journey finding my voice, but you've always stood by me even when I've been impossible;**
*You're all awesome.*

To my readers and devoted supporters:

Your encouragement has played a key role in me putting pen to paper again.
*Thank you for believing in me.*

Rogelia Euson, this one is for you.
I hope you enjoy.

And to my favorite distraction—you were undoubtedly my greatest muse. *You've* served your purpose of accompanying me to where I needed to go.
Thank you *endlessly.*

# *To my Mom,*

You've encountered my art and passion and guided me
through my toughest times. I thank God for giving
you such a strong soul in order to deal with me.
Thank you for the borrowed strength
when I needed it most.

*To my daughter, I hope you are as fierce as Bria, but
know how to relax and have fun too.*

# Prologue

*This time, I'd gone too far.*

I let my emotions get the better of me, acting on impulse instead of using my head, and now, here we were. I should have just stayed in bed with his arms wrapped around me, completely safe from all this mess. But I was too restless to do so. I should have ignored the damn call that had ultimately triggered everything, including my rash decision. I should've allowed myself to be showered with kisses— enjoying a second round of love-making.

The way he took me tonight had surprised me. My body trembled so hard while I came to an explosive climax, I could've sworn I was experiencing an earthquake. It was insane. What if he was solely mine? What if I'd believed him when he had claimed there was no one else?
Having a tongue that yearned to taste me and lips that gladly left a trail of hot, damp kisses on my skin was invigorating—not to mention arms that loved taking me into them. That place was second to nothing.

*"Love"* …. how crazy was I to use that word when describing what this man did to me? What would it have been like if I'd dated him correctly or even admitted to being into him? I couldn't understand it myself, but I had a thing for this guy, and it felt okay for me to skip past the bull. Him showing me that he could take directions as well as command the lead was beyond words. I could hardly contain myself. The build-up was so intense, it rocked my body like the drumline of a good Soca rhythm.

"Stay here," Trevor said, making me remember where I didn't want to be. I clamped onto his arm. Now was not the time for me to be expected to let go or be brave. I couldn't have him risk his life for mine, showing my disapproval with a head shake. This was the wrong time for me to find myself without words, yet I was too afraid to speak. I wouldn't let go. I'd only now realized that I needed him.

My favorite part about knowing him was looking into his eyes and feeling no fear to be me. He didn't care how much of a headache I was. He took me like a shot of whiskey, straight with no ice, and savored the taste, baring the burn, which sent him into a delighted frenzy. Now those same eyes were looking at me with fear, trying futilely to reassure me that everything was going to be alright. But I was too much of a realist to believe that. I knew from the beginning what I was getting myself into. I never imagined he would share the same fate. But what did I expect from a man who was continually trying to save me? I would seriously trade in a kidney to have his body forcing mine into the mattress rather than be here.

My curiosity had gotten me into a lot of things in only one year, but this situation, I couldn't see myself wiggling out of. I should have trusted him, but I didn't, and now I found myself looking past him and staring straight into the barrel of a gun.

# Chapter 1
# Brief Recap

I moaned in content and stretched a bit, exposing my feet to the slight chill in the air. My toes curled, feeling the difference in temperature from under the duvet. I smacked my tongue while I collected my thoughts. I exhaled, feeling entirely at ease like a weight had been lifted. I needed the release. The tension in my neck was completely gone.

I jolted, brought to the realization that my state of relaxation was brought on with help, and from what I could see, I was not in a familiar setting. This alerted me to my last conscious activity. I swallowed hard and began turning my head. Taken by a masculine scent, I tensed, then slowly maneuvered my way from the man snoring on the bed. He groaned, making me freeze. My heart accelerated thinking I'd woken him. I was relieved that he only repositioned himself by turning toward me, making his front visible to me. I began rising to my feet. My eyes were wholly captivated by the unknown man whom last night had refused to unmask himself during our night of intimacy. I must say, it had added to the thrill of it all—what a way to start my new year.

He stretched, and that shook me from my trance, reminding me that I needed to get out of his apartment. I began quickly but silently gathering my clothing and slipping into them. I took in the space that was all male. Dull, white shades hid the room from the outside world.

The area was barely furnished, having only a bed and a nightstand where a lamp and picture frame rested. I took a few steps closer and zoomed in on the pictures. There was a woman wearing glasses and an oversized sweater cuddled on a couch, reading a book in a black- and- white image.

I immediately knew it was this man's lover. Feelings of anger started to engulf me, and I stopped to look over at him lying on the bed. He'd used the curtain of last night's festivities as an opening to cheat on his partner. Sure, I didn't ask questions on the way over here—I should have. But I was left to assume that he was single, even if he did cover his face. I mean, anyone could have claimed him at any time last night, so where was she?

I headed for the door, only to stop in front of a hanging mirror. I took in the light-skinned person about to take the walk of shame. She held me captive. Her hair with ends colored burgundy was no longer in the cute librarian bun she'd taken so much time brushing and packing with gel. It was now an untamable mess of dangling curls. But this woman was no mess.

She held a Ph.D. in psychology, yet her passion for photography would be the reason she would make the journey back home to St. Maarten to work for a magazine company. She also intended to take some courses on journalism and English literature. She would then combine her love of pictures with complementing words, which would make people fall in love with reading all over again. It was also sure that she would take some time out to give back to the youths. Her plate was full, her life meticulously sketched out, so the last night of dumb fun was okay by all accounts. *That would be in my author's bio if I were to make one*, I told myself, still

2

looking at the woman in the mirror. I heard a noise coming from the bedroom and knew it was time to make haste and leave.

"Moments later, I found myself looking through the metro window on my way home. And as I'd mentioned before, that was the last I'd seen or heard of him." I bowed for my audience, almost losing the towel wrapped on my head. Reflexively, I grabbed at it, centering it again. "That's what I'm gonna share tonight."

"Oh, wow, you were such a slut," Mich said with a smile. "A poetic slut, no less," Kayla added. "Wait. Isn't a poem supposed to rhyme?"

I rolled my eyes. My friends, who were a massive part of the reason I'd ended up sleeping with the guy, were now busy judging me for it. On this night, Mich and I had set up an exaggerated presentation for Kayla to get over a fella she'd loved but lost. The idea was to sleep with someone and never see him again because we were all heading back home to St. Maarten.

The girls and I had made a proper acquaintance when we had been bunched together in the same student complex in Amsterdam.

Kayla—dare I say, my favorite of the two—was the last to make the trip back. She was enjoying the sun, sand, and sea and took every opportunity to gain back her tropical color. Besides having been recruited at a job fair by an auditing bureau to be a junior auditor, Kayla's life was well-managed and very routine.

This was a side effect from trying to be everything to everyone else and not staying true to what she wanted. Her previous relationship had suffered because of it. I wouldn't say she was boring, though—more like, controlled. I was glad she had found a man who allowed her to be herself. Bryan was her future; she'd stressed t h a t on numerous occasions. She was waiting for him to propose. The plan, which was mostly sketched out for Kayla on our last girl's night out together in Holland, was simple. She was to be hooked up with a total stranger, get laid, and then send him packing the following day. We'd all experienced something of the sort. However, my story was the most repeated.

Mich—the one who'd concocted the plan—was the shortest among the three of us. She was anything but basic. Her almond eyes would make men do anything to be with her, but she never kept them around long enough, so why bother learning their names? Her skin, a creamy honey tone, was flawless—which was only a distraction. You first had to deal with her tongue. She'd had a diploma as a registered nurse specializing in geriatrics. I could imagine the ill treatment the elderly clients were receiving under her care.

"Yeah, I can see why you want to go to the Poet's Lounge," Kayla said, flopping back into the chair. She sat observing the slice of baked dough covered with cheese and sprinkled with ham in her hand before taking a bite of her pizza. She then sat up and peered through the window, probably wondering if outside was as quiet as the inside portrayed it to be.

My apartment sat on a hill away from the noise of the island's center. The road here was not perfect and would make anyone who valued the shocks of their vehicle stop and think twice before

4

visiting. This was the second time since being back that I'd moved. My previous location was a tad too big and expensive for a single tenant. It was quiet here, and neighbors kept to themselves—an added bonus to the place.

I remembered the slight nerves I had gotten having to pack all my belongings into boxes. My new home was smaller, but from the moment I'd shut the door, which allowed no noise in, and had gazed through the window, I was sold on the space. Adding modern furniture and colors made me return to its comfort after my long days of work. As for my friends being here—clouding the silence with the sound of music pitching from a Bluetooth speaker box connected to Mich's phone and taking the opportunity to leave crumbs on my chair—I had invited them over so they could update me on any changes that were happening in their lives.

It had been a while since we'd hung out together, and we'd agreed not to let our busy schedules get in the way of our friendship. Chillin' was mandatory at least once a month. My life had split in so many ways; it was hard to believe I was trying to find time for socializing. And I was trying to do that in the most inexpensive way I knew how— over pizza, my favorite go-to snack.

"Come on, guys, don't be like that. It'll be fun, I promise!" I unwrapped my hair. "So, what do you think of the color?" I said, my hands presenting the new look.

I had decided to tone down my appearance by bleaching out the burgundy color and going with a copper tone at the ends instead.

Mich shrugged. "Not your color." I rolled my eyes. "I

5

like it! Tamed, but still—"

"Boring—Edgy," they said simultaneously. "Well, I can't do anything about it now, so deal."

I flipped on the hairdryer, drowning out further debate on the topic. I sat listening to the poetic speaker reciting her original piece on the strength of her soul and the beauty of dreadlocks, speaking genuinely about the injustice she'd had to endure because of it. Being a curvy woman, Ms. Johnson had also made herself a target by the way she decided to go about her artistic expression. Her story held me captive as she described her troubled life growing up.

She was fantastic—a true testimony of strength. She started with a depiction of her former self-image and how she'd thought less of herself—comparing the person she is now to the self-loathing husk she was years ago. She associated that to being heavily influenced by the man she loved at the time. I listened on as her words inspired those sitting in the glow of dimmed lighting on cushioned velvet chairs while they enjoyed their drinks and snacks. Paintings of the poet hung on the walls, portraying how multi-talented she was when it came to creative expression. Her piece tonight was like so many this evening because of the theme for tonight's spoken word challenge. The tone of the night was mostly one-sided; I'd agree—some would say a bit feminist being t h a t a large number of the crowd was primarily women. The men who did attend were also incredibly supportive.

Everyone showed their approval and support by clapping. My girls failed to show, but in some way, I was glad for it. They would have undoubtedly been talking instead of being silent, and I didn't need them spoiling my place of recuperation. Once a month, I would seek haven here to recharge my batteries to be able to take on this male-dominated world. It was beautiful, being surrounded by so many women of strength and courage. I was especially humbled speaking with Ms. Reyes, one of the cultural icons in our society. Her cheerful and positive spirit was refreshing, which made me consider writing a piece on her for the magazine's next centerfold. Tomorrow would be the start of a very hectic year for me. But I was looking forward to the challenge.

The evening was over, and after making light conversation with Ms. Reyes, I was now making my way to my office. It was a tad late on this Tuesday evening to be going back to the office, but I wanted to find out what package had arrived for me after I'd left my second job at the *Daily News* earlier that day. As planned, I had landed a job at the local newspaper company and had built quite a reputation for myself.

I was an all-rounder. I had started from sorting the paper to proofreading and had gotten the opportunity to have my little opinion section in the lifestyle section of the articles where I would respond to readers on things; they often sought clarification on. Being a photographer was the icing on the cake after the courses I took on journalism. That combination sealed the deal. I was quickly tasked with reporting and filled a position as one of the editors, politics being my main focus—which was my favorite thing to do, I soon realized.

The office was almost void of people, but the printers were going full force to ensure the papers would be ready. I took a moment to speak to one of my coworkers, who had to collect the package from the front desk. She informed me that there was no return address, and that made me quite curious about its contents. It was nearing election time on the island, so the rats were out, and parties thought they would be able to use me in their ploy to embarrass one another.

Unlocking the door to my office, I made way to my desk, which was littered with papers. The package rested on a pile I noticed looking over while hanging my jacket on the rack. The coffee stain on my blouse had its own story to tell about the day if the redness of my eyes didn't give me away. I sat back into my chair and closed my eyes, taking a moment. The faint sound of police sirens played in the background. I hung my head back in the direction of the window situated directly behind me.

"Breaking news," I mumbled, opening my eyes again. An audible exhale preceded me picking up the brown envelope marked "Shane"—which was one of my alias names. Mail directed to this name usually had a more serious tone to it. A smile crept across my face at the thought of the naughty content I would be privy to. Believing I had a mischievous twinkle in my eyes, I unfolded my reading glasses. "Oh, my, this won't do," I said, tilting my head to the side while rotating the photo. My smile was turning into an agape mouth. "The Mrs. is not gonna like the position her husband was in," I said under my breath. "Lucky for him, I am not *that* kind of journalist," I concluded, feeding the copied images into the paper shredder. I paused, and then gave my neck a slow rub while exhaling.

A chuckle escaped me thinking of the pictures once more. It was a thing here for political parties to do their best at discrediting one another, but I preferred sticking to the facts. That was surely an attempt by an individual, maybe even a lover holding a grudge, wanting to defame the person by taking things public. That sort of hanky- panky, I preferred not to get involved in.

I turned on my computer and headed into the kitchen for a mug. I would need two cups of coffee tonight if I was going to make my deadline. The work I had to put in was unimaginable, but I loved the demand of me that came with it. I cradled my mug as I sat waiting for my computer to start up properly. It was slow, and I told myself on several occasions that I needed to buy myself an external hard drive. Now started, I began to scan through emails from writers seeking help with their lives.

My "Gabby Listens" advice column, which I mostly had fun with, was a hit with the community. It was a welcome addition that brought a not- so-serious tone that relaxed me. One email in particular stood out to me. I'd answered so many letters having the same sorts of problems. My response would surely be automated. I decided to give it a full read. Ms. " Probably Cheated On" was seeking advice on a suspected cheating boyfriend she was with for over three years. She couldn't put her finger on it but knew something was up—just in the way he was recently acting, and of course, he'd changed his phone etiquette. *A red flag if any*, I thought.

I continued to read as she described how, in one instance, he was overly sweet and attentive, and in the next, acted as though he wanted to get rid of

9

her. And of course, he would end calls in front of her instead of answering them—another warning sign. I closed my eyes and smelled the coffee before opening them again.

I shook my head, wondering why some women who already knew their man was cheating chose to stay and continue as if they didn't know, how they accepted cheaters based on the length of time spent in such a relationship, arguing that the good times outweighed the bad. Where did their strength lie? Was her unfaithful man holding it hostage so she wouldn't be able to get up, dust off the filth, and walk away?

It never ceased to amaze me how some women and men forgave and threw their full understanding at a so-called repentant partner, miraculously forgetting all the uncertainty and grief they'd been through. I guessed they reasoned it better than being alone on an island where there were two to three women to every man. You might as well hold on to yours, no matter how much of a dog he was. Gladly, I'd met a few women not wanting to settle for anything less. "No judgement," I said on an exhale.

I started to reply. I was trying my best not to come off as judgmental—or worse, sarcastic. It was hard. I'd even remembered a not-so-pleased reader assuming things were easy for me to say because I'd never been in love. He'd then ended his mail with, "How can you write about things you've never experienced?" The comment had me stumped for days. I was fighting a mental conflict within myself. I wondered when and how I began making light of certain people's life struggle—especially seeing my educational background. It was unethical for me to do so.

After discussing it with Kayla and realizing that not everyone would like what I had to say, I eventually apologized for the way I'd responded, forgave myself, and moved on. I mean, my findings weren't all based on assumptions or widely fabricated. They held merit. And who in their right mind wanted to hear my experience with love? Anyway, I typed a response and sent it along with the letter from "Probably Cheated On" to the chief editor. "The other emails will have to wait," I said aloud. I went ahead and finished up the more pressing articles I had to complete. I then switched off my computer and stretched before hitting the light switch and grabbing my jacket before exiting my office.

# Chapter 2
# **Introductions**

"Hi, Mrs. Duncan, Ms. James. I would love to talk, but this time I need to get out of here, like right now. My friends are waiting."

Church was unimaginably long today, but I knew it had more to do with myself and the girls making it home way too late from the Festival Village. Why we'd insisted on attending this morning service was beyond me. I don't think the preacher appreciated s sitting there with shades on, hiding our bloodshot eyes. Nor did the congregation enjoy listening to and following Kayla as she led the worship service somewhat off-key.

My ears bled on every lousy note. And let's not forget about the giggles met with shushes. I couldn't help but think the message was directed at me. Again, whose idea was it to attend church after spending a night jumping and waving in the Festival Village? I already felt like the message was directed at me with the frequent gazes thrown my way. The preacher, I knew favored the political party with a candidate I was constantly butting heads with. I didn't expect her to use her podium to go into what she described as blasphemous writing and false portrayal. The message was surely for me. Me voicing my opinion on the radio was seen as the sin of the week. I must have stepped on some toes with that interview. She wasn't even disguising the fact that people like me were who she thought was wrong with the country. Now it was time to be held accountable by two of the members. I was also sure to be reprimanded for my friends' behavior as well.

"Your friends can wait a few minutes 'til you hear what we have to say," Mrs. Duncan scolded.
I held my breath and braced for it.

"We heard you on the radio."

"Yes, we did," Ms. James chimed in. "We loved it!" Unexpected, but a relief. I was able to breathe again. My joy melted into anxiety. These two elderly ladies had, for some reason, adopted me since I'd joined the church. Their opinion of me weighed more than I cared to admit. It felt good having them look out for me and take care of me. Being able to collect meals apart from when I did so at my grandparents' home had saved me loads of harassment in the kitchen. That comfort, however, came with the condition of being scolded by them when they saw fit. This felt like one of those moments. I swallowed hard and waited.

"Darling, it's so nice to hear young people go in on the mistreatment of the senior citizens," Mrs. Duncan said, her facial expression stern. "We think it's commendable."

"Sweetheart, when you come over today, we will tell you more about our struggle," Ms. James said before turning on her cane to hobble away.

"Wait! I can't help today." I rubbed at my head. I was up for a headache.

"Why not?"

"I have a thing with the children later on that I for sure can't miss," I said, my expression apologetic. "Oh, okay, well, do find the time to pass through sometime this week."

Mrs. Duncan reached out and touched me on my cheek with her palm and rubbed at my face. It

13

was one of my favorite things to experience. I felt calm. She then turned, took Ms. James by her upper arm, and they both began to make their way out of the churchyard. Their friendship had been tested throughout time. It was nice to see it hadn't broken their bond. I hoped to be so fortunate with my friends.

*She's beautiful.* I sat and observed her as she gracefully moved across the stage, her dance nearly perfect. I was so nervous. She had a few mistakes here and there that were just plain adorable. Aniah, one of the foster children who had pretty much the same story as I did when it came to her parents, had been talking about her dance recital for weeks and had made sure I'd sold all her tickets. Now it was time for her to express herself through music. The audience erupted, clapping and cheering after they'd concluded their choreographed piece. I found myself on my feet, yelling her name, tears of pride welling in my eyes. She'd located my voice and started to wave vigorously at me. The recital had come to an end, and Aniah was busy running around with two friends of hers. I was on cleaning duty with some other guardians.

"They were so breathtaking. I loved every part of it," one of the ladies said.

"Yes, it was something to watch. I'm glad I didn't miss out," I said, picking up and sticking some empty plastic water bottles into a garbage bag.

"Which one is yours?" the lady asked. I stopped and took a moment to look at Aniah. "That one." I pointed at her.

Oh, how that sweet, little thick-haired, tiny-eyed, four-year-old powderpuff girl brought me joy. She was a handful at times, but assertiveness came with survival, seeing she was the youngest of the bunch. I'd had the privilege to be her big sister when I first started volunteering at the foster home. She was cautious, not wanting to open up to me in the beginning, but I understood why. I saw myself in her so much. I believe some of my characteristics were also beginning to rub off on her. Well, I hoped at least the good ones were.

"Ah, very nice," she cooed.

I smiled and continued my garbage patrol.

Being part of the big sister program at the foster home was one of the most rewarding things I had going for myself. It was destined, I thought, seeing how close I lived to the place. On their way to school, the kids would sometimes stop in and check up on me before they continued on their way to catch the school bus. I'd been such a devoted helper at the foster home that they'd signed off on me having a handful of the girls over at my place every last Friday in the month, just for a few hours so we could chitchat. I'd even bought a projector so we wouldn't always be stuck inside my apartment but could watch movies outdoors when we felt like it. The hardest part of the evening was saying goodbye to Aniah, who would always have some trick up her sleeves in an attempt to stay—which wasn't allowed. "Don't forget, you owe me ice cream," Aniah said with her hands on her hips, catching her breath from running. She then shot back off, running from the girls she was playing with.

15

"So, did you like it?" Aniah questioned while wholly focused on her ice cream on our way back to the foster home. "I loved it, sweetie. You were my favorite one there, darling," I replied in my best uppity voice. We both giggled. I gazed at her through the rearview mirror and saw her finished with her ice cream, now wiggling around and unbuckling her car seat.

"Aniah, please keep still and buckle back up!" I ordered, watching her lean over the back of her chair. A honk and flashing of lights alerted me that I was, unfortunately, being pulled over by the police. "Of course, they can't catch escaped prisoners, so they pick on the little guy," I mumbled under my breath. I sat still until the officer had reached my car door. I then rolled my window down. "Yes, was I doing something wrong?" *Besides being a law-abiding citizen*? I thought to myself.

"Give me your license."
I went into my purse to honor his request. I then handed it to him. He looked at it, then at me.

"Ms. Pantophlet, you should be more careful. You wouldn't want the things that are precious to you getting hurt." I thought he was referring to Aniah not being buckled in, but his following line told me otherwise. "You should work on knowing when to hold your tongue and stop feeling the need to voice yourself," he said, very cynically. I immediately knew he was referring to the interview. I scanned the officer misusing his power and wondered whose orders he was under. "Be careful now, and drive home safe," he said, handing me my license. I drove off, watching him through my window as he headed in the other direction.

I focused on keeping a composed appearance while I dropped Aniah home. I then realized that I was overly disturbed by what had happened and decided I needed to be calmed before calling it a night. My mind was all over the place. Was he acting on his own, or was he just a messenger? I wasn't settling at all and found myself dialing Kayla, but to no avail. I then made my way over to Mich. Mich's mom opening the door wasn't surprising, seeing that they lived together—having to wait for Mich on the couch for a bit, however, was. She wasn't home yet, but it wasn't long before she came stumbling in. I went to her.

"I thought you were home," I said, helping her inside. I was a tad agitated that I was led to believe she was available. An intoxicated Michelle heard me anyway.

"Well, thanks to you, I am now," she replied. She tripped and giggled at herself for nearly falling. "Are you drunk?" I asked the obvious. "Because I could use a sober friend."

"Goodnight, Mom!" she yelled into my ear, damn near deafening me as we passed the living room area. "I'm good." With her arm resting on my shoulder for support, we headed into her bedroom. She flopped onto her bed and started relieving herself from her stilettos.

"What a night," she said, falling backwards onto the width of her bed. She took a moment before raising her elbows and giving me her attention. "Now, tell me. What was so important that it couldn't wait until tomorrow?" The look on her face made me wonder. Why was I even wasting time here? I was hesitant for two reasons: was I reading

17

too much into the situation, and would she even remember our conversation?

"A police officer threatened me tonight! And he did it right in front of Aniah." I started pacing. "Threatened you why?" She sobered a bit and sat up straight. "Because of the radio interview, I'm guessing. I don't think people are happy about it." "What, the one where you went in on that man? What's his name?"
I stopped pacing and answered.

"Curtis." "Wow..."

"Normally, these things don't get to me, but Aniah was there, and I had to play along for her sake, but..." I was drained. My mind had already taken me through every possible scenario— none with a happy ending. "Okay, well, settle down now. Look, if you don't feel safe, you can stay here tonight. There is plenty of space on my bed," she said, tapping a spot next to her.

"I don't know."

"It will be fine," she said, fluffing the pillow. She then gestured for me to come. I walked over and sat next to her. She placed her hand on my leg. "Don't let this guy scare you from doing what is right. He has no control, and he's trying to intimidate you. But there are more people out there who believe in you."

I gazed at her, seeing the sincerity in her eyes. Mich and I had our moments where we would argue like enemies, but sometimes, she surprised me. "Thanks." I released a sigh of relief.

"No prob, hun." She got up, went into her adjoining bathroom, and started removing her earrings. I watched as she did. "So, where were you coming from?" I inquired, sensing a change of topic lingering in the air. She turned and gave me a sly smile before redirecting her gaze to her bathroom mirror.

"I was out with a friend." She was now removing her makeup with a tissue.

"Really? Which friend?" I stood and went over to her night table. I picked up and started examining a little box I'd noticed.

"Ah, Bria, tsk-tsk, you can't help snooping, can you?" My brows dipped as I thought about how untrue that statement was. I then caught myself still holding the box. I quickly put it down.

"Fine, I don't need to know." She peered out the bathroom. "I didn't say I wasn't going to tell you." With a slight frown, I followed her movements as she came waltzing out in her bra and panties and ended up on the bed. Slipping out of her shoes, she said, "Well, there's this guy who thinks he has all the right words."

I grinned. "They all think that they do. But continue." "Okay, so, I'm utterly annoyed by him, and he knows it." She smacked her tongue. "He finds out where I work, sends me flowers, lunch, jewelry… thinking he can buy me over," she said, drifting into her own little world while playing with a necklace around her neck, which I knew she was referring to.

"Yeah?" I feigned surprise. "Yeah."
I exhaled through my nostrils. Subsequently, I shook my head.

"What else?"
"Well, the rest is history. He's still working for it, but I'm not about giving it up too soon."

19

*Since when?* I was stunned. "So, is there more you want to tell me about this guy?" I wasn't the least bit interested in hearing the rest, but I was obligated as a friend to play along.

She got excited like a schoolgirl about to dish on her crush after doing the Facebook stalker routine.

"Where do I start?"

*Why did I ask?* This was sure to be long.

"So, like I said, he's charming, owns his own business, he has kids…"

"Same mother or different?"

"Different." *Red flag.*

"But he's good with both."

I'm going to need a bigger flag for this one. "Go on." "Look what I bought yesterday," she said, jumping from the bed all excited. She returned with what I thought was a netted handkerchief. "What is that?" "Just a little something I picked up," she said, fidgeting as she did. "Did I mention he's French? He's talking about taking me to Guadeloupe. He's gonna give me spending money so I can get all that I'll need to make the trip fun for the both of us."

"And this is what you picked out?" I said, still trying to figure out what it was I was holding. "It's a sample I plan on teasing him with. I haven't shopped as of yet. Hardworking businessmen need playtime too, right? He's such a freak!" Mich continued about this secret lover with a bit of a temper.

Crazy, because at the beginning of the conversation, it seemed as though they'd just met. She was already planning on going away with him to a country where she couldn't speak the language to save her life. That girl lived for love stories, yet

20

always ended up in nightmares. By the time I'd gotten home, I was mentally exhausted. Tomorrow would come with its own new challenges. But as of right now, "I need to get some rest," I said after checking the time on my phone.

My eyes could barely stay open. I did my rounds of checking the front and then back door once more to be sure it was locked and headed into my bedroom, also locking that door.


"Shit, shit, shit, shit, shit!" I cursed, swerving like a mad woman in traffic trying to make up for some of the time I'd lost after getting too comfortable celebrating the fact that I'd landed the job as the photographer for the wedding of Mr. Harrigan and his soon- to- be wife. There were so many other photographers vying for the position, so I had to sell the couple on how perfect their images would be in the most sought- out magazine throughout the Leeward Islands, having their picture on the cover page. They were very well known, and this was sure to put me up there among frequently sought- out names in the field. The wedding, I'm sure, would be attended by local celebrities and power players in society. So, rushing out of the confirmation meeting was a no-no. However, I was now scrambling to get to my second, yet very demanding, job at the newspaper. I had an interview scheduled, and my boss wouldn't appreciate being scooped by the competitors.

Curtis Bryson was determined to get his story out there. Especially since I was blasting him on multiple radio stations or personally writing articles on him under my alias name, 'Shane.' The unsuspecting sucker would be meeting me in person today, but I would go as myself pretending to be standing in for Shane, who had an urgent meeting to attend. I was curious to find out if he had figured me out.

It had been two weeks since my intimidation, and I was guessing he was doing damage control, trying to assess how much hostility I still held toward him, or he was wondering if his scare tactics had worked. They hadn't. Something he'd probably realized from the piece in today's newspaper sent in by Shane. If he underestimated the situation and thought there would be no hard questions asked, he would be wrong. Today would be his day of reckoning. My studies in psychology had given me an advantage in deciphering a person seeking to withhold information, or even trying to lie about their real intentions. Over time, I started to just cut to the chase when asking questions, and that became annoying to some as a party trick.

My friend, Kayla, would warn me preemptively before taking me with her to social events. I saw nothing wrong with my candidness and thought people would find it refreshing to have an open and honest conversation with a stranger. But that was countlessly proven untrue—especially when it came to the male species. Digging too deeply into their psyche was never appreciated. Still, I enjoyed doing it. This Curtis fella was going to be a real treat for me today. I'd been waiting to call him out on every discrepancy concerning his campaigning methods. I'd studied and prepped for it, and his day of reckoning had arrived. Nothing would be off limits, as he had agreed over the phone for full disclosure.

Hurrying into the office, I was also wrestling with my clothing, trying my best to seem unruffled. I wanted it to come across as if I intended to keep him waiting. My leopard-printed pencil skirt, white top, and blazer with gold accessories and pumps were warning signs to all men who thought there was anything easy about me. Tying my hair up in a bun to give off the impression of me not taking any crap would serve as the first signal. Nope, he had no idea what he was in for, and if he knew better, he would keep all his sexist remarks at bay.

I walked into my office and was taken aback finding someone standing with his back to me that I knew wasn't Curtis due to his framework. The man I was to question was heavy-set and shorter compared to this well-built, taller man—the man now with his attention directed outside my office window. I was overwhelmingly curious.

"Are you usually late? Because it certainly doesn't speak well of you." His smooth voice added to my curiosity of wanting to know exactly who I was meeting with today.

"And you are?" I asked, taking the focus off my tardiness and onto the stranger fully suited up, standing with his hands in his pants pockets. He had yet to face me and was taking his precious time to turn in my direction. He inhaled deeply and audibly as if ready yet kept his gaze to the window. I was annoyed having a stranger in my office refusing to identify himself and quite possibly snooping through my stuff. And then there was the question of why my prey had sent a stand-in who probably had a brain the size of a peanut and knew nothing worth mentioning. "I don't have the time for shenanigans, whoever you are." I headed over to my desk and slammed the newspaper on it. "Make it fast."

"How rude of me. My name is Trevor Mathews." He finally turned and introduced himself. His expression held an indifferent calmness while he played with his cuffs. He then held out his hand to shake mine. I stood, observing the gesture while my body ignored it. Sensing my displeasure, he withdrew his hand. "I don't see why you're so upset. Shane sent you. That coward."

"Shane is anything but a coward."

The man now facing me looked extremely polished. His temperament relaxed, seeming casual yet professional. He was well-groomed with a light mustache. With a quick flick of his wrist, he spun his watch before making sure his cufflink hadn't slid loose. This was not an uneducated fool or mere stand-in—this was someone Mr. Curtis thought fitting enough to handle me. I adjusted my guard and advanced with caution. "And what exactly does that mean?" I asked, referring to his ending statement. "You find me as a woman incapable of coming up with reasonable questions?"

His eyes narrowed, scanned me, and took me in. I fidgeted, wondering what had crossed his mind. "Hmm, I think we both know that is not the case—Shane." That surprised me. My brows spasmed. Had he guessed, or had he been playing with me from the beginning?

"My name is Bria, but you can call me Ms. Pantophlet."

"So, you're saying you're not Shane, but

24

you happen to know how she would handle things. You're that in tune with her. Then I'm disappointed." "Look, I don't have the time for this. What do you expect to happen here?" I folded my arms over my chest.

"What do you *want* to happen here?" Again, he took me in. What was wrong with this guy? I was over it.

Avoiding further eye contact, I went into my desk drawer and started jotting down a note I wanted to remember. "The exclusive as promised." I readjusted my posture by standing straight. "If you can't, then I'm afraid we've both wasted each other's time today." I exhaled, dropping my bag onto my desk. Silence suddenly filled the space. Our eyes locked, his confident stance unmoved by my angered stare. My office phone began to ring, yet I refused to look away. He would not be winning this standoff. "Aren't you going to answer that?"

I waited a few seconds longer before plucking the phone off its hook. "Bria speaking." I listened for a bit, still holding eye contact. I blinked rapidly and looked down as if to focus on what was being said. The caller on the other end managed a smile out of me, and I looked to my unwelcome visitor, finding a sly grin on his face. "One second. Look, I'm going to have to disappoint you and your boss today. Something more important than his side of the story just came up. Please find your way out." He took a moment, then went for his suitcase.

"Oh, and this," he said, handing me the engraved desk plate with my name on it before making his way to the door. "Nice trick. Placing a fake nameplate." My angry eyes made contact with

25

his and dared him to say another word. I followed him to the door, making sure to slam and then lock it on his exit. I then made my way back to continue my conversation on the phone.

# Chapter 3
# **Unshaken**
**Trevor**

I'd been challenged before. But nothing had prepared me for the woman I'd faced off with today. I couldn't put my finger on it, but I was sure I'd met such a being in my past life. It was the only explanation I had for coming across so unruffled and walking out of there unshaken.

"You've survived, I see. How did it go?" Mr. Bryson asked, finishing up with some papers. "You could've given me a heads up," I said, walking farther into his office. He was a heavy-set man with short limbs. He sat there in his executive leather chair, wearing a knowing grin on his face and a khaki-colored suit with a stain on the jacket. He'd hired me a few weeks ago and assigned me as both his PR manager and legal advisor—jobs I'd thought would build my portfolio and boost my image. However, regulating how the world perceived Mr. Bryson was taking a lot out of me. He was continually portraying questionable behavior, which gave new meaning to the word "flexibility" in a job vacancy ad. Keeping a low profile was all I'd asked of him for two weeks, yet he'd somehow managed to catch the attention of Ms. Pantophlet within two days of my request.

I only wondered how often I would be bending backwards to get him out of trouble. His sanity was becoming a topic within the halls of the government building. People asked if it was just so that his name would be engraved in the minds of voters come election day.

"Ah, Trevor, can you lock the copies away

27

in the safe and pass me the folder in there?" I took the stack of papers from his hand and proceeded as instructed. I went into the safe and saw the folder he was referring to. It was labeled "Bria Pantophlet."

I turned, and he gestured for me to open it. I started to scan the files and saw that Shane was hyphenated. I understood at once.

"So, you knew it was her? Why didn't you say anything?" "I wanted to see how you would handle things." I looked on, expecting further explanation but got none. "Now that you've made contact, how do you suggest we proceed?"

Dropping my hand holding the folder to my side, I first exhaled, going through potential suggestions in my mind. That was the question. My first instinct was to avoid any unnecessary contact with this journalist he so-called couldn't stand the sight of, but that was proving impossible since he appeared to welcome the attention. Ms. Pantophlet had the resources and open access to places he frequented. She was always popping up, which led me to believe that she was being tipped. I should have done my homework before taking the job. Now, I had no other choice but to play along.

"I would let her in and use her for free publicity, both good and bad. Don't fake anything to quiet her. She would see through us, and that will only backfire." He just sat there in his chair. I could tell by his facial expression—the way he dipped his brows and clenched his jaw—that I'd pitched him something he thought plain ludicrous. I was beginning to think he would throw me out. He took more than a moment before responding.

"You know if we do that..." He rose to his

feet. "I would need you to keep her under control," he said while walking over to his window, forcing his hands behind his back.

He saw nothing wrong with the impracticality of his request. "Can't someone else do that?" I said, trying to hide my distaste for the babysitting detail I was being placed on.

A burst of laughter erupted out of him that was mocking. "You were named top of your class in political science. Surely a little woman such as Ms. Pantophlet would be nothing for you."

*Nothing for me*?! I'd had hell finding out who exactly the person was that was defaming my client. It was a challenge getting people to give her up. But there always seemed to be someone willing to talk as long as they had the right incentive. And once I'd found him, Curtis made sure that motive was met. He had ordered some digging of his own to be sure. But it was only then in her office after she'd defended this mysterious Shane that I'd confirmed she was, in fact, the person I was seeking. Not an older woman, which she'd led people to believe. Now I was being given the task to control her. It was remarkably tricky just holding a conversation with her. I honestly didn't know how to proceed.

"I can handle her," I said, more to convince myself. "Good! Keep me posted on what's going on," he said, now making his leave. At the end of my workday, I headed to the gym. I'd had some upper body exercise to do according to my training schedule but skipped out and decided to just run on the treadmill. I threw headphones on and made my way into the workout space, stepping onto a machine. *Control her.* "Ha!" I said aloud. The person next to me turned, and I then realized I might be a little loud and needed to lower my voice a bit or stop talking to myself in public altogether. I started the machine up and began with a light jog for a few minutes before increasing the speed on the machine.

This woman was a brute—harsh and abrasive. There would be no need to handle her with care, assuming she would go along with the concept. It made better sense not to tell her. I'd gotten a fair amount of info on her, but some details were missing. I would have to find them using different means. My thoughts were of her, from wondering what made her tick to why she had a hatred for men. "Another man basher."

I got home, took a shower, and planted myself in front of my computer. I started the search on Facebook, figuring she wouldn't be putting personal information on herself out there. My file on her also had information on the people she was usually spotted with. I decided to search for them instead. She must have shared stuff once or twice on their pages.

I was sidetracked after a few minutes of scrolling through one of her friend's pages. There was something politically interesting. I clicked on the link and found that the article had a surprising amount of likes and shares. *This woman could rule a nation*, I thought, seeing the comments of approval and replies she had received. She was well supported. That was certain.

I now understood why Curtis needed her kept under control. She was on the brink of starting an uprising if need be. He was not the only person she'd gone up against. I remembered her focusing in on

30

someone during her radio interview I was told to listen to, so finding his name among the rest was anything but unexpected. I continued to scroll and found her way of writing unique and engaging. Her readers were surely entertained as well as misinformed, based on what I knew. How easy it was to fool the general public.

A knock on my door broke my attention from the screen. I'd almost forgotten I was expecting company tonight. I logged off and went to open the door for her. "I figured you wouldn't have gotten around to cooking, so I brought something."

"You cooked?" I asked, knowing the answer. She giggled. "Now you know that would've taken up time I'd rather spend dealing with you." "Understood," I said, moving aside so she could enter. A pause would be placed on this whole thing concerning Ms. Pantophlet. At least for tonight. My meal for the evening had arrived, and I was planning on enjoying every bite.

## Bria

The day started like none I'd had before. I was running around in preparations for our upcoming voluntary efforts happening in just a week. Every year, the foundation for the kids, which I was now serving my first year as president, would receive a grant from the government and other organizations to hold an event where the community got involved. It was our way of letting people see how grounded our foster children were, reminding others that they

31

were quite capable and openly willing to contribute to the island. This would then reassure people that their placement into any family they were adopted into would be positive. They just needed a loving home in return. Some people seemed to have the idea that all foster kids were problematic and didn't deserve such treatment.

The foundation had been up and running for over four years now with very few hiccups. The major project pitched this year was themed "Build a Child a Home," which would require organizations and different companies' involvement. The idea was for them to donate either their services or workforce in helping us build a community home where the children could then go to do their homework and other afternoon school activities that would help them along their way in life. I'd already gotten several groups to sign on and was now impatiently waiting for the call concerning funding. My first errand for the day had been to visit the Department of Social and Youth Affairs, who then sent me to the Ministry of Finance concerning the hold-up.

I headed into the building and made my way to the respective division. My purpose known, I was then instructed to sign in. The lady at the front desk advised me to have some coffee while I waited and take a seat. I sat there for almost forty-five minutes before being told that the respective person wouldn't be able to meet with me at all. I was then called into a side office by an unidentified woman. She sat, having no issue taking a personal call, speaking on someone else's uppity behavior while I sat opposite her. I was fuming. I had to tell myself that it was for the children.

I took a beat to calm myself before retrieving copies of already submitted documents out of my bag. "That won't be necessary," the dark-skinned, hair in a low bob cut lady said, holding up her hand, halting me. She still hadn't ended her call. "I know who you are and why you are here," she said with the phone resting on her shoulder.

I froze, wondering if her knowing me was a good or bad thing. Without taking her eyes off me, she whispered something to the person on the other end of the phone, chuckled, and then ended her conversation with, "Exactly, bye."

I was waiting in anticipation of her next move. Her elbows were resting on her desk, and with her fisted hand supporting her head, she stared me down with a facial expression that was wooden, her eyes extremely cold. The woman engaging me in a stare-off was not to be assumed friendly, but I had no time for this. Once again, I unzipped my bag to collect the papers. "Ma'am, you mention knowing me and why I'm here. Can you please give me an update on the progress of the funding? When can I expect—" "Expect!" she shouted, stunning me. "You will 'expect' nothing."

By now, you could imagine it being damn near impossible for me to hide my annoyance.

"What is your problem?"

"I don't have a problem. You, on the other hand, need me. So, if I were you, I wouldn't show myself in here." There I had it— another civil servant who'd had a little taste of power and forgot that her job entitled serving others.

I wondered if her given position surrounded nepotism because professionalism was obviously out the door. It was becoming the norm where parties in power would select and place people they knew into influential positions to trump those who opposed them, blocking progress for the island. I was so over it.

"Look, I just came to inquire about the funding for the project."

"There is no funding," she stated, shocking me. My eyes widened in surprise.

"What? Why not?"

"Not like I need to explain. But to keep it simple, there are more important things we could do with the money." She smirked.

This was unbelievable. I'd sent in the request on time, and if I'd suspected not getting through, I would have weighed my options. I felt the delay and had considered the possibility that the ministry might be stalling, but to be denied outright was just a thought I'd numerously shaken from my mind. My kids would suffer, and I felt that it had more to do with me as an individual than there not being enough in the government coffers for social affairs such as this. The anger boiled within me.

"Thank you," was all that I could say. I rose to my feet and made my exit, hearing her on her phone again before I even got out the door. My vision blurring, I had mere minutes to make it to my car without anyone stating the obvious of me crying. I bumped into someone upon exiting and didn't bother to look back at the person referring to me by name.

I sat defeated, face down, crying in my car, firmly gripping my steering wheel as if having the strength to break it. I sat back, my face heated up in disappointment knowing I'd undoubtedly failed the children. Thoughts of Aniah sitting behind a computer in what was to be their place for remedial lessons were turning out to be unachievable. I had run out of time.

I closed my eyes and took the time to gather myself. I needed to think straight; allowing a potential migraine to send me hiding from light wasn't going to do me any good. "There must be a way," I muttered. My phone began ringing, prompting me to get it. The number was foreign. I hesitated before answering. I offered a somber greeting before the person on the other end introduced herself as a member of the Finance Ministry. I didn't feel the need to be ridiculed over the phone and decided to put an end to it at once. "I know you think your opinion here is important, but guess what? I matter and so do my kids. So, fuck off!" I yelled before ending the call.

With a bag of groceries in hand, I got home, still a bit flustered from what had happened. I rested my purchases on the counter and started unpacking them, my mind racing, trying to find a solution to my problem. Maybe it wasn't too late to raise the remaining amount needed to cover the cost, and maybe entities wouldn't mind working for free for such a cause. I just needed to put my thinking cap on and figure out a way to pitch it to them. I sighed, pulling out an avocado I wanted nothing more than to enjoy with a piece of bread. I went for a knife and sliced it, only to see shades of black inside. Disgusted, I dumped the whole damn thing in the garbage. I turned on the faucet to set water to wash my dirty dishes in. Maybe a glass of some cold orange juice would drown the craving I wouldn't be able to satisfy at the moment. My phone rang. I recognized the number, so I went ahead and answered.

"Hi, Ma." "Hi, sweetie, how did it go?" my grandmother asked. My actual mother only knew of me in her womb. She died giving birth to me, and my dad didn't find it necessary to be in my life after that. I stood, recalling the memories of how my grandparents loved me as if I were their own. From making sure I never went to school without two slices of jammed bread and a glass of warm milk in my stomach, to cheering me on while I participated in a math Olympiad at school.

The day I'd left for high school was the hardest day of my life. I wondered if I would miss the remaining years of their lives while I was away. I was more than delighted to have them at my graduation ceremony in Holland. I'd lived a few months under their roof before getting my place. They'd given me the deposit for my apartment and had gone furniture shopping with me. They played an essential role in my life, and I would walk through fire for them.

"Nothing yet, Ma," I replied, answering the question posed on whether the funding came through for the project. "But I know it's going to happen." I clenched my eyes, knowing saying anything further would alert her of the lie I wasn't even fooling myself with. She was equally frustrated, mumbling something incoherent. I was sure it was a curse word. "Don't worry about it. I'll figure things out," I said, reassuring her. I didn't need them stressing about things at their age. "How is Paw?" I asked, referring to my grandfather. "He's fine."

I giggled upon hearing that he was out working on his car again that hadn't moved in years. Both of them had their own thing, which kept them going. Washing clothes almost every day was hers.
"Ma, don't worry. It will happen. It has to!" She agreed, insisting that I should trust God's plan.

"Yes, I will," I said, then said my goodbyes before hanging up. I knew He had something for me, but for now, I would have to come up with an idea to make things work. "I got this."

I finished washing up. I flopped down into my desk chair with my head tipped back. Defeat tore through me. Despite how much I wanted to cry, I knew I had to focus on finding a solution. I took a minute, closing my eyes so I could block out everything, seeing only the dark space between my eyes and eyelids. I exhaled slowly through my mouth, inviting the calm needed for me to enter my creative and resourceful place.

My senses were heightened. I could feel the sun's rays that streamed into my apartment, filling my pores with vitamin D. The sound of my porch gate squeaking triggered my internal alarm, which caused my eyes to fly open. I wasn't expecting anyone. I glanced through the window to make out the silhouette of who was trespassing. I rubbed at my temple and waited for the knock at the door before making a move. It was Jamila, my outgoing, athletic, extremely talkative, and kind-hearted friend whom I'd gotten to know after moving into my apartment.

"Hi," I said, greeting her at the door. She was average in height and mocha colored with hair similar to mine. She looked out for me, and I had no reservations doing the same. I was more than fortunate to have such a woman as my neighbor and friend. "Hey, how..." She trailed off. Her brows creased with worry.

"What happened?" she inquired. My eyes were probably puffy and hadn't cleared up from crying, I gathered from her line of questioning.

"Ah, nothing. I am just having trouble with my seasonal allergies," I lied, more because I didn't want to go into it at the time.

I had no problem with dumping my political baggage onto her. It was one of our mutual interests, but when it came to my kids, I was overly sensitive. Jamila could get just as emotional about anything that affected life negatively. The foster children were exceedingly dear to her heart as well, and her knowing what had occurred today would set her off for hours.

I didn't need that right now.

"Okay," she said cautiously. I patted at my eyes, then found my gaze on the envelope in her hand that I asked her to deliver for me. "Did he sign it?"

"He kinda forced it back into my hand before I could get out the door after scanning it," she said, handing me the envelope. With much frustration, I took it and threw it onto the chair.

"He'll come around as soon as he realizes that he wants this just as bad as I do."

"Bria, maybe you should go talk face to face." I

shushed her with a look. Her gaze fell to the floor. Honestly, I didn't have the energy to explain why I didn't want to see him physically. I just wanted him to remain in my past. Resting my hand on her shoulder made her look at me.

"Thanks anyway," I said, feigning a smile.

That seemed to work. She perked up and started staring at me with a grin on her face. "What's up with you?" I said, surprised by the sudden change. I then started back to my living area. The silence made me turn to face her. With her phone clutched to her chest and her demeanor, I knew it was something she was bursting to say. My issue would have to wait until I cleared my head enough to start working on a plan B—for everything. The sound started soft, then peaked before exploding into a shrill, eardrum-popping shriek. I had to plug my ears with my fingers.

"Girl, settle down and tell me."

She shook her head in agreement, and I uncorked my ears. "I got the job," she said, holding onto my arm while catching her breath. She then yelled while jumping in the air a few times. "Well, it's a part-time catering gig as a waitress, but still. It's something. And from the look of it..." She squinted, focusing in on the info she was skimming through on her phone. "It has the potential to grow into something more."

"Wow, that's great!"

"Yeah, I'm just waiting for them to send a schedule," she said, sticking her phone into her pocket. Just then, her phone pinged again. Smiling, she pulled it out and checked it. She sobered. "No, no, no, no, no," she said, going over and flopping onto my couch. "What?!" I responded, concerned.

"I just got the schedule. I have to work tonight." I was a bit confused.

"Isn't that what you wanted?" She didn't look up. She was still going through her schedule.

"Yes... it's just that I have my nephew to take care of tonight. He's been looking forward to me taking him to the movies all week." "Okay," I said cautiously. "Wait!" She bit into her lip. She then started with the plan she was concocting in her head.

"What are your plans for tonight?"

"I'm not doing it," I said, walking away from her. I was charming, yes, but in a controlled atmosphere where a trusted handful found my sarcasm delightful—not offensive. Throwing me into a nest where attitudes and egos raged was bound to raise my pressure, and I would not hesitate to explode. Someone was bound to get hurt.

"Please fill in for me." She followed me. I observed briefly, looking back at her. Her head was tilted to the side, her palms pressed together, pleading.

"I'm not a social butterfly, Jamila. I thought you knew that by now."

"Come on. You might even get a story. It's your dream setting. A bunch of elite socialites."

"I don't do customer service. I'm not friendly."

"It's catering. Just stand, smile, and serve."

"I don't want to. You know how some people are—snobby, think they're better than everyone. I might say something."

"Please, I need the money."

That stopped me. I knew she was financially

strapped at times, probably more than I thought. The last thing I wanted was to make things more difficult for her by not assisting where and when I could. Maybe this was what I needed to regain focus. Perhaps there, I'd obtain clarity. I turned and found myself gazing into puppy eyes with pouted lips meant to break me. I exhaled.

"Alright, fine! But there'd better be something good," I said, scolding. She was all teeth.

The black-tie event was set in the home of one of St. Maarten's high rollers. In my best black skirt and white pinned-up shirt with loaned black tie, I stood serving fruit punch at the function Jamila was supposed to work but couldn't. I smiled as required, a smile which vanished as quickly as it came. It had only been an hour, yet my pinky toes were going numb from being squashed inside a shoe that I hadn't worn in months. But it was the only pair of shoes which matched the strict dress code I had to follow. I kept having to remind myself that I was doing this for a friend, so I needed to stick it out. I must say, it was interesting. Seeing high society, mostly referred to as the elite, walk in having not a care in the world with not a fight in them for a worthy cause. Jamila was right. I was sure to overhear something. If it was worth reporting was yet to be determined. My mood changed, seeing Mr. Bryson. He strolled on by gripping his date by the ass and didn't forget to smirk at me. Disgusted and distracted, I never saw Trevor, who now stood directly in front of me.

"So, you wear many caps," he said, gaining my attention. "Hi." I gazed straight past him, thinking that would be enough of a blow off. "I'm sorry, 'Jamila.' Undercover? "Again, I ignored him, keeping my eyes on Curtis.

I was nudged by my co-worker, who was charged with serving the welcome champagne for the evening. She'd introduced herself as Samantha. I blinked as if coming out of a stupor. "Punch?" I said with what I can only imagine was a forced smile. Trevor licked his lips and took a glass of champagne before continuing on his way.

I was getting itchy standing in place for what I felt was more than an hour and welcomed the instruction of me having to walk around and serve drinks. I flowed through the crowd, pressing ' tape' on my little recorder hidden in my sweater pocket. With conversations somewhat whispered, it was evident that the "elite" also gossiped and did it shamelessly. My gaze found Curtis by himself, talking on his phone before slipping away from the crowd. "Well, that's not where the toilets are," I mumbled on my way to finding out just what he was up to.

The hall he disappeared in was short but had several doors to choose from. I proceeded with caution. I saw a door slightly ajar and figured it was where he must have entered through. I placed my ear against the door, listening for sounds. Hearing nothing, I opened it and entered. The room was only lit by the moonlight streaming into it. I advanced further into what was a home office. I was careful not to bump into anything, having to curve a corner to meet the office desk.

"Well, I'm here, I might as well make the best of it," I muttered. There must be something useful here. Not that I would put someone's business out there, but just out of sheer boredom, I headed to the desk and quickly started sifting through papers found in the drawer. I squinted my eyes, trying to read the documents. "Ow," I groaned, tensing and grabbing firmly to the desk chair as a pain seared through my lower abdomen.

I held my breath for a few seconds and then released slowly. There was a pulsation of pain vibrating through my lower torso, which had become more frequent. Finally, I calmed myself. This had become a new concern, but getting to the source of my distress would have to wait. "It's okay. I'm okay," I said, reassuring myself. I would have to find time to get that checked. I shook the negative thoughts forming in my head and tried to redirect my focus on the task at hand. I swallowed hard, briefly pausing to gather myself.

*Give me something worthwhile,* I thought while continuing my search. My thoughts were interrupted by the sound of someone fiddling with the doorknob. My heart, which was coasting in neutral, shifted into drive, stepped on the accelerator, and had begun flooring it. I hustled to get the documents back into the drawer, wondering why I hadn't locked the door. I surveyed the room and found little to no camouflage. I propped myself between a filing cabinet and a wall and hoped that they would be satisfied with only a peek inside the room. I held my breath when I heard the approaching sound of footsteps…

# Chapter 4
# **Prickly When Provoked**
**Trevor**

It was evident that someone was in here, and I knew exactly who that someone was. I didn't bother to turn on the lights, heading right around to where she would be, finding mangled papers with a few shoved into the desk drawer. I exhaled, already exhausted with all of it. "Ms. Pantophlet, come out from behind the cabinet!"

I stood patiently, waiting for her to reveal herself, which she took her time doing. "You're not supposed to be in here," I said, followed by a deep huff. Calmly, she stepped from her place of refuge. "I was looking for the restroom and—"

"Enough! I don't understand how you haven't been locked away yet if this is your way of doing things. Such a nuisance." I shook my head in disappointment.

She was everything I was warned she would be and more. For some reason and by someone's doing, she'd been purposely ushered into an unsuspecting homeowner's place, under the guise of a waitress, with the intent of creating a stir in the community with her little gossip column in the newspaper tomorrow, I assumed. I was so furious with myself for giving her the benefit of the doubt. Her gaze failed to meet mine, and I was pleased she felt some shame. I reached for her hand and pulled back immediately, feeling the instant electric charge on my fingertips. We both gazed at each other. Irritation was visible on her face. I took hold of her.

"Let's go!" I said, showing her the way to the

door, insisting she walk in front of me. "Make sure to grab your things when you get out. Your services are no longer needed." I stomped on behind her. I was pleased to hear someone else testing the knob. I would be handing her over immediately.

My breath caught when she abruptly turned and grabbed me by the collar. I observed the bend in her lips and the crease in her brows before she yanked me down to meet her. I was equally blindsided by Bria's lips being forced against mine. She took me by the hand, forcing me to wrap myself around her. Surprising myself, I didn't protest and stepped closer. My hands latched onto her, pulling her close.

A kiss that started as intense mellowed out into something passionate. My lips parted, allowing her tongue to enter freely into my mouth. I took her in. I felt her peaks and knew she was equally as turned on as I was by the harshness of it all. Her hands slid up my chest, playing with my buttons and undoing them one by one. I felt the chill of her fingers against my hot skin. My basic instinct was to take her here and now on the floor.

Then, without any warning, she shrieked and pushed me, abruptly breaking contact, which made me stagger back like a drunken fool. "What the hell—" I managed to watch her make a speedy exit out the room. I was left wondering why she would cut such an explosive session short. She ran past the man intruding into my "happy time" with Bria.

"Sorry, sir, but they sent me to find you," the man said, appearing a bit shaken himself. I pushed past him and went in search of her. I was dumbfounded coming back out into the opening, finding her well composed, serving drinks as if

45

nothing had happened. But I understood it now. It was all an act. One that was dependent on me playing the part of a man fondling the hired help. She'd done so well, I too was convinced and was still trying to regain my composure.

## Bria

"So, where were you?" Samantha, the champagne waitress, queried. The question was posed a second time in the hopes of registering enough to draw a response out of me. I stood there rubbing at my hand where that fucker's touch had zapped me, leaving quite a sting. I needed to catch myself. My actions a while ago had surprised me. That couldn't have been my only way out, yet I'd chosen to proceed in that manner. But it had worked. Now I just needed to make it through the remainder of the night.

"How about that one, do you know her?"

We were playing a sort of 'guess who' game, testing our knowledge of who we knew was well off. I was forced to converse but welcomed anything that would help me appear unshaken. I turned in the direction indicated by Samantha. My eyes first fell on Trevor, who stood with a champagne glass cocked to his lips, conspicuously gawking at me. That made me a bit self-conscious. It got worse when the person Samantha was referring to followed his gaze and landed on me. I just knew something was about to happen.

The modelesque, striking-as-hell woman had an arm looped into Trevor's, staking her claim to him. She was the type that probably got away with shit eighty percent of the time because of her beauty. It was strange because I still couldn't connect the dots of who she was. I was nailing this game before now, when my mind went blank, stunned by her appearance.

"I know her, but I don't *know* her," I said, still struggling to make her out while sizing up the woman waltzing over to us—her high slit showing one of her incredibly toned legs.

For some reason, I felt a slight resentment. Of *course* that was the type of woman Trevor dated. No wonder he was such a tight ass. I shook the thought away, reminding myself to save judgement until I'd made her out. "Quick, tell me about her."

"Ms. Jasmine Caines is a stuck-up socialite who clawed her way out of the ghetto, yet now thinks she's better than everyone. Want to know how she got where she is today? Mostly by lying on her back! Now she acts like she's royalty, going about as if people have forgotten about her."

Go figure. "So she fits right in," I said, my eyes fixed on her approach. "Ms. Pantophlet. I see you managed to squirm your way into this event." I was taken aback—one, because she knew my name, and two, she was trying to faze me.

"I'm sorry, you are?" She bared her teeth, then ran her tongue quickly along with her upper fangs. This I found pretty unattractive for a woman to do. She then crinkled her nose at me. Was she jeering me on for some fight? "Punch?" I rolled my eyes and reached for a cup. She scoffed at me. "Believe me, I don't want anything from you. Like you can't have anything that's mine."

47

Right then, Trevor pulled up beside her, making it clear to what she was referring to. "Is everything okay?" he asked, wrapping his arm around her waist with his eyes fixed on me. He licked his lips. I was repulsed and was sure my face didn't hide it. His hand dropped from her waist and dug into his pants pocket. He then cleared his throat. She wrapped her arms around him and buried her chin in his shoulder—such an attention seeker.

"Everything is perfectly fine. Not to mention classy," I said with obvious sarcasm, hoisting a glass to the both of them before washing my throat with its contents. "Think nothing of it, sweetie. I was suggesting to this here news lady to work on her sources. Her pieces are just too gossipy."

"Excuse you." My frown deepened.

"I'm sure you've heard how trashy you came off on the radio, let alone in the papers."

"Why, because I see through the propaganda?" I asked. I really couldn't care less about her opinion, but something about the moment had me engaging in defending my work. I was ashamed to admit she was getting to me.

She feigned a smile. "Do I have to spell it out for you? You're obnoxious. You write pure sleaze in your so-called 'Gabby Gossips' column, and your presence is unwanted here. You are so ghetto black." I wasn't overly surprised by her rudeness and didn't flinch. Figures such a pretty shell would be rotten inside.

Some people didn't like what I wrote. I knew that and had used it to power my creativity. But it was unfair to have all my work seen as rubbish. I gave good advice. Calling it "sleaze" was farfetched and insulting. And how the hell did she know who was behind "Gabby Listens"? My eyes were burning through the snitch standing next to her. "I'm more than that. I'm a journalist. I don't write sleaze, and I do things that are not just about me," I said mockingly. "But I don't blame you for being misinformed. Your source is unreliable and can be easily manipulated. Why don't you pick up a paper sometimes and read it? It's not that hard. Don't be a sheep." I narrowed my eyes, challenging her to try and match me with words. That was a definite trigger, seeing her tilt her head to the side while she sized me up.

"Child, you will never reach my level. You'll keep orbiting around those who are capable, hoping to feed off of us like a fucking *maggot*. You call that writing? Please! Give a monkey a pen, and he'll probably do a better job than you. You need to know your place." She shook her head and took me in before slicing me with her eyes. "Knowing people cringe in disgust whenever you enter a room," she concluded, going in for the kill. "You're so simple and annoying. I honestly think you don't know better."

She'd figuratively taken off her earrings and pumps and was ruthless with her attack. Her offensive words flowed like silk from her tongue. I was ashamed to admit that I thought her surroundings would keep her packaged neatly and subdued. But it made no difference. The gutter w i t h i n her had shown itself, ready to devour whoever thought she wouldn't defend herself in a battle. She'd ripped me another hole, so to speak, and it was now a matter of punching her in the throat or running away from just being bitch-slapped.

Furious, I found myself breathing deeply as I took the champagne flute from Samantha's tray, throwing the contents in Trevor's face. He was clearly to blame.

"Christ!" "Oops, spasms," I fibbed.

"That would have been a more proper response, my dear. But you're too uppity to know that. You should try harder to hide it," I said, slamming the emptied flute on the table. I looked full into Jasmine's face, who was gawking with her hands up. I'd splashed her a bit, and it was rewarding.

"I'll see myself out." The exchange was isolated enough not to cause too much of a stir. As composed as I could be, I walked away with my head held high. Her words had affected me, but there was no way in hell I would let them see that it had made a dent.

"You've been distant lately."

"I know. My job has me all over the place. I'm just so tired at the end of the day," Jerome, my slightly muscular, tall, dark, sexy, on again- off again lover said, trying to feed me an excuse of why he'd stopped texting me for over a month. The thing is, I knew why. He was off on vacation with his main woman, and before that, we'd fought on the phone about what I'd meant to him—a question he'd refused to answer. He then hung up on me mid-conversation as I struggled to push for the answers I knew I wasn't ready to hear. Crazy enough, I was the one who'd initiated us being here tonight. I couldn't believe how much Trevor's date had gotten under my skin, and for some reason, I'd immediately texted Jerome who had quickly responded and agreed to meet up.

I'd made his acquaintance while he was doing some work at the magazine company. He and a few others had come to install a new air conditioning system. They'd left such a mess behind that I found myself confronting him the next time they came around. While doing so, it was hard not to soften as I fell into eyes that held me captive. It was one of his features I'd found myself focusing on when he contacted me a few days after to schedule a portrait picture he'd wanted to be taken. I booked my friend's studio and had fun asking him to pose for me, watching as he awkwardly tried to follow my instructions. His laugh was also one of the things that made me want to know him better. I would have never thought I'd get stuck on something so loud and obnoxious. It just made me smile.

I felt nothing abnormal after he'd called wanting to know when he could pick the photos up. But when I think of it now, going over to his apartment to personally hand them over was unprofessional, yet not without consideration. I knew what could have happened, and it did. He took the opportunity to pull me in and place a kiss on me that had him asking if I had issues with asthma. He'd left me breathless. My clothes were off shortly after that. There was nothing romantic about us, and compatibility had already been ruled out.

While I'd sat waiting in the car outside the motel for him to arrive, I thought about how average the sex was and how we certainly didn't

51

match up. I thought maybe I was blocking my orgasm, and he deserved a few more tries to get it right.

The radio was my company, and an old soul jam started up, which I was sure had touched many emotionally and had most certainly kept its fair share of women in relationships they should have ended within months of conception. Laughably enough, such songs had also played a massive part in my reasoning to still hook up with this guy. Some behaviors were just harder to unlearn. "How tired?" I asked, wondering if he was making time to fulfill any other sexual favors.

"Don't worry," he said, reaching over, cupping my neck. "I saved some energy for you." He came closer, and the feel of his warm tongue unlocked my lips. Sounds of our kisses filled the space. I felt him unbuttoning my blouse, and I allowed his hand to enter. He rubbed against my breast nestled in my bra. I relaxed and focused on his touch. I must admit, I was moist from just that. He broke the kiss and stepped out of the car. He gave the hood a knock on his way over to my side of the vehicle.

I stepped out and joined him. My skirt folded up, and his hand cupped my buttocks. I shifted my panties to the side and guided him into me, his stiff cock unhesitant. I started to work his pole while he held both my breasts before gripping me around my waist, helping my motions. I found him watching me, and that added to my pleasure. My head went back, and I picked up the pace, riding him. The satisfaction was overwhelming. I just loved the way he felt. I thought it was inevitable that I would be reaching my climax.

He was huffing, his pumps becoming forceful. I knew he was enjoying himself. I felt the first inkling of my rise, and a smile raced along my face. This was finally it. This was my moment to release like I'd never had with him. We would release together. *Oh, my, I might get pregnant*, I feared, but the thought faded with one of his thrusts into me.

"Shit, B r i a ," he moaned, his movements lacking control. I couldn't believe it as he held me tight, stopping my flow. His f o r e h e a d was resting on my chest. He took a moment to catch himself. "You can come off now," he said, all smiles. My mouth fell open as I shifted from him.

He broke the silence with his laughter. "Baby, you just know how to work me." He didn't know how to return the favor.

"Well, no need to go up there now," he said while redoing his zipper and pants button. He was referring to the room I had already paid for. "Later," he said before planting a kiss on my cheek. He then hopped out of the car and headed over to his on the other side of the lot.

I was completely disoriented and had no words. Was I in some parallel universe where relationships had evolved so much that he would think it was okay to just up and leave? Was that the norm these days? I started fixing my blouse and skirt. I then stepped out of the car. Clutching my door handle, I watched a group of young men as they walked past me. One pointed at me with a smile on his face. He nodded as if to say, I was the boss lady.

My cheeks grew warm.

I'd never thought about possible spectators. It was completely irresponsible for me to allow that to happen, especially in this day and age where everything was considered fair game when placing stuff on the internet. Although my windows were tinted, there was no way someone would take my car as being rocked by the wind.

My reputation would surely suffer a hard blow, and all that I was working on achieving would go down the drain if I were caught on camera doing something not even worth mentioning.

I would have to show better restraint. This was never to happen again. Not with someone who didn't respect me enough to keep things behind secured doors.


"Do we have everything?" My question was directed to Ricardo, a T.V. news reporter who covered all the parliamentary sessions on the island. We had made it back from getting a couple of cheeseburgers from Kevin, who owned the food truck located on the parking lot at the census office a few blocks from where we were heading. Ricardo was busy wiping at a smudge created by his haste to devour the burger before making our way to parliament. He wanted to do things differently. He was fed up with the standardized questions his boss insisted on him asking. The people were also tired of begging for their leaders to stand up for what's right. The place where we all called home was in disarray after a storm had passed through, revealing all our vulnerabilities and shortcomings as a country.

The people wanted straightforward answers and not the usual run-around from our representatives. I was all for it when he'd asked me to assist him as a news reporter. I thought he was taking a significant risk. He knew I wouldn't be holding back with my questions and assured me that I didn't need to—he was "counting on it," he said with a smirk.

Those ministers were in for a treat today after having reported back to the parliamentarians. In the council of ministers' press briefing, they would find themselves faced with more direct questioning. It would then be time for them to cut to the chase because I wouldn't be going easy on them. Ricardo was busy checking the cameras as we prepared ourselves to head over there. I was excited about the opportunity to try something new. I was getting comfortable being a writer and had hoped that this would open doors to so much more.

On our way by foot to our destination, I noticed a few people gathered around a radio, already tuned in to hear what was going to be done about workers who'd lost their jobs. The people needed a hero, and the usual candidates were either paid out or placed in a high position where they were then hushed. It was sad to see how over the years, some powerful contenders who'd used their platform to inform the people of their rights, now stayed quiet and no longer fought for a cause they claimed to be passionate about.

Unfortunately, it was the way things turned out, and they were reduced to mere puppets doing as they were told. Some even had a hand up their ass. I remember being told once how "if I ever decided to return to St. Maarten and all I wanted was a job, things would go good for me. But as soon as I wanted to contribute and have a voice, I would be entering the political arena." I had eventually understood what that person meant. I could barely voice any opinion and not be seen as a troublemaker.

Up in the parliament building, we'd set up our cameras to film. Dressed in my lucky pink jacket, a white V-neck printed t-shirt and jeans with my hair pulled back tightly in a bun and wearing my glasses, I was all business, taking down notes to ask the prospective ministers.

"Hello, Ms. Pantophlet, or are you here as Shane?" I recognized the voice immediately.

"I'm here as whoever will get some honest answers out of these people, Mr. Mathews," I said, not bothering to look up. "Ah, honesty, I didn't know you did that," he said, finding a seat next to me. If only asshole lapdogs like him got to me.

I kept my focus and held my tongue. Instead, I adjusted my glasses and leaned forward. I flipped over a page in my note pad and started on another question. He was looking over my shoulder.

"Reading glasses or—"

"Do you mind?"

I turned to face him, plucking my glasses from my face. I didn't care for any four-eyed references, so if that's where he was going with things, I was shutting him down right now. "Yes, I wear glasses. Big deal. Now keep your childish comments to yourself."

"Tell me, how do you plan on twisting your truth today? I mean, so that I can get a head-start on my rebuttal for Mr. Bryson," he didn't hesitate to ask. I guess he smelled a rat.

"You tell me, what do you think? Is he going to be the usual blow bag today, or is he going to have his own opinion and not showboat saying what he thinks the people want to hear? After all, the session is streaming live. He has a good audience outside already. Great opportunity to work on his re- election."

I rose, not wanting to hear another word. I went and found another seat where I could concentrate on the task at hand. That idiot Trevor was in for a rude awakening when he finally got to see who his boss was firsthand.

After a few hours discussing an urgently called agenda point, the session had come to an end. They'd barely touched on the topic of unemployment. The chairlady adjourned the meeting, and I immediately picked up my microphone and zoomed in on my first target. Before I could utter a word, there came a big crash downstairs. We headed to the entrance and saw the security guard pushing back people as he tried to get the door closed.

"What the hell is going on out there?" I said, running back and heading to a window for a better view of things. There was a mob on the street. Could it be that the people had finally organized and were ready to protest?

"I have to get out there. I have to let the rest of the island know what is happening," I said to Ricardo, who had found himself at my side.

"But how? I don't think they will open the door. It might cause them to storm the building."

"Okay, so the conventional entrance is unavailable, but there must be an emergency exit somewhere," I responded, heading over to the securities post.

Everyone's eyes were focused on the screens inside the hall. Ricardo had already pointed his camera to record what was happening and had even hung his microphone through the window for audio. A grim picture was being painted, which had gained all onlookers' attention. People had made placards, and many were busy blocking the streets. A group of restless delinquents were rocking a car, attempting to topple it.

An interview with this crowd would be expected. *And I was the one to get it!*

I pulled a guard aside and asked for directions to the emergency exit. I then began to inspect my recorder. I headed in search of the staircase. "Where do you think you're going?" This damn Trevor guy had forcibly grabbed my arm, halting me.

"Ow," I shrieked with attitude. "Are you trying to break my arm?" I fought to secure my limb, but he wouldn't let go of me. "Your arm won't be the only thing you get broken today if you go out there." His face was intense.

"What do you care?" I said, struggling. "At least I'll be off your back," I said, this time wrangling my arm away from him.

"Tempting, but that's not how I'd pictured getting rid of you." We held each other's stare. This guy was not about to stop me from getting the scoop of a lifetime. "Get out of my way!" I commanded, giving him my back. Again, he grabbed hold of me.

"You're too damn stubborn. You're not going anywhere." He yanked me into him.

"Who the hell do you think you are?" I puffed.

"Right now, I'm the assumed asshole that's trying to keep you from getting hurt," he fired back, amazingly angrier than I was. I started to fight against him and found myself with my hands locked behind my back. "Let go of me!" I screamed, completely outraged.

"Not a chance."

"You are indeed an asshole!" I assured him, still futilely fighting with him. He spun me around and pinned me against a wall. He then pressed his torso against mine. I screamed. *What the fuck was he gearing up to do to me?*

"You fucking pervert!"

He adjusted himself and twirled me to face him. He then placed a hand over my mouth. I bit him. "Jesus!" he screeched while pulling his hand away. "Let go of me," I demanded. "What the hell is going on here?" an unfamiliar voice called out. I felt a sense of relief. "Sir, please, help me," I began, completely breathless, squashed between Trevor and the wall. "This man is trying to assault me sexually!"

"Is everything okay, Trevor?" the security guard asked, unamused.

*Why the hell was he addressing him? And by his first name?!!*"Yes, I'm detaining this young lady from making a big mistake by going outside."

"Okay, just ease up a bit," he said, his tone revealing worry. I couldn't believe what I was hearing. I screamed in a fury. "You got a wild one on your hands," the security guard added with a chuckle. "You don't say."

"I'm going to fucking kill you when this is over," I said, unwilling to give up the fight. "Please go easy on me in your newspaper post," he jeered. I screeched again. I couldn't believe it. He held me captive for a while longer until the sound of sirens was heard. His warm body was pressed against mine. His face was extremely close. I felt his breath on my neck as he tried to settle himself. The muskiness of his cologne was penetrating my senses. I was beginning to forget why I was there. This was uncomfortably awkward.

"Know that this is only adding fuel to the fire," I said, wondering why I was again breathless. I had given up the struggle for a while now. He exhaled, and the warmth of his breath appeared to be melting my protest. "I understand fully, but you'll come to thank me."

The guard returned and informed us that the police had finally gotten things under control. Only then did he slowly begin to release me. I took the time to straighten my jacket. He stepped back, and I folded my fist and took a wild swing at him, decking him square across his face. He staggered back while holding his jaw and cursing under his breath. We both were hurting, but I didn't care. Hastily, I strode away.

I left the building and headed straight to my apartment to take a shower.

## Trevor

*My god, what a right hook!* I thought, dabbing the corner of my lips with my tongue, still tasting blood. The tightness I was feeling while flexing my jaw was telling. She had that waiting for me. No one warned me of the possibility of her becoming physically abusive. And to make matters worse, I was now being tortured by having a cold pack pressed against my face.

"Where does a woman learn to punch like that?" I asked, fidgeting from the chill of the pack. Veda was getting extreme joy out of seeing me like this. She wouldn't stop laughing after hearing I'd gotten a lick that took me back to my childhood. "Serves you right. I mean, what were you thinking physically restraining her?"

"What I was thinking was that someone needed to control her before someone got hurt. I didn't think I would be that someone." Veda laughed, causing me to look at her. She wore bright lipstick and had traced her eyes with a heavy, dark pencil, which made the brown of her pupils pop. Her hair was cut low and curled on her scalp with skin naturally tanned and smooth as caramel. She was untamed yet wore a pinned-up skirt suit showing she was no pushover. "Why didn't you block it though, Mr. Karate?" she suggested, referring to the Tai Chi classes I took as a young boy into my teenage years. I would clearly have to pick it up again.

"Anyway, you're lucky you got off with just a warning tap to the face." "A tap! The woman almost dislocated my jaw," I said, stunned by her comment. "You're not saying anything to make me dislike her," she said, showing too many teeth for my comfort. I yanked the cold pack from her hand and rose out of the chair I was commanded to sit in. "There is nothing funny about the situation. She's clearly deranged."

Veda, my cousin and closest confidant, was

61

my greatest ally since we were kids. We'd grown up together like brother and sister. People never believed that due to her Indian features. Her mother, my aunt, a born St. Maartener, and her father, a migrant from India, loved each other with an undeniable passion that birthed a semi-disciplined woman. We'd literally lived steps away from each other and found ourselves in the same class through primary school. It was only after high school when we'd chosen different study paths that we'd split up. We did, however, keep in touch. We were both back now, being productive members of society—her as a social worker and me fully equipped in law. I'd even conducted a few classes at the university on the topic of political science and was now working for a very influential politician as his advisor.

Things were going great for me until he'd assigned me to keep Ms. "Nasty Right Hook" under close surveillance. This, I was beginning to understand. She just wouldn't leave him alone. From her articles in the papers to radio interviews, his name always seemed to be rolling off her tongue. It was like she had a crazy crush on him.

"Look, the way I see things is like this." She came and stood next to me. She then took me by the chin, which made me flinch in pain, and rotated my head so I would face her.

"You guys have already started off on the wrong foot. And if you are expected to get near her and not have her put a restraining order on you, you need to make things chill between you two. You need to tame that dragon lady." Although she was breathing heavily and profusely cursing the shit out of me, "dragon lady" was not quite how I saw her today. My eyes couldn't help falling on her chest as it moved up and down. I caught myself mixing the warmth of my breath with the air against her skin just to calm the goosebumps that kept showing themselves on the upper part of her cleavage. I was super perverted with it. Maybe I did deserve that right hook.

"And how do I do that?" I asked, trying to get my mind from telling me I should have reached out and touched her breasts while I had her against the wall.

"Ahhh." "What?"

"Nothing," she sighed and found herself sitting on the arm of the chair. "Okay, let's do this. It looks like I'll have to teach you about women."

"No, just difficult ones like yourself."

She stuck her tongue out at me. Childishly, I returned the gesture. She then flicked me her middle finger. "Oh, classy! Is that how you treat an abused man?"

"Listen…" She shook her head and rolled her eyes. "You need to do something that will grab her interest while forcing her to be in your presence. Then, you can work your charm. Show her you're not the bad guy she thinks you to be." She stood and started gathering her things. At the door, she added, "Try to be suave and smile with her. Who knows, maybe it might work," she said, then left me to my thoughts.

The concept was simple; pretending I was sincere would take some skill. But I already had a gimmick in mind, I just needed to extend the invitation. I would read through the file I had built on Ms. Pantophlet and see how I could use things to my advantage. She wouldn't see it coming.

# Chapter 5
# **Unbridled**

## **Trevor**

*Huh, she made it*, I noted with a smirk on my face, watching her from above deck. She'd come onboard with others being brought here by a scheduled dingy. She'd immediately started taking pictures. According to the file I had on her, she was also into photography. I'd taken a look at some of her previous work and figured she was worth the money she was asking. Luckily for her, our first pick had a standing engagement.

I was curious to see her in a different work setting. I hired her through a friend of mine, knowing that she wouldn't have accepted my invitation. I knew she would be interested in coming on this chartered yacht as soon as the guest list was known—which I made my friend slip on purpose.
She also made use of the plus-one ticket I'd added just in case she might feel odd being here by herself. Women still went out in groups, this I knew.

"Well, I better get to work," I said to Jasmine before pecking her on the cheek. I then stood, took a sip of my beer, threw the half- empty bottle away in the trash, and went to greet Bria.

Today was extremely hot. The brief walk down and around persons who would describe their drunken state as 'nice' was a tad off-putting. But the idea of having young, eligible voters, some influential, on board convincing their peers to sign on to a particular party or candidate was just ingenious on my boss's end—or diabolical. I'd reached around and now stood to the back of her. I was hesitant. I released a breath. *Here goes nothing*, I told myself, swallowed back the nerves, and then stepped to her. "Ah, now who invited my biggest fan? Ms. Pantophlet, we meet again."

She mentioned something witty under her breath, and from how her friend reacted, I knew her claws were out. I looked down at her right arm and found myself playing with my jaw. I cleared my throat. She was still snapping pictures. Bria didn't bother to turn and face me.

Awkward and feeling a bit out of place, I decided to focus on her friend, who was still taking me in. "Hello, I don't believe we've met. I'm Trevor Mathews," I said. My eyes were switching from Bria to her friend. She didn't give me a name, but I figured it would eventually slip out sooner or later. She was all teeth.

"I see that unless women aren't walking around almost completely naked, don't expect you to put money into it," she said while reviewing the picture she had just taken. Was she tagging me as a sexist now?

"It's all in good fun," I responded, treading cautiously. She turned, giving me a quick once over.

"Mr. Snazzy, don't you look nice?" she said, making me grin while accepting the compliment.

"Thank you. I'm here on business." I wore white linen, which was nothing special, but I guess compared to the men here mostly in boxers and or mariners, I appeared a bit overdressed. "Business, huh?" she said, finally turning to look at me. A cluster of her hair tangled in her eyelash. The kink of her curls was so fitting for this sea excursion. Her

65

lips, however, thinned out, which made me straighten and wait for another jab at me.

"Well, if that's the case, I'm sure you won't mind answering a few questions I didn't get to ask at the press conference the other day." Curious, and on my toes because she was going about this in a very professional way, I nodded, deciding to play along. I figured I could handle her.

"Why would I?"

"Great! Just let me get my recorder out. I wouldn't want to misquote you on anything," she said, pulling the device from her fanny pack. Her first question was a snap— an inquiry on newcomers heading into the political race.

"I think it's wonderful. New, knowledgeable people, new ideas. We should get some legislation passed," I stated with confidence. Her eyes locked on to me. She shook her head, feigning interest. She was not sold on my response. Something was surely on its way. I gulped.

"Yes, true. It does make you wonder about the old crooks—I mean, veterans—such as your boss—running around. Do you think if re-elected, he'll opt for staying within the executive branch of government to fulfill his agenda and keep covering things up?" She said like it was nothing. Did all that roll off her tongue? She didn't take a breath *or even pause*!

My mouth went dry. I stuttered and fought for words. Her chin lifted as she claimed victory. "Oh ah, wha—what was that? Nothing," she chided before sticking the recorder back into her pouch. She turned fluidly, giving me her back before brushing her hair behind her ear. She then picked

66

up her camera that hung at her neck and began photographing again. I shook my head in frustration. Oh, she was cunning. I had to be more careful with her, I realized. A fact I already knew. I found her friend staring at me with her brows up and her mouth open. I'd admit, Bria won that round. I took a moment to collect myself.

"And you, what are you wearing?" I said, clearing my throat. I had lost her attention, and I must say it was bothersome knowing she found me not worth her time.

She took a few more snaps before responding with, "Nothing you would find appealing. Thank God." She then turned to me, expressing her lack of enthusiasm for the topic by rolling her eyes. *So childish*, I thought.

"Goodness, you are such a sour puss. It wouldn't kill you to wear a bikini now, would it? Hey, you might even attract a man," I said, knowing it was a low blow, but I didn't care. I didn't like her attitude. Her head snapped.
"Shove it, you pompous asshole! I am working," she said before bending to retrieve something from her camera bag.

I felt a sting in my pits. Her response was rude, but I found pleasure in knowing I had ruffled her feathers, which was interesting. A mischievous smile cracked my face. "And the gloves are off," trickled out of me. I rubbed at my temple.

"You know, I don't like that you are so comfortable calling me names, Ms. Pantophlet," I said, smiling.

"Names that perfectly suit you. Besides, if I recall correctly, you started it," she retorted. With that, she was right, but I wasn't through with her just yet. I took a breath.

"Look, it's just that I didn't take you for a bathing suit kind of person. It's something special seeing you try to dress the part."
My last comment caused her to turn. I found my hands lifting to protect myself in response. What a coward I must have appeared to be by doing so. "What, were you expecting the burqa or hijab? Because none of that is going to happen."

"What?" I asked, not quite following her.

"I am not about to throw one on and do as I am told," she added, which I found inappropriate.

"That is quite offensive. I would even go as far as saying insulting to the culture they belong to and the women who wear them proudly. I expect better from you," I said, utterly displeased with the words she chose to refute with.

She rolled her eyes, turned on her heels, and made her getaway. I too departed, leaving her friend to find entertainment elsewhere.


*That woman is wound too tight. Not even on a trip filled with people wanting to have a good time could she lighten up*, I thought, back at the bar now having a cold one. I mean, how did she get good photos if she didn't know how to draw emotions from her subject? I'd requested another beer and took my time to savor the taste.

Insane! Veda knew nothing of what she spoke. This woman was just not to be satisfied.
It had taken me a few minutes to realize that the

music had stopped. I turned and saw people peering over the railing. I became alert and found myself moving through the crowd. I needed to know what was going on. I looked over to the lower deck and saw Bria making a spectacle of herself. I found myself racing down the staircase to get to her. "What the hell," I said in aggravation under my breath, hurrying toward her.

On arrival, I was dumbfounded and disgusted by the behavior being portrayed by Bria. She was making a total fool of herself, and cameras were out taping the mess. She was carrying on about sleeping with the guy she was confronting, and everyone, including him, found her sexual confession hilarious. "Bria!" I growled between clenched teeth while grabbing firmly to her arm, whirling her around to face me.

"Is this what you do when someone refuses to sponsor you, you throw a drunken tantrum?" My statement based on what she was scolding him on.

"You don't understand. *He started it.*"

"Yeah, he started it," I said in disbelief of how she was not holding herself accountable. Thoroughly enraged, I clenched my jaws and released a long breath from my nose. "You need to get off."

"What, you're throwing me off the ship?" she said, failing to look at me, gawking around at those laughing at her.

"An attendant will bring you to shore," I said, gesturing to a mid-weight man I just knew would have trouble controlling her.

I didn't want to hear a thing and had learned

my lesson. *This babysitting patrol I am on stops now*, I thought. The man whom she was verbally abusing didn't regret seeing her leave. He gave a gesture signifying his content for the way I'd handled the situation and didn't hesitate to continue to degrade the women accompanying him by tastelessly touching them.

I nodded and walked away.

People started to clap, adding to the shame of her actions. At least, I hoped she saw it that way. A path was being paved for me as I made my way back to the bar on the upper deck. Music filled the open air again, and those present continued as if nothing had happened.

From the upper deck, I saw her board the small boat, refusing the hand of the attendant. They were taking her away. Today was unacceptable. What the hell was her deal?

I ordered a black label, then took a seat.

"You okay?" Jasmine asked, coming up beside me, rubbing my shoulder.

"Yeah."

"Okay, I'm gonna go socialize a bit. I'll be right back. You did well," she concluded with a pat on my back.

I took a swig of my drink; I cleared my throat from the burning that followed.

"I saw the whole thing. You kicked her off the boat, wow! You did that to a woman you just won't shut up about. Savage!" Veda said. She was holding and sipping on what looked like a pina colada. "Not now, Veda," I said, rubbing my forehead.

"You weren't joking about her being intense

70

though. But what could've set her off like that?" "She set herself off," I said, turning and looking her dead in the eyes. "This woman is bad news. End of story." "Well, I don't know how you'll get back into the friend zone you were already not in." She chuckled. "Oh, maybe send some flowers. That should help. I can see her dumping them already."

Flowers? Never! She wouldn't know what to do with them. I could see her biting the heads off the bouquet. *Who would believe I was considering it?*

I don't even know why I was thinking of smoothing things over. She was the one acting up. "Veda, please, the last thing I want right now is more of her." "Hang in there, boo," she said, patting me on my back before leaving. "Can you believe we got her to do that?" a fellow said before taking the empty seat next to me.

"Nice," his friend responded. "And her reaction—you dun know, priceless. Let that gyal go 'bout she business. She picture-taking skunt."
"I don't know who brought her, but time to get paid!" one of them said before they both began to laugh.

The guys were clear, and I now understood. Bria had been provoked. I'd judged her without knowing the whole story and now felt heaviness in my stomach. I felt despicable knowing I'd played a part in embarrassing her. But who had put them up to it? A question I was sure not to get the answer for. I exhaled harshly. I was not moving in the right direction when it came to smoothing things over for my boss. This was surely strike two. "Shit!"

71

It looked as if I was continually searching for ways to get her in my presence. I hoped this wasn't to be the precedent I was setting for myself when it came to her, but how could I expect anything less? Her temper was constantly flaring up, causing her to misbehave. Her conduct was just unacceptable. However, this one was on me, so I would go about my approach differently. After all, it was my job to keep an eye on her, which meant she needed to accept me into her space.

I'd gone and sent an email identifying myself as the one who hired her as the photographer for the boat trip. I went ahead and requested the photos. There was quite a bit of back and forth—me mostly insisting she come to collect her payment in person. I'd stressed my willingness to pay the full cost for whatever number of photos she had taken, and she'd finally agreed to swing into my office last minute. I felt a cold sweat building while I sat at my desk. She was in the building on her way up the stairs.

I watched as the seconds ticked away on the clock and felt like a man on death row waiting to be taken to the electric chair. I knew she was going to bring the fire. I swallowed hard, trying to calm myself. I took a few deep breaths.

A rap on the door startled me, making me jump out of my seat. I wasn't even aware that I was that fearful of a confrontation with her. I gave my jacket a quick tug, ran my hands down the length of it, and then tightened my tie before making my way over to the door. Again, she did a hurried knock, adding an impatient "Come open the door, please," while rapidly turning the knob only to find it locked.

A hard rap on the door followed just before I opened it, finding her turned fist in the air.

She rushed past me, stopping midway into the room. She stood with her arms folded. The glare in her eyes intensified by the dim lighting made by the solely lit bureau lamp on my desk, which was the only light source on at the time. I'd unknowingly staged a scene for drama.

"Where is my money?" Her question was so direct, I flinched. "I'd like to see what I'm paying for first, if you don't mind," I said with a stammer. I needed to collect myself. She dug into her bag and produced an envelope that she smashed onto my desk.

"These are photo samples, and here is the USB with the digital versions," she said, placing it softly but with attitude on my desk as well. She then returned to her glare, this time with her head slightly tilted to the side, a raised eyebrow and her nostrils flared. Meekly, I made my way over to examine the photos. I was not about to challenge her.

I came around and sat, pulling my chair under my desk. I offered her a seat.

"I prefer to stand." Her words were said between clenched teeth. The tension in the room was unmistakable.

My eyes slowly made their way from her face down to the envelope on my desk. I took my time taking them out, which she found warranted an audible exhale. I must say, that got to me a bit. I slowly started looking through them and found myself smirking. They were impressive.

My eyes fell on one that was blurred. "This one is a bit dull." She exhaled again, sending my blood to boil. Why was she acting this way? I was still a

73

client, regardless of what had happened.

"It's the effect I was going for. I was isolating the object in front," she said, pointing. "See, it's sharp," she said, popping the 'p' in the end.

"I'm not paying for it," I said, putting emphasis on my last word. I then pulled out my checkbook and started writing, finding it fair to deduct for the unwanted picture, although that wasn't our agreement.

I plucked the check, which was yanked from my hand before I could get out a thank you. "Whatever," she mumbled on her quick leave from my office, making sure the slamming of the door echoed in my ears.

# Chapter 6
# **Safe Space**
**Bria**

"Girls, girls, girls, please, a little softer," I stressed, trying my best to contain the smile racing across my face. It always got crazy loud when it was movie night at my place. Having the foster girls over was a treat for me, which I probably looked forward to more than they did. The pizza was on its way, and I was sitting on my couch trying to untangle the frizzy mess that was Aniah's hair. She was complaining every step of the way, and it didn't matter how easy I was trying to go. To her, the slightest tug hurt. My braiding technique was also up for questioning seeing the standing braid I'd just created.

"What superpower do I have?" Aniah asked, her question connecting to the Marvel film we had finished watching. The remote was now in someone else's possession.

"You have the power to make a mess and not clean it up," I said, instantly laughing at my wittiness. "Seriously!" she replied, completely unamused.

The other girls were all distracted using the Wi-Fi in my apartment to post on Facebook, listening to music with headsets on or lying on the floor watching a reality television program. They were all over my apartment as if it were theirs. It was hard getting anyone's attention right now, but I had no issues with it. "Did someone order the pizza?" Mariska, one of the big girls, asked while face down in her tablet.

*Do people enjoy reading paperbacks anymore?* I thought to myself, seeing her flip through the digital pages of the book she was reading. Just the smell of a book was enough to get me excited. The feel of the pages at the tips of my fingers as I waited to turn the page or enter the next chapter was amazing to me. And the culmination of a story where the reader is finally satisfied with the future of the protagonist—glorious.

No tricks, no vampires or werewolves, just give me something real that I could relate to. This was only my view, of course. At least some youths still picked up something that encouraged reading. That alone was a victory for literature.

"Yes, I did. One beef and one BBQ," I said in search of the hair moisturizer.

My phone pinged, and I took that quick moment from struggling with Aniah's hair to see what the message was. It was Kayla reminding me of the doctor's appointment scheduled for tomorrow. I swallowed hard thinking about how I wasn't looking forward to it. I had gone to my general practitioner a few days ago, and after hearing what my complaints were, he immediately wrote me a referral to see my gynecologist. The urgency of it had me thinking the worst, and my stomach churned every time I did. I hadn't entirely made up my mind on whether or not I was going or rescheduling.

My phone rang. It was the pizza guy informing us of his arrival in a few minutes and that someone should come outside.

Without being asked, Aniah leapt up and broke free of my grip of her hair. She ran to the bedroom, announcing on her way that she was going for my wallet. I exhaled and shook my head. She was up for any task that put a pause on this combing process— no matter how brief. I rose from my sitting position on the couch and met her at the door, where she handed me my purse. The pizza guy was now knocking, and that excited her further. She made a rushed move to open the door for him. She opened the door, and to our surprise... there stood Trevor with his fist in the air, ready to knock again. The frown on his face vanished and was replaced by raised brows after his eyes went from mine to Aniah's and then back to me.

"You're not the pizza guy," Aniah stated before looking up at me for confirmation of her observation, drawing Trevor's eyes back to her.


## Trevor

There was nothing in her file about her being a mother, so I wasn't at all prepared for the face-off I was having with a disappointed miniature version of Bria.

"No, I'm not the pizza guy," I stuttered, a bit uncomfortable watching this little person with pretty, brown eyes in a Disney princess printed pajama and a disapproving glare measure me up. *This was surely Bria at her age*, I thought. I was somewhat intimidated, I'd admit, by a girl with a full afro, no older than four or five, and I couldn't help a slight curve to my lips at the notion.

"Why were you banging on the door like that if you aren't the pizza guy?"

"Aniah, please go inside." "But the pizza—" she whined. "Will be brought right in when it arrives,"

Bria interjected.

The little girl held my stare, and I was rendered speechless by the power she surprisingly possessed over me.

"Aniah," Bria said, making her flinch. She made a sudden move, and when she did, the comb that was clinging to her hair fell with a thud to the ground. The child bent to pick it up.

"Is this how much hair you pulled out of me?" she said with utter surprise. "We have to have a serious talk about your combing skills," she said. Her lips pouted, and with a frown on her face, she plucked the hair from the comb and rolled it into a bunch in her fist before showing it to Bria while intensely gawking.

I could no longer help myself. The laugh that was building while witnessing the exchange was too much and had managed to escape from me. It was an uncontrollable, hearty cackle that lifted the heaviness of the day I was having. I needed this.

They were both staring at me now.

With a fist to my mouth, I coughed a few times trying to regain my composure. "Hi," I said, trying to break the awkwardness. I did, however, feel a little less intimidated knowing there was someone out there who Bria was probably no match for.

"What are you doing here? You are not welcomed," she proclaimed, steering the little girl back into the apartment. Her defensive tone made me remember that we weren't exactly friends. I took my time to wonder again why there was no mention of a daughter in my extensive file on her.

"Is she your daughter?" I asked, going in search of an answer without further thought. The words were now registering in me as being quite nosey. "Who wants to know?" the young missy bellowed from afar, gaining both Bria's and my attention. A blare of a car horn drew Bria's eyes back in my direction, but she was now looking past me. From inside the house, a shriek of joy followed. Bria brushed me aside and headed toward the car. I watched from one scene to the other. In the apartment, other girls were coming into view. This confused me more.

*Who were all these children?*

Knocking at my arm on her way back inside, Bria then rested the pizzas on her dinner table. The girls flocked. It was pleasant but strange, observing Bria in this setting. Her personality and energy were completely different. Surrounded by this group of youngsters, her aura had adjusted and calmed amidst the chaos that was happening as they scrambled to collect their slices of pizza.

"You want one?"

I gazed down into the wide, beautiful eyes of the child who was quickly becoming my favorite. "Aniah," Bria said soberly, "he doesn't 'cause he's leaving."

I hadn't realized I had drifted into the apartment. I was surprised by the tranquility I was feeling here—albeit I was being kicked out. "Here you go, Mariska," Bria said before directing the following to me. "Leave now!" she stressed at me while handing another slice to one of the adolescents. "I can't. I have news..." I drifted, realizing the connection to what I was actually doing here and what was happening now.

"I came to inform you personally that the

funding came through for the Build a Child a Home proposal you submitted."

She stopped midway through handing another girl a slice. Her gaze was questioning my involvement. The girl took it from her hand. "And how do you know about that?"

"I was speaking to someone about politics, of course, and your name came up. He is a fan of your work—said they had called to apologize about the wrong info given to you concerning the funding. It wasn't declined; it was just waiting on the finance minister's signature," I lied. She wasn't buying my story. "They were trying to reach you."
There was still no word from her as she looked on. Her eyes were piercing. My throat went dry.

"But you weren't answering. Maybe something is up with your phone," I said, completely uncomfortable. I knew her phone was working perfectly fine. Matter of fact, I'd told them to get her on the line straightaway after she'd bumped into me on her way out of the building all teary-eyed that day. I'd strongly voiced my opinion on the department's work ethic. I was completely disgusted, finding them laughing at the situation. I'd done a follow-up and found the request had been approved. Bria merely needed to sign and collect.

I now understood why she was so distraught. She was fighting to get things done for her kids. These had to be the foster children mentioned in the submitted proposal.

"Good to know," she replied. Her eyes fell to the floor, and I saw a hint of hope in the curve of her lips. She then raised her head, and her brows dipped before her eyes directed me to the door. I made my leave, wishing all a pleasant night. My now favorite of the children there, Aniah, handed me a slice of an already bitten piece of pizza. With a smile, I took it and bit off a piece in front of her.

I then left.

Standing at my front door, unlocking it, I replayed the image of Bria sharing out pizza dressed in pajamas. A grin cracked across my lips, thinking how, for the first time, I might have met the real Ms. Pantophlet. She was all about the children regardless of all her other aliases and caps she wore.

"Children," I said, shaking my head as I entered my home. She was passionate about doing things for children, and even though most of her file reported on the trouble she found herself in from time to time, they all had one connecting factor. They were for the betterment of the next generation. That was the one thing that gained her full attention, which I assumed only her closest friends knew about. It was amazing to see. She just lit up having them around her.

"Wow, I didn't see that one coming," I muttered, shaking my head, admitting to myself that I had come down too hard on her from the start.

Dropping my keys on the kitchen counter, I then switched on the light and made my way further into my apartment. As always, the cleaner was expected to make a thorough sweep of the place, which she always delivered on.

The apartment had all the necessities. Nothing extravagant like the colored chair pillows which I'd noticed at Bria's place or the lamp that stood next to a single person's chair draped with a blanket located in the corner of her apartment. My dining table wasn't set with matching tableware as though home-cooked food was to be served. Nor did I have candles of different shapes and sizes placed together on runners solely as décor. My curtains were plain, brown like most of the furniture in the room, and served their main purpose—keeping harsh sun rays and prying eyes out. Nothing was redundant. There were no vases with a few artificial flowers in them or colored stones. None of that found a place in here because I was all about practicality.

*It is quite boring now that I've compared it to her space*, I thought as I stooped to place my suitcase on the floor next to my home office computer. Sticking out from under the table was a storage box that, to my recollection, wasn't left there by me. My curiosity engaged and my senses alert, I proceeded to open it. The contents consisted of papers, Polaroid pictures, and strangely enough, a video cassette. Examining a few papers and seeing who they were mostly directed to, I was confused and wondered how and why it was delivered here instead of being dropped off at Bria's.

## Bria

The day was hot and humid. Sweat beaded on my forehead. My underarms were damp, and my feet were overheating in my boots. My eyes closed, begging for a gust of wind and some cold passionfruit juice to wet my throat, but there was none, yet it was worth it. The Build a Child a Home project continued into Sunday as expected. I was thrilled to see so much of the community lending a helping hand for such a worthy cause. From concept to breaking ground yesterday, I could honestly say I never thought it would be so inspiring.

The children would be excited to see how many people wanted better for them. I for sure didn't take it for granted. The last few months were spent convincing organizations of the value of such an initiative, and having the landowners sign on without hesitation was tear-jerking. Their legacy was certain and would impact the lives of many to come.

Now the work had begun on building a center that would function as a second base for children where they could expect warm meals and equipment to guarantee their evolution in society. I was in high spirits, which my friends teased was a rare phenomenon. Work was on-schedule, and no one was slacking. Things were running smoothly. I thought of going over the architect's plans for the structure. I wasn't sure if it was an annoyance or the sweep of heat that took hold of me, but seeing Trevor in slacks accompanied by a female making their way over generated a slight irritation within me.

"It's for the kids," I whispered to myself. "You invited him?" Kayla asked over my shoulder. "No, I didn't. It's just hard to shake a tail," I said with a frown. "It's too hot to get into anything with him today." Kayla grunted in agreement, then walked away.

"Blessed morning, Bria."

"No rest for the wicked, huh? Figures," I said, hoping it sounded light enough, and redirected my attention to the plans. When did things get casual between us?

"Noble causes get me out to wield a

hammer," he replied.

I did my best to look extremely occupied, hoping he would take the hint. "Or a way to try to impress. I see you're never short of… choices." My attention briefly fell on his company. She released a light laugh. "I'm sorry, this is Veda. My cousin." His gaze was intently on me. I felt like I had swallowed my tongue.

"Oh, uhm."

"Who do we report to? She's also here to help," Trevor stated, his facial expression straight. I turned and found the woman smiling at me. I pointed in the direction of the project manager.
Veda left in his direction, but this Trevor guy, oh my goodness. He wouldn't budge.

"I see you have the plans. May I have a look?" What did he know about building stuff? His hands were probably smoother than mine. I quickly reminded myself of the good day I was having, exhaled, and then without a word, handed them over. I turned on my heels and started to walk away. "How long do you estimate it taking?" he asked, following behind me. "A few months, the real work will start tomorrow. These two days are just for the sponsors to get their pictures taken." "Nice, I bet the kids are excited," he said with glee in his tone.

*Why was this guy cozying up to me?* "We all are." I turned to face him. "Look, I don't mean to be rude. But if you came here to help, grab a shovel and start digging or something. I don't have time for small talk." "Got you," he said, looking me dead in the eyes. I made a move to turn but was halted by the gripping of my wrist. Aggravated, I turned and looked down at my arm, which he then quickly released.

"Bria, there is something important I need to show you."

What was wrong with this guy always insisting on having special time with me? Couldn't he sense I didn't like him? Wide-eyed and utterly irritated that he was a constant bug, I flapped my hands at my side.

"What now?"

"It's in my car. Please come with me," he said, not waiting for me to accept.

I followed behind, wondering why from the first moment I'd met this guy, he was so determined to make life difficult for me. He was constantly popping up, and as I could tell, he didn't like me too much either. Yet, he insisted on being around.

His presence was starting to make a negative impact on my mental state. I mean, it had to be unhealthy having someone around who gave you a weird feeling in your stomach every time you saw them. I had to put a stop to it right here and now. I grabbed at his hand only to be zapped by static. I flinched and quickly released him. I rubbed at my hand. He looked down at my hands before going to my face.

For a second, I forgot what I was going to say. "Bria, regardless of what you think of me right now, I need you to see what I have for you." His docility took me by surprise. Mmj vHe turned, opening his car door, and produced a box. He went around and rested it on the hood of his car. He then gestured for me to come and take a look. My hands were sliding off my hips. I slowly made my way over to his side. He removed the lid and stepped back. I drew close and picked up the video cassette marked 'school play'

85

from the box. I was becoming weary, wondering what junk he'd brought to me.

I shuffled through the papers and briefly froze as my eyes fell on a picture. I went for it. I didn't know what to make of the faded photo of me taken during my kindergarten class picture day. I pulled out another photo. This one with me sitting next to my grandmother as she read the Bible. "Where did you get this?" I asked, knowing only of one group of people who would have them.

"It was delivered to me," he said flatly.

I continued my examination, which consisted of copies of my school report cards, swimming diplomas, summer camp certificate, and the list went on. It was my childhood in a box, handed over to someone I could hardly stand.

"Where did you get this?" I asked again, this time with hostility. "I told you."

"You're lying!" I accused. I knew there was more to it. My grandparents, who were the only ones sure to have stored all of this, wouldn't have just handed copies over to a total stranger. My breathing panicked, I raced back onto the grounds in search of the right person to report my absence. I had to get out of there. I needed to check up on my only surviving family members. If this was yet another threat by someone showing me they knew how to get to me, I had to protect the innocent people in my life.

My grandparents must have let an intruder in posing as a friend of mine. My heart picked up speed. I grabbed the storage box, flinging it onto the passenger seat of my car, and then drove off in search of my relatives.

Foot on the accelerator, I wondered about Trevor's timing and how chipper he was on his arrival. He was becoming more rooted in an obvious plot to frazzle me. But I couldn't help but wonder if he was just a pawn because of his slight hesitation in showing me. He must have considered it would be a shock to me seeing him with things that would be considered personal."

Within twenty minutes, I'd arrived at my childhood home in Cayhill. The box was resting on my lap. I unhooked the wooden gate and trekked the path leading up to my grandparents' house. I was greeted by two Chow Chows wagging their tails. Kneeling, I gave them a quick scratch behind their ears, then headed up to the porch where my grandfather was sitting. He released a cheer before making an effort to stand. First resting the box on the floor, I then went to him and helped him to his feet. I gave him a hug, relieved to see him unscathed. I then asked, "Where's Ma?"

"You know she's out back, washing clothes," he complained. "Of course," I beamed, feeling more relief enter my body. I gave him a quick peck and headed around to the back of the house. Toward the bottom of hanging linen, I spotted her legs, then heard the humming of a church chorus. My grandmother was in her world as she reached into the clothes basket and, with a clothespin, clipped a pillowcase onto a line.

I stood there for a moment, remembering how I as a child would be right there helping. She would do her best to not balk at the sight of me struggling with a handful of her clean, damp clothes with probably one of them dragging on the floor in my effort to be of assistance to her.

"Hey, you," my grandmother called out to me.

I took a breath. Resting the box on the ground, I then moved toward her, my arms automatically going up to take her in.

"Ma," I greeted, embracing the warmth that came with her. "We weren't expecting you until tomorrow."

"I know, I just couldn't wait," I said, trying not to alarm her. "Aren't you supposed to be busy with your project?" "Yeah, but something came up," I said. I walked over to the box. "Come look." Due to a past injury resulting in a broken hip, she took her time limping over to meet me.

"That Trevor guy I mentioned to you before had this," I said, looking up to her. "He must have come here and maybe gotten the opportunity to steal stuff. Because those cowards would do anything to get to me, but don't worry..." I tried to reassure her, seeing her paralyzed and staring into the distance. Her face filled with worry. "They know better than to harm you."

Hearing my words did nothing to calm either of us. "Ma, it's okay," I said, thinking I should've stepped more lightly into the topic of their home being intruded. I took her into my arms and felt her body stiffen. I swallowed hard and started rubbing her back. I kissed her on her wrinkled cheek and again spoke words that assured their safety.

"Tell her, Victoria," the voice of my grandfather added to the tension of the moment. He only called my grandmother by her name when it was urgent. I wasn't sure how much he'd overheard. But if he was referring to her letting Trevor in, then there was certainly no cause for her to blame herself and withhold the truth from me. It was an honest mistake.

"Tell me what?" I asked, releasing her slightly, still trying to reassure her with my eyes that everything was okay. The worry on her face was now mixed with anger directed at my grandfather.

"It's time for the truth," he said unwaveringly. My arms broke completely from her as I curiously waited to hear exactly what was not being told to me. "That container isn't ours," she began, her eyes still on my grandfather. "No one was here." She then looked at me and released a deep breath before adding, "It must have come from your father," she said, taking my breath away.

My whole life, I'd been lied to by the people I trusted most in the world. After my mother died while giving birth to me, my devastated father was overwhelmed with grief and got mixed up with some bad people. They'd been in contact with my father this whole time—something my grandmother stated casually as if I'd never asked about him before. I'd gotten extremely emotional when given a number to call him on and a postal address of wherever he was in the world where they forwarded copies of my life to him. He was constantly moving.

The tears that had been flowing since my grandmother revealed the news about my father disappearing after being released from prison had subsided. "Why didn't he take me with him?" I inquired, which was answered with, "he feared I wouldn't be safe with him."

"Bullshit!" I exclaimed, drawing attention to myself. "Calm down," Kayla said while rubbing my back. "So, are you going to try and contact him?" I shrugged, honestly not knowing what to do. Kayla had decided that the news deserved a stiff drink and suggested we meet up. I was going strong on my umpteenth shot of something I was having trouble remembering the name of.

"Wow, your father is somewhere out there and trying to make contact with you," she murmured, gazing at the upside- down bottles lining the bar wall. "That was the question, though. Because if so, why didn't he just leave it on my doorstep?" Again, the tears came, knowing he was around yet refused to meet me personally.

"I don't know… trying to protect you," she stated, treading cautiously.
"By giving my enemy info on me," I barked back, then tossed back a shot. I beckoned to the bartender who then refused to top me up.

"Maybe he thought Trevor was your boyfriend." My face alarmed her of me not being okay with her choice of words. She then quickly added, "You have to make up with your grandparents, by the way. You can't hate them for trying to protect you." I swallowed hard and cringed, fighting back the feeling of an upset stomach. "I know. I just needed…" I released a breath.

They were wrong for hiding things from me for so long. But I understood they would figure I would go in search of him no matter what I had on my plate, and I guess they didn't want that extra burden on me. "Aw," I groaned while holding my side. The pain must have thought it to be a perfect opportunity to let me know I had other issues to deal with.

"Still in pain? What did the doctor say?" My refusal to make eye contact spoke volumes. "Bria! You didn't go. I reminded you. Oh, my goodness, what is wrong with you? This could be serious," she whined.

"I know. I know. I got caught up. I will reschedule," I said apologetically. "You'd better. And I'm going with you this time," she said, her brows lifted, daring me to protest.

I turned to the bartender and gestured for another drink. He gave me the "you're done for the night" look and continued with someone else. "How are things with you and Bryan?" I asked, directing my attention back to Kayla. I needed a change of topic. "I don't want to talk about that." Her eyes fell on her glass in front of her, and I wondered how disconnected we had grown from each other for her to not want to confide in me.

Kayla exhaled. "Look, I know there are lots of questions running through your mind right now. But this is your father. He's alive. What are you going to do about it?" She was right, but what was I to do? If my father ran because he had problems with some bad people, wouldn't I be waking the dead searching for him? *I mean, how deep in trouble was he in if he had to run?* I wondered, watching a faded picture of my dad holding me as a child in his arms. I smiled, thinking he might really want to make contact if he actually had photos of me since my youth. I was torn between wanting to meet him in person and quite possibly revealing his whereabouts to whoever might still be out to get him. Unbalanced, I slid off my bar stool but made it look like I was making ready to leave.

"Don't tell Mich, okay? I need to figure things out first." You know I won't," she said, gripping me and helping me to my feet.


## Trevor

I peered through the window and to my astonishment, saw that it was Bria making the commotion on the other side of my fence. I sighed and released the curtain. I wondered how she'd found out where I lived. "You don't think I know you're in there? Let me in!"

"Who is it?" Veda asked, coming up beside me, drawing the curtain, making it more obvious that someone was home. "I see, it's your other half," she said, gaining my glare before walking back to sit on the couch.

I corrected my stance and went to open the door. Outside, I then gestured for her to come in. A whiff of alcohol trailed behind her. "Thank you," she stopped and said with attitude. She then politely greeted Veda.

"What have you come to accuse me of now, Bria?" I sourly realized I was still offended about being called out as a liar.
"It's crazy that I can pinpoint the exact moment when everything started to fall apart in my life, and it all began with you." She pointed.

"You're drunk," I started, wondering why I'd even chosen to entertain her.

"Oh, this is going to be good," Veda said, taking a sip of her peach iced tea and cozying herself on the couch. Her eyes wide, she began popping peanuts into her mouth.

"Look, if you've come here to curse me in my home, there is the door." "From the time you kissed me at that party, my life has been one big shit fest," she puffed, ignoring my request.

"This just got even more interesting." Veda's brows were raised in curiosity.

I huffed. "I—" My finger pointed towards my chest. "You kissed me!" Bria came stomping over to me.

"No, you walked up to me at midnight and kissed me, sir," she stressed. "Since then, I've made one bad decision after another." I was lost, having no idea what she was speaking of.

"You have been around the block." Her hands waved me off. She flopped down into the couch next to Veda, who offered her some peanuts.

"I like her for you. You're both stubborn and don't listen to reason, and that cancels the other out." *"Shut up, Veda."*

"He doesn't understand me," she said, shaking her head, "and it's infuriating."

Veda was all teeth while she sympathized. I, on the other hand, was done with this tipsy Bria. "You need to—"

"New Year's night in Holland, we slept together," she said to Veda, and just as if a light bulb had been switched on after taking in her words, Veda exclaimed: "You're the girl!" She gasped before throwing her hands over her mouth. She then gawked

93

at me. I still hadn't figured out who she was in my life, and Veda picked up on that.

"Remember the masked party? She left before you woke up!" That's when the memory came back.
"When did you figure that out?" I asked, stunned, remembering the night. I'd awoken the next morning embarrassed to turn and face her.

"The party at the Villa. The way you kissed me and the taste of what you were drinking that night. They were the same."

"You guys have been busy," Veda teased.
Bria continued.

"Plus, the picture of you and your partner on the nightstand. All of it jolted my memory." She shook her head. "You men disgust me. You have a woman somewhere probably making sure you're well taken care of but don't think anything of sticking your hot pastry strudel into someone's toaster."

I would never feel the same about the snack again. "Wow, she and I weren't together at the time."
"Conveniently separated, right? What was it, you guys argued and broke up for the night?"
She knew nothing of what she spoke. The sting of finding Nicole with another man in my home reopened the scar left there. I'd come home a few days early from a trip she'd encouraged me to go on and found a man relaxing in my apartment. He didn't even know who I was and had challenged my appearance in my own home.

My friends thought I had wallowed long enough and started taking me out to meet other women. One of those nights was when I'd hooked up with Bria. The following morning, I arose regretful about using her to get over my previous lover. I was

94

somewhat relieved not to have to speak with her or find her in my bed. Shameful to say, it was all about sex.

She got up and aggressively made her way to me. Pressed against me with a finger in my face, she scolded, "I hate you for using me... but I must admit, I was using you too," she confessed before her body gave in. I grabbed her and struggled a bit, moving her over to the couch again. For a little person, she sure had some weight on her.
"You sure know how to leave a mark on a woman."

I looked down at Bria and wondered how someone with such a peaceful glow when sleeping could be so frustrating when awake. I swallowed, wondering if I should rest her in my bed.

"What are you going to do with this one? I vote we keep her," Veda said, answering her own question. Now really, what was I to do with a woman determined to make my life sour yet gave me good chills when she got worked up and close to me?
I released a frustrated gust of air.

"Hand me my phone."

We made our way into my bedroom, her giggling at the fact that I'd refused to unmask myself. She then asked to use the bathroom to freshen up a bit. She left, and I wondered if I should go through with it. I'd never seen her before until tonight, but the kiss... that made me want to experience her.

Moments passed before she reappeared, standing in the bathroom threshold. Her eyes were narrowing in on me. She licked her lips, and the thought of her warm tongue gliding over my erection made a wave of sensation wash over my entire body before heading straight to my tip. I flexed. My rod was raising as if summoned. It yearned to take a plunge in her waters and to add to it. My conscience shut down, realizing it had no say in what was to happen tonight.

"What would you like me to do?" she asked, but I held my reply. *She will find out soon enough*, I thought. I watched her sashay over to me. I swallowed and then made my move toward her. I passed my hands along her neck. My finger and gaze followed the cut of her jacket, finding the uncovered bulge of her cleavage.

She gripped softly at my hand, still at her neck. Her eyes were mesmerizing, the only flaw being a small scar under her eyebrow. I traced a finger into the hollow of her neckline.
Her lips parted as if to say something but only quivered as she released a subtle gasp. She tilted her head down, and I watched as her fingers slowly undid her jacket buttons. I spread open the jacket, finding a simple top. My fingers slid under it, and with little effort, it found itself on the floor.

Her bodice exposed, a lace bra was all that hid the raising of her chest. A grin ran across my lips. I took her breasts into my hands, enjoying the sight of the division between them and the warmth of them. My eyes found her watching me as I undid her bra from behind. Her plump breasts popped free with a little wiggle. I wanted them in my mouth immediately. I wanted to feed on her while listening to her moans of delight and explore all of her wet caves. I took her taut nipples between my fingers and rubbed at them. Impatiently, I gripped at her pants and harshly unbuckled them, then walked her back to my bed. My hands palmed her ass while doing so. I forced her down, making her sit on the edge of the mattress. Unassisted, I stopped to undress.

Her fingers tapped at the outline of my enclosed shaft before diving into my briefs and withdrawing that which she sought. The warmth of her wet mouth made me tremble as she engulfed me. I gripped onto her ponytail and guided the rocking back and forth movement of her head. I enjoyed the repeated plunge.

The remorse of using this stranger had fled, and the feeling was replaced by an indescribably warm and incredible, mind-blowing build-up. I wanted to explore the folds of her as well.

With one final plunge that sunk into her throat, I then retracted. I arched her back, sprawling her legs open after relieving her from the remnants of her clothing. My head dipped between her legs, my saliva mixing with her juices. I drank from her well of abundance. Her body was tensing and releasing as I greedily fed on her. I was intoxicated by her moans of pleasure.

I then broke from playing between those lips with my tongue and climbed on top of her. Hastily, I slid into her—the feeling overpowered my senses, making me jerk back. I slowly reentered, allowing myself the enjoyment of her warm interior—the folds within accepting of my thrust.

I delighted in the scent of her skin as I sporadically laced her with kisses.

She grazed my flesh with her nails, and that excited me further, releasing the carnivore within me. My speed increased, and I began pelting her insides with gyrated thrusts.

I knew I wouldn't be able to last any longer, but I couldn't have stopped even if I wanted to.

My breath was caught in my throat as I bucked and released, giving her all of me.

I awoke the next morning finding my lover for the evening had left my cave without the need of giving me her name. I had greedily found pleasure in a stranger—a feeling I had wanted to relive on numerous occasions but couldn't because of the circumstances surrounding our rendezvous.

That was how I first acquainted myself with Bria. My razor- sharp memory recalled that night while stroking the seam of my trousers. My body was now needing me to finish what the thought of being with her had started. I headed to my bedroom, knowing I needed a shower. I would be imagining the water that ran down my body to be the soft touch of her fingers.

# Chapter 7
# **Misplaced Memories**
**Bria**

I was in danger of having my heart break from its protective caging. The generator started up with a roar, and a fresh burst of light illuminated the yard. I peered around the corner and saw that they all were gone. But where?

I'd followed a tip suggesting to come here. The informant had said that I would have a front row seat to illegal handlings. "Under- the-table sort of dealings" was how he had phrased it. My snitch's identity had been a mystery to me. His voice was distorted by some covering placed over his phone's mouthpiece.

My curiosity had gotten me into some tight spots before, but nothing like this. Down at the boatyard, where I'd snuck in undetected, I'd found cover beneath an occupied boat lift. I'd stacked a few crates, making me harder to spot. After hiding there for well over an hour, I was beginning to think the tip was a prank.

I was about to call it a night when I heard voices. One was the security guard on duty who was also in on whatever was going on. That I reasoned after seeing him shake hands with the person tipped as the one I should keep an eye out for. They were all up to no good. I had already started snapping and needed that perfect shot of the three men. I'd stopped to change the lens when the argument started. Something about not getting enough money to finish the job.

A fired shot shifted my reflexes into gear, sending me ducking for what little cover I could find behind the crates. I tried to still my breathing. I couldn't remember if I'd yelped and was hoping I didn't alert them of my presence.

I took a chance and peered from behind the stack. I saw the guard lying on the floor, wincing in pain. He wasn't dead—yet. I then watched in horror as the man with the gun pointed it at his victim again. That's when the electricity fell out— my eyes being denied making me a witness to someone's murder. I retracted back behind the crates. My body was stiff, as if part of the set. I shut my eyes and tried not to imagine what was to happen next.

Somehow, I'd found myself at the police station reporting the episode. The officer at the window told me to take a seat while she sent a team over to the boatyard.

"That's when you stepped into the picture. I didn't hear or see anything else. I must have blacked out," I said, opening my eyes, finding the detective's hard gaze on me. I took him in, concluding he was either someone who took his job seriously or someone not to be trusted. Either way, I had to choose my words wisely.

"So, you were trespassing?" he said in a Curacaolinean accent. I realized I was being interrogated not as a witness but as a caught lawbreaker. Getting hysterical, I said, "I'm telling you someone was shot, and all you heard was me being there, uninvited!"

"Lower your voice." He clenched his jaw.

I had probably made more enemies here during my journalistic career than friends, so I heeded his warning. The phone on his desk rang, and he answered it. His eyes were intimidating me all the while. His conversation ended; he then left me in his cubical. Goosebumps danced on my skin, making me rub at my flesh to chase them away. I sniffled, subsequently rubbing at my nose. They had taken my camera and could find pictures, so it was hard to claim I'd fabricated the event. I would be requesting my mandatory phone call.

The detective returned and with him came Trevor. "You're lucky. The owner isn't pressing charges, so you are free to go," he said, looking down at me. "I don't understand. What about the crime?" I was confused. I wasn't here fessing up about going onto private property. There was a possible murder at play.

"We found no further evidence of wrongdoing other than your trespassing," he huffed, tired of me. "But my camera. I took pictures," I persisted.

"There is nothing on your camera that corroborates your story, Bria," Trevor stressed. "Only a few black images. It's like you left the lens cover on," he stated, leaving me with nothing left to say. Arguing was futile, so I conceded, allowing my escort to lead me down the stairs where Kayla was waiting.

"Oh, my, are you alright!?" Kayla came running toward me. She held my hands before taking me into her embrace. "Who told you I was here?" I asked, still in her grip.

"Gyal, this St. Maarten. By now, everybody

101

knows you got arrested. The paparazzi on that!" she said, releasing me. I concurred. Bad news traveled fast on this island where everyone was their neighbor's keeper—unless called as a witness involving a killing.

"Yeah, funny how there is nothing to back up my story," I said while being handed my camera and other belongings.

"I don't know what you thought you saw, but if I were you, I would stay clear of trouble. Don't let me catch you anywhere near that boatyard again," the detective warned and then left. The story left in that yard would come to light sooner or later. But for now, I would settle my nerves and find something else to keep me busy.

"I licked it, so it's mine," Mich said, throwing me with that comment. "Oh, god, we can always count on you to be completely inappropriate," I said, rolling my eyes in disgust.

"Or totally myself. You need therapy. Seriously, you're tense like all the time. Besides, I know he's going to love this," Mich said, grinning from ear to ear.

I nodded, hoping not to have to see another animal-printed ensemble. So far, everything Mich had bought came with the expectation of them not leaving the hotel room. It was clear the kind of company she was to be. She was excited about the trip she and this mystery boo were going on. I was starting to wonder if he was a fabrication of her mind.

All this talk of traveling reminded me of my recent trip to Saba to conduct a photo shoot. The change of scenery was well needed. Anything that would relax my mind was.

My sleeping pattern was disturbed. Although my body was tired, I would find myself waking up as early as 2:00 a.m., unable to fall back asleep—frozen in my bed watching the scene I'd witnessed at the boatyard dance like shadows on my wall. And worse, there was no way I'd forgotten to remove the lens cover. It was surely a cover-up— even the source of my intel I questioned. I was obsessing, and it was getting to everyone around me. I was disappointed when my boss at the newspaper company instructed I let it go and take a few days.

I needed to refocus my energy. And a day out with the girls would aide that. "Wasn't Kayla to meet us here?" I said, trying to change the subject.

Mich was never down for politics with me, and to be honest, I had my fill of it as well for the week, but I sure didn't want to go into her love life either. Every time she brought it up, I would have to fight back comments and my thoughts on the matter. I really didn't want to be a bitch about the way she chose to live her life, but supportive was something she wasn't going to get out of me either. I was pretty much over the conversation and hoped she took the hint.

"I have no idea. She's been M.I.A. quite a bit lately," Mich said, sticking her clothing purchase back into her shopping bag. Mich had miraculously been the first person here after a day of shopping. I was impressed that she'd made it at all. She had taken a bus and had asked if I would be kind enough to drop her off on my way back. She was turning into a responsible and reasonable woman, and that was saying something. I thought maybe, just maybe this guy was good for her. But something wasn't sitting right. I just couldn't put my finger on it. He was a bit too perfect on paper for my tastes, and the constant praising and doting over him was nauseating. Every move she made surrounded him. "Yes, but the spa day was pretty much her idea, and it is almost time."

"Do they wax here? I can do with a Brazilian."

"Oh. Look. Kayla," I said while getting to my feet. I really couldn't do Mich any longer. "Hey guys, sorry I'm late. Something came up, and I had to settle it. What did I miss?" Kayla said, exhaling. "Nothing," I quickly interjected, not wanting Mich to start up again. "We are up next," I added, going into my purse in search of my gift certificate for this place given to me a few months ago by my boss.

Mich, Kayla and I made our way to the counter and announced our appointment. The front desk clerk scanned her agenda, made a check in it, and then led us to the back where we took off our sandals. Ready and oiled up for our foot massage, which was an added pleasure, we sat chatting about every and anything.

"What's that on your leg?" Kayla asked, drawing my attention to the spot she was pointing to on Mich's upper leg. Her pants had shifted up, and with that, a hell of a bruise came into sight on her thigh. "Oh," she said hesitantly before shaking her head. "That's nothing! I bumped into a bed outside a room while flying out to get assistance for a patient who had fallen." Her hand passed over the spot before pulling the pants leg down to cover the mark. "Oh, okay. I guess that happens," Kayla replied. Her gaze was locking with mine. I thought about digging for more details but was certain further questions would be dismissed. My gaze went to the floor.

"Oh, guys, before I forget. I received this the other day," I said, relieved I had something of value to say in the awkward air space. I went into my bag. I produced and handed Kayla a letter which was sent to congratulate me on my foundation being nominated as one of the selected groups remaining in the running for limited funding.

The addresser had reached out to organizations who catered to children in need following a previously held discussion concerning the funding initiative. We were then told that all who met the criteria would be notified and mailed the submission guidelines for the final selection. The two best-suited applicants for the grant would be announced at a later date.

"Okay," she said, scanning through the information. "So, congratulations are in order," Kayla said, handing Mich the letter to read.

"Not just yet. I still have to pass the finals. Exciting, right? The grant will help do so much for the kids." "You'll get it, that's for sure."

We continued to enjoy our pampering session. Mich dominated the conversation with talks of her mystery man. I was more than relieved being on the outer end, having Kayla between us. I smiled, glancing down at my phone, which was alerting me of an incoming call. The caller ID made

105

me a bit nervous. I picked it up. "Hello...?"

"Good afternoon, this is Doctor Smith's office. Is this Bria Pantophlet?" a feminine voice queried.

"Yes, it is."

"Please hold for the doctor."

I looked over to the girls, giving them my best unconcerned facial expression. It was only then that they seemed alerted. I waited as the call was being transferred. My throat was so dry, which made it hard for me to swallow. My eyes jumped from the shelves filled with different nail polishes to a woman walking past us in a robe, clearly on her way for a waxing.

"Is everything alright?" Kayla asked.
With a quick nod directed at her, I then shifted sideways and continued to wait. The pit in my stomach was becoming more discomforting.

"Hello, Ms. Pantophlet? Doctor Smith speaking." "Yes, any word?" I asked, not wanting to give too much away. "Your results came back, and I would like to discuss them with you in person."

I reminded myself to breathe.

"Can't you just say it over the phone?" I squeezed my eyelids shut as every negative thought forced its way into my mind. "I'd like to do this face to face, Bria."

"Oh, good," I whispered while fighting back the tears. Jerking, my breathing was not cooperating at this point.

"Bria?" Kayla's concerned tone registered in my ears. I started reaching out for her in search of support. The thoughts that consumed me were taking

106

my breath, and I felt dizzy. The doctor was setting an appointment with me—a date I would rather not keep. I hung up and almost knocked the pedicurist down on my way over and into Kayla's arms. I doubt I was coherent enough to explain what the call was about, but Kayla and Mich seemed to have gotten the gist of the conversation. This was turning into a shitty month all together now.

Stepping out of the spa and while making way to our cars, our path was being obstructed by a woman struggling to wrangle in three small children. We stepped aside, only to have her block us again. The woman appeared completely overwhelmed, her expression mixed with anger and desperation. She was clearly at her wit's end, struggling to keep it together.

Her focus was on Mich, who attempted to walk past her. "These are his children. You're not the first, and you won't be the last," the woman said, now fighting back the tears.

"What's going on here?" I asked. Mich's face was void of empathy.

"You have to see that what you're doing isn't right. He keeps hurting his family." Mich continued over to the passenger side of my car, all the while ignoring the woman.

"Mich, what is she talking about?" Kayla questioned this time. "Let's get out of here," Mich said, refusing to be held any longer.

"You're heartless and a fool if you think he's gonna stay with you. You don't know him. You're in for a real treat!" the woman yelled as we entered the car.

After taking a quick glance over at Mich sitting with her arms folded in my passenger seat, I turned on the ignition. Her hardened demeanor spoke volumes. She was not up for questions. She was not going to answer to anyone. But it was clear as day. Mich had found herself entwined with someone else's man. She must have felt completely embarrassed, having us witness her being called on it. She was indeed not the last to be taken and blinded by the words of a cunning and deceitful lover.

Since the confrontation, days had passed with us not hearing a peep from Mich, and that alone was alarming. It wasn't like her to ignore calls, and she was a compulsive text junkie. We anticipated at least a text slip-up out of sheer habit. Her not blowing our phones up with viral messages was not in her nature. Kayla suggested we head over to Mich's mom's place. Mich wasn't too thrilled about her living arrangements and had on numerous occasions, voiced her complaints about her mom treating her like a child. Those two were constantly at it.

We stood patiently, waiting for the sound of latches being unlocked to still. And when the door opened, we greeted Ms. Maccow with a smile, which was countered by a cold "what do you want" stare.

"We are here for Mich," Kayla stated. "You think I don't know that!" She turned and left us at the door. After a brief hesitation and us giving each other the "look," we both giggled and shook our heads before proceeding inside. I was more than taken by surprise by the scene unfolding in Mich's room. "Are you seriously still going through with it?" Kayla asked.

This was absurd. Mich was packing after what had transpired outside the doors of the spa. "You're actually still planning on leaving with him," I voiced, trying to register and make sense of it all. I rubbed at my temple, quite certain of the headache that was to occur.

With her mouth agape and eyes wide, Kayla stood fighting for words to add.
"That asshole is fucking playing you!" I barked, not caring to censor anything. "And God knows who else. Mich, think this through. Do you want to be *that* girl?"

It was just too much. Sure, there were women out there doing their best to break homes, and I questioned whether it was their true intent at times. Women got way too much credit for being the sole reason families fell apart, and not enough blame was passed on to the men who went seeking a bit of spice in their sex life, but witnessing this was ridiculous.

"Women lose their men all the time and become salty. She's no different," Mich said, stuffing her suitcase. "Is he married?" I asked, which she ignored. I grabbed her by the wrist, forcing her to face me.

"We all know marriage isn't final these days," she replied, breaking free of my grip and then continuing to pack. "That makes it right then," I said, appalled by her comeback. "You're into breaking homes now." "Look, it's not like I was trolling him on

109

the internet. We are way past that."

"Yeah, but he's been lying to you this whole time about it," Kayla finally added.

Fed up with our inquiries, she flung the towel she was about to pack at the bedpost. She then closed her eyes and rubbed at her temple. "No, he hasn't. He told me," she said, opening her eyes and locking us in her gaze.

The room fell completely silent. I was shocked by her statement. How could she know and still go through with it, and did it even take a whole heap of convincing? "You knew about her, yet pretended you didn't?" She watched me, confirming everything.

"He also told me how things are so stagnant between them—he feels like he's living with a roommate. He's not even sleeping with her."
How could she believe the lies he was feeding her so he could have his cake and eat it too?

In the corner of my eye, I saw Kayla bow her head and move away. This was not the time to mince words or hold back from talking some sense into Mich.

"You think you're gonna be the one to set this man free and he'll do what he has never done in the past?" I said, trying to knock some sense into her. "

He's not going to move out of his comfy apartment to live here in your mother's home with you. The man's long-time woman—his children's mother or probably his wife—told you there were many just like you. She knows, and she's still with him. He's playing both of you."

"Bria, please!" Kayla said, a bit stunned at my bluntness. But this shouldn't even have been a discussion point. "No, let her speak," Mich insisted.

"She needs to open her eyes."

"It's not like you would understand. You only know how to repel men."

Unbelievable! Everything I was saying was falling on deaf ears.

"Well, at least there will be no word out there about me being easy once they threw money at me," I said, my expression hard. "You're an on-call whore. Have some dignity." She ignored me.

"Mich, you're a nurse. Just think about all that he is exposing you to. Let alone his family issues," Kayla tried to reason. "He loves me, and I love him regardless." She continued scooping up clothing and harshly sticking them in her traveling bag. "Do you not see how wrong this is? He's making you crazy," Kayla cautioned.

"God, you are so stupid," I stated under my breath. "Funny how someone with your issues still finds time to judge others," Mich said with her back to us. Word had gone from someone's mouth to her ears. "How long have you been waiting to say that?" I asked, gazing over at Kayla, the only one who knew of my mess. Mich was certainly counting the days to drop the bombshell.

It was tense. And I for sure wasn't about to go running with my tail between my legs. This fight was a long time coming. Mich thought she could say just about anything with there being no consequences. She would be proven wrong today.

"Bria, please just answer your phone," Kayla said, her eyes pleading.

I hadn't noticed, but indeed my phone was ringing. I refused to break my stare and without doing so, retrieved it from my pocket. It was Trevor. Not quite the person I wanted to speak to at the moment. Grabbing the phone from my hand, Kayla picked up. "Yeah, hello?" she answered. "Yes, she's right here. Hold a minute," Kayla said, handing the phone over to me. This added to my irritation, and I locked eyes with her, but that didn't seem to faze Kayla as she challenged my glare.

"What?!" I answered, utterly over his constant interference in my life.


He had asked to meet me at the Emilio Wilson estate where he was finishing up a business meeting. Still fuming, I stood on the premises ahead of the suggested time, wanting to know what he'd found. I headed to the museum to read once more on Mr. Wilson himself and all those who came to the island with the desire of either taking or reclaiming it. The pieces on display, either made of wood or rusted, had found their final resting place within these walls, built by an outsider wanting to make the estate more appealing to visitors. There had been constant debates concerning whether it was in the island's best interest to excavate yet another plot of land in the interest of tourism. A debate that went quiet after locals were welcomed to zip down what was advertised as the steepest zip line in the world.

Very few held the sour taste in their mouths of what our country was slowly becoming—an amusement park for travelers. I preferred not to get into it because I too enjoyed the thrill of being strapped in and zipped down the hill, all the while praying not to fall out.

"Hey, Bria." I turned, shielding my eyes behind shades while looking in the face of Trevor.

My last performance at his home had not sat well with me. I recalled the evening well enough, seeing that I wasn't entirely wasted, yet I was way too loose to stop from making a fool of myself. I told myself I would need to get a grip on my emotions and let go of whatever grudge I held toward Trevor. It was the only sure way to stop myself from acting up. And then there was the fact of him knowing how easy I was when we'd slept together. Oh, why did I divulge that bit of information in the presence of his cousin?

"You wanted to meet with me," I said calmly, trying not to give my agitation away. "Yes." He cleared his throat and made his way to me. "I had to check the authenticity of the info. The source had to be trustworthy," he said, opening the brown envelope found in his hand. During our phone call, he had mentioned pulling some strings in order to locate my father. I tried finding old articles, searching with keywords hoping to get a hit on my dad, but dug up nothing. This man who was hardly even an acquaintance had procured more information on my dad than me, and I didn't know what to say to that. Right now, I just needed to know if his source would lead to any discoveries. I waited for him to produce what was enclosed. He leaned in, and the smell of him played on my senses.
Thrown by it, I stepped back.

I saw his eyes land on my chest, and like a reflex, I immediately held my breath in an attempt to stop the rise and fall motion. I folded my arms and rested a hand over the hollow of my neck. I pretended to play with the pendant hanging from the silver necklace found there. My fingers were concealing the area where my pulse could be registered. I then swallowed hard, hoping he didn't pick up on my discomfort.

I was doing my best to act normal, but I was failing miserably. His eyes narrowed as he took me in with intensity. "Did I catch you at a bad time today?" he asked, which I shrugged off. I then encouraged him to stick to the reason we were here. "He isn't far," he said, slow and cautious. "I just need to lock in a definite location."

I started through them and narrowed in on a few lines that were highlighted—my father's last known address being one of them. His current location was indented.

"I can accompany you?"

"That won't be necessary," I said, my mind racing. I turned and headed for the exit, leaving him standing there.

"So that's where you are."

"Are you hearing me?"

I was entranced. Of course I'd heard him. It's just this guy was really bad at jokes. I knew I shouldn't have come here, but I was pressured into making the appointment. Now here I was, in front of my doctor, being forced to listen to this mess.

I'd been suffering from almost unbearable pain for weeks and having the added symptom of spotting nowhere near my time of the month had raised even more concerns. That day at the spa, the girls insisted I check with my gynecologist.

Kayla, who had even attended my initial

114

checkup, stood guard in the waiting area, making sure that I didn't skip. I now sat with cold toes, wishing there was a back exit. And then, there was my social life, which was a mess and quite upsetting. It was official. *My whole being was off balance.*

The fight with Mich, who regardless of all our warnings, still flew out to meet her lover, had me questioning if she only went through with it to prove me wrong. This was a smart, educated woman. She undeniably saw the red flags. Having to take separate flights because of some hocus pocus last-minute meeting with a client should have shown her a few more.

This guy knew how to work it. I was surprised Mich even mentioned that telling piece of information to Kayla. She was undoubtedly up for a rude awakening. And finally, the call from Trevor concerning his follow-up with the lead on my father. We had a scheduled dinner date in order to discuss what more he'd dug up, and based on the little information he'd given prior to him calling me again, I'd already made travel arrangements. I just needed a few more specifics.

My kids were the only aspect of my life that wasn't spiraling out of control. Other than that, I felt as though I was on a rollercoaster ride and about to lose my lunch.

"What are you saying? That I won't be able to have children? This can't be happening. How could I feel so healthy and suddenly, this happens!?"
Things just weren't adding up.

My gynecologist had been reaching out to me for almost a week. I kept pushing things back. Oh, why did I decide to do this now? I had a plane to catch the next day, and I still hadn't finished packing. "It's not that you can't. That's not what I'm saying." He sighed. "The pain that you've been experiencing was your body giving you warning signs. We have to operate."

"Why, though? Won't that cause scarring and mess things up more? The pain isn't that bad. You're leaving my body parts right where they are!"

He sighed. No longer facing me, he went over to the ultrasound machine and held on to it as if seeking support. It was too quiet for too long. I needed him to say something promising.

"Bria, this is problematic. Infertility can happen next because of it." His words touched me and seemed to have saddened him. He paused. The air conditioning tried its best to dry the tension sweat beading at my temples. Hearing I had fibroids was manageable, but me not being able to have children was just plain unacceptable.

"Garry?" I said. My voice was barely audible.

I sat wanting him to look me in the eyes and tell me everything was going to be alright. I was hoping to talk to a friend I'd had many conversations with in this very room. It was weird to Mich that Doc and I had built a friendship—especially since he'd seen all up in me as I laid spread open and at my most vulnerable.

On my first appointment with him, he'd walked into the office that day and found me with my hands folded and legs clamped closed. I sat completely tensed on his examination bed, watching as this much older man sifted through the files my previous doctor had left behind. My mind had made him out to be a pervert—which he wasn't.

116

I am more certain that our lengthy conversation that day had to do with the fact that he'd seen my anxious stance. I was hindering him from doing his job. We'd bonded over a comic bit we'd both seen, "Laugh till your Belly Buss." He'd made reference to one of the jokes that fell short, and I'd instantly picked up on what he was talking about and started laughing.

"Bria..." He turned to face me. "If we do something now, you'll go on to make lots of children of your own." His voice was calm and reassuring, but I still wasn't at ease. "Doc, I can't do this now. It will have to wait until I get back." I dug into my bag in search of my keys.

"Are you going on vacation?" His line of questioning was probably posed to figure out scheduling for the operation he wanted me to undergo. "Not quite. I got some personal things I need to get sorted out."

"Okay. Well, let me know when you get back so I can set things up as soon as possible."

"Yes, Doc," I replied, avoiding eye contact. I stood and threw my bag straps onto my shoulder and headed for the door. "And Bria, don't think I won't know when you do," he said, halting me in my tracks.

With my back still toward him, I managed a grin. Seemed as though he too had a tracker on me.

My bags were packed, and I was ready to be taken to the airport by Kayla, who was running a bit too late for my taste. What was with her these days with time? She'd become so unreliable. I checked my watch and decided it best to get a gypsy driver. I couldn't believe they were more dependable than my friends.

I retrieved the number of my go-to gypsy driver from my refrigerator door and gave him a call. He would be here in less than ten minutes. I scanned my room again, wondering if I'd forgotten anything. My red laptop bag, which I'd gotten as a Christmas gift from a past lover, would double as a handbag and had all I needed to confirm my identity and hopefully match the man assumed to be my father. It would be an emotional trip. That's for sure. I didn't tell my friends I was doing this, which would've probably given me much-needed support, but I couldn't. Life was having its way with them as well. From Mich blindly bending over backwards to please a man who was using her while she mistook his intentions, to Kayla who was also constantly unavailable and hiding something that I couldn't put my finger on. My intuition was telling me I'd better back off and let them figure things out.

I could honestly say, I needed time away from them myself, but when I got back, I would most certainly get them together for a talk. I had a few things of my own I needed to discuss. And leaving things the way I did with Mich hadn't exactly given me sweet dreams. My mind flashed back on the news I'd recently gotten from the doctor. I was still struggling with it. Life was drastically changing for me, and I felt like I could barely keep up. I needed a distraction. However, this was probably not the right kind. Nevertheless, I had to do it.

My phone was ringing. It was time to go. "I'll be right out," I said to the driver.

I took one last look around my apartment to see if anything was still plugged in that shouldn't be. My landlord wouldn't be too happy discovering her place got burned down because of a forgotten connected cord.

It was all good and time to leave. Things would go on pause here, but I would be back. "Trevor's lead had better pay off," I said, grabbing my camera bag before exiting.

Flying… how I'd come to hate it. What a stumbling block it was for me in my quest to see the world. I'd always wanted to travel to exotic places, but the fear of take-offs, landings, and just the in-between airtime had always been the deciding factor in whether I would or not. Short distances alone had me on edge, and I would find myself contemplating swinging by the pharmacy for a sedative. This journey, although about an hour and a half away, would be intense no matter what.

"Would you like something to drink?" the airplane stewardess with a Spanish accent asked me after she'd handed me a bag of packed oatmeal cookies.

"Apple juice, please."

She poured some juice into a small plastic cup, and after thanking her, she quietly moved along.

I had almost forgotten about the communication barrier that I might be faced with in Santo Domingo. And unfortunately, I knew very little Spanish. I didn't put much thought into it, assuming there must be plenty of people who spoke

English that would be able to direct me to where I needed to go. The woman sitting next to me, whom I'd already heard speaking both Spanish and English, was a perfect example. I took a few breaths trying to settle my mind, which was constantly trying to block images of me going under in an operation room, thoughts of my friends getting into trouble while I wasn't there, and of course, the latest political development happening in my country. Curtis was up in the polls as being one to be re-elected.

He was hiding something. I just couldn't figure out what. I knew he was up to no good, and for the life of me, I couldn't understand how Trevor of all men would be helping to cover things up. It didn't seem to fit with his character. There was a chance that he didn't know, but that was slight. I had to get into Curtis' office to search for clues. There must be something there. Things just didn't add up, and I didn't care how much Trevor mentioned him being one of the good ones. I knew that to be false.

I shook my head, wanting to stop focusing on all the things I had no control over. The expectation and circumstances around meeting my dad came with its own set of woes.

He could reject being part of my conception and want nothing to do with me, or this trip could turn out to have even more devastating revelations. What if I had missed out on his presence here on Earth? My heart couldn't take losing him twice in one lifetime. I had little to no time to prepare myself for that harsh reality.

# Chapter 8
# Off Balance
## Trevor

Setting things up last minute to get here was a hassle. I'd insisted it necessary to come here to keep my eyes on Bria while she snooped around— arguing how God alone knew what she would be able to uncover that might somehow fall back on my boss. But following a woman who would be furious seeing I had followed her here, who would object to me accompanying her, would prove my worth in her eyes.

Her plane had already landed, and she was probably waiting to be cleared by immigration. I was finally one step ahead of her. The thought of how far I would go to keep an eye on her crossed my mind. The answer to that surprised me no less.

Standing alone in the busy arrival hall of Las Americas International Airport watching individuals, families, crew attendants along with businessmen and women get on with their business and the vacation schedule was what I was doing for the past half hour. I didn't want to be distracted in any way and miss Bria. Yet something about me just waiting for her wouldn't come over very well. I could bet on that. I had to do something and quick, I thought, scanning the place for something that would make it seem as though I wasn't there because of her. How would I explain this? How would I explain knowing she was set to arrive today when she hadn't uttered a word to me? She was sure not going to buy this being a coincidence. She had already dismissed any further assistance from me. I needed to work on my lying—

one of the things I truly hated when it came to her. I swallowed past the dryness in my throat. I was getting nervous, and I didn't understand why. What was happening with me? Did I even have the stamina to keep up with her here? This feeling was getting out of hand. I needed to gather myself.

I bent over and went into my briefcase. I could at least have my phone in hand.

"Lady, all I'm asking for is some simple directions. You don't have to be a snob about it."
I stood and tied the voice to the figure my eyes had fallen upon. Bria and who I suppose she would describe as an uncooperative local were going at it as they came down the ramp, and from the sound of the conversation, neither of them knew what the other was saying. They were drawing attention to themselves, and the last thing I needed in another man's country was to be locked up due to me finding myself having to defend Bria because of a brawl. "Can you please just listen and stop…!"

"Yo no comprendo, yo no comprendo, por Dios hija, deja de hablarme en ingles por favor," the lady pleaded, trying her best to get through to Bria. "Try to understand what I am saying and stop with all this blah-blah-blah."

It was somewhat hilarious. But I don't think Bria felt the same way. She seemed a bit more agitated than usual, and it was time to break this thing up before authorities got involved.

"Hola, recibí esto de aquí. Ella se pone nerviosa cuando vamos a viajar. Pienso que la voy a dejar."
"Tienes que decirle a ella que se relaje, y que no sea tan agresiva."

"Yo se; Este viaja era para que se relajara." "Pero no funciona, que lo cura."

"Si." I turned and looked at Bria before giving a quick smile, admitting to not only her but to myself that it was a crazy situation. "Adios!" I shouted as she walked away. I laughed and exhaled audibly as she sauntered off and away from what could have translated into a hostile scene.

"So... I'm crazy, huh?" Bria commented, smacking me in the stomach. She knocked the air right out of me and made her way to the exit.

"Next time, I'll settle for a simple 'thank you,'" I murmured and kept pace behind her.

"'Thank you'? What are you doing here? I think you are really taking this stalking thing to the next level. 'Cause spying on me in a different country might give me a reason to have you killed!"

"Spying?! Why does this have to be spying? I got here before you did and—"

"And what?" she said, abruptly turning to face me. "Waited for me to show up? That's still considered spying."

I had no words, and from the look of things, she was nowhere near convinced by my poor acting skills. The fury in her eyes told me she wasn't up for any bullshit. I was not to be the one getting a beatdown from Bria on what seemed to have quickly become one of her bad days. Something was going on with her. And it wasn't only about meeting her father on this trip.

"Are you alright?" I asked, hoping the sincerity in my voice would ring through. She stood staring at me. I wondered if I should retreat while I

123

still could.

"Why are you here?" she said, unwavering. "And I want the truth."

My heart was pounding. Only she made me nervous and unsure of myself for some reason. I wondered what my facial expression gave away. Oh, God, help me.

"The *truth*."

"Yes," she retorted.

I swallowed hard and briefly looked away, only to return to her hot stare.

"The truth is…" How was I to say this without my ass being served up on a platter? "That I wanted to see if this lead was really worth pursuing. And I thought you could use someone who actually knew the country and had a few ties here. I came to help… If you'll let me."

She stood quiet. Damn, she was hard to read. "I can help," I stressed.

Her lips parted, and her chest raised as though about to speak. Yet, she decided not to and looked away. "Okay."

"Okay?" I was a bit shocked.

"Yes, you can stick around, only because I might need help." She exhaled. "What other languages do you know?"

"French… and some Dutch."

"Alright, then. I need a taxi to my hotel so I can dump my bags and get started." She handed me a piece of paper she had retrieved from her bag. It had the name of a hotel on it, which I recognized. It was a good distance from where I was staying.

"I think… I mean, don't you think it would save time if we stayed in the same place?"

"No!"

I exhaled. I knew there was no point arguing. She was persistent and had already given me a win for today. I shouldn't push it.

"Let's get you to your hotel then," I conceded.


"What he's saying is that he doesn't recognize who we are talking about," I stated, but this seemed to have caused more anxiety in Bria. This I could tell by the agitated look on her face. She was about ready to make the man eat the paper she had in her hand. She was also damn near close to printing and hanging copies of a missing person's poster of her father.

The thing is, the copied image she had was so blurred, it was hard to make anything out. It was all she had of him. She was already fighting back her frustration, and to make matters worse, it had begun raining.

"Bria!" I shouted while trying to catch up with her. She was trudging behind the man attempting to escape her—her potential murder victim.

I took hold of her hand and spun her to face me. "Bria, he doesn't know."

"He must know something. He just needs to look closer."

It was heartbreaking. I was watching her fight back the tears all because of this failed trip to find her father. It was more than I could stomach, and it was all my fault.

First, there were government agencies. They just weren't helpful at all. There was no missing person's report at the police station on the name Bria had given. There was no file at the census either, and immigration—just forget about it. He was a ghost if he was ever here, and if he was, he sure wasn't a legal citizen, so finding him was impossible.

Then, we had to track down a man who we were told knew him. The so-called tip. But this guy was also hard to find. We'd spent two days on that alone, and when we'd finally found him, all that stood in front of us to be brutally interrogated was a scrawny, homeless, scared man who knew absolutely nothing. Bria was so blinded by disappointment t h a t she couldn't see past it.

"I understand your frustration but losing it now won't help anything." She tried freeing herself from me, but that made the unthinkable happen. Bringing her hand back to her side made the wet piece of paper tear. I stood paralyzed.
"Oh, my fucking god!" she shrieked. My hands hung loose, barely gripping her. "No…" she whimpered.

My heart sank, watching her pout like a child who had broken a favorite toy. I gravitated back to her and then pulled her near.
"He knew something," she whimpered into my neck.
"Just let it go, Bria," I murmured, trying to calm her.

"No, I won't let it go!" she snapped, aggressively wiggling free from me. "Need I remind you that we aren't here on vacation? That guy might be hiding the truth," she stated, her hand stretched out, pointing in the direction he ran off in.

She was heaving, breathing out of control. Her hand flew to her forehead then slid down, covering her eye and most of her face. She turned, giving me her back. She was not the kind to show weakness, and this was beating her.

126

She went to her knees, then to the floor.

I couldn't stand to see her like this. I'd gotten her excited about possibly finding her father here. I was the one who had given her hope only for her to be confronted by this reality.

There was an emotion building in me, and the sight of her slowly unraveling was just too much.

"Get up," I barked in anger. "Get up off this damn floor and let's go!" I went to her and began forcing her upwards.

"No, stop!" she yelled.

She started to fight back, and that was exactly what I needed from her. She was a fighter, and defeat wasn't going to have its way with her. Not on my watch.

"Just stop it!" she said, trying to escape my hold. "You want me to stop? Show me you got this because I know..." I trailed off, turning her to face me. My hands were grabbing firmly to her shoulders and my breathing deepened, struggling for control. I scanned her face. Her eyes were flooded with tears, and her nose flared a bit.

"...I know you are stronger than this. So whatever is going through you right now, I need you to beat it!" I gave her a quick shake on my last word. We stood there, pelted by raindrops. She dropped her head, and for a second, I thought she was going into it again. Instead, I heard her chuckle.

"Who would have thought..." she said.

I tilted my head to the side to get a better view of her face. "Thought what?"

"That I would need you." Her admittance shook me. I felt a warmth flowing through me. To feel needed by her was something I didn't even

127

know I wanted until this very moment. That caught me off guard. "You could've just asked. I could've told you that long ago," I said, attempting to ease up. She laughed.

"Okay, Mr. Cocky." She wiped at her face. I brought her into me, feeling her submit to my embrace. "Isn't this considered a conflict of interest?" "What?" I asked, not wanting to let go just yet. "You looking out for me," she murmured. I swallowed hard. *This is what it's supposed to be*, was the thought that ran through my mind. "I don't see it like that."

"How do you see it then?" she asked, pulling away. The rain had subsided, leaving us drenched. "Well, some people would see me allowing you to get soaked like this as me hoping nature does the job for me."

A laugh erupted from her. This made me beam. "Well, it's gonna take more than a cold to do that…pneumonia, maybe," she suggested. I laughed. "Come on, let's get you dried. I can feel you shivering now."

"Good idea."

We made our way to her hotel by taxi. The driver didn't seem too pleased about us stepping into his car sopping wet. I promised to give him something extra for his trouble after he'd dropped me to my hotel. He complied with the request.

I now stood at the bathroom faucet grooming myself while replaying the day in my head. She needed me today. A smile graced my face before quickly vanishing.

The lead I had gotten was pure bullshit—a wild goose chase. This would need rectifying by the source. That would have to wait until we got back, but for right now, I would get ready for our last night here.


Standing at the front desk of Bria's hotel, I asked the receptionist to ring her room. I stood, waiting for her to answer. She'd refused to stay in the same hotel as me, stating she only needed a place to sleep, so a pool like the one found where I was staying was considered unnecessary. But this was not where I'd pictured her checking into. The place was remarkably dingy and overrun with insects everywhere. I stood frozen watching a colony of ants dismember a cockroach near a trash can. I wondered what the rooms were like.

I'd expected a flat-out "no" when I proposed we have dinner a few hours ago on the phone but was pleased when she responded with a "yes," which shocked me. She hadn't given me a hard time of which I was prepared to debate the pros of getting a healthy meal in at least once since arriving here. We'd been hitting every food truck, and I was beginning to think I was the only one feeling the effects of excessive junk food binging. My body was going to rejoice having tasted a salad tonight.

"She said to come to her room," the receptionist conveyed, then gave me her room number. I wondered if Bria had decided to bail on my dinner invitation.

I shoved at my blazer sleeves and headed to her room. The hall was long but narrow and a light flickered, warning of a faulty connection. Who had recommended she stay here and why didn't she just pack up and leave after first entering the place? Or worse yet, smelling it! It was like they used an old mop and hoped bleach was all that was needed to mask the overpowering smell of heated garbage. The air conditioning was also not working properly. I'd reached her room and gave the door a good knock. I'd concluded that I would contain myself and not pass half the evening insisting she not spend her last night here.

The door opened and standing on the other side of it still fiddling with her earrings was Bria. My gaze drank her in. She wore a turtle-necked, all-white jumper pantsuit having some sort of a cape-like feature connecting to the back as shoulder covering. The outfit highlighted her curves but not in a promiscuous way. Her hair of defined kinky curls was more playful than usual yet tamed in an open-bundle ponytail. Lips subtly glossed. Eyelids dusted with little diamonds. She was simply exquisite and took my breath away.

She surely didn't belong here. It took me a few moments before realizing I was staring and hadn't greeted her correctly.

"Good night," I finally articulated, watching as she now did a hop on one leg while struggling to place her second pump. "You needed me?" She grabbed hold of me for support.

Instinctively, I held her hand resting on my shoulder. "Don't worry, let's go."

Purse in hand, she pulled her hotel door shut, making sure it was locked before strutting past me in the direction of the elevator. Without a word, I followed suit. *I might just not say anything that would cause conflict. I would enjoy tonight*, I thought.

## Bria

The glow of the day was fading, reminding me that it would soon be the moon's turn to light our paths. I could really do with a drink after the way it began. Sitting in a taxi, Trevor seemed to have lost his words, yet at the corner of my eye, I caught him smiling to himself a couple of times. I wondered what that was about. Since he knew the place and could communicate better than I could, I had little trouble doubting he would have a good restaurant in mind. He had astounded me hearing him speak the native language as though it was his mother tongue. I wondered what other surprises he had in store for me. He'd made it through the weekend without getting on my nerves. He was very cautious not to make things seem as though he was monitoring me. He must have figured I knew that was what he was assigned to do since he was constantly popping up where I was.

"Where are we?" I asked, stepping out of the taxi. "La Puerta del Conde. You will like it here," Trevor stated while stepping out of the cab. He then pushed the door shut.

"Oh, nice."

He was an asset to have around, I'd admit. My get-out-of-trouble card or key that opened doors that would normally be double- bolted locked. Far from home, he had proven yet again his value. I could breathe easier. Why did I think traveling alone with basic knowledge of the country and close to no Spanish in my vocabulary would be a good idea?

Anyway, I was here with him, my multilingual guide. I must say, he was a very interesting character. I felt relaxed and decided to capture the moment. I withdrew a disposable camera from my purse and started snapping.

"Do you always have a camera on you?" he asked, bringing me back to this reality.

"Most of the time, yes. But this I bought in the electronic store around the corner from my hotel." "Have you ever taken pictures of me when I wasn't looking?"

I gazed at him and noticed him lick his lips and swallow, doing his best to come across as if it didn't matter to him. I'd taken many shots of him, more than I cared to admit. I allowed the question to go unanswered before taking aim at a woman stepping out of a bookstore.

"So, what do you think about the place?" Trevor asked, walking next to me in a tee and blazer with jeans and white sneakers. I observed that he went for a very relaxed look, which was something I'd never seen him do.

"It's nice. The history behind it intrigues me. I wish I could see more," I said, taking a few more shots of my surroundings.

"Ah, she smiles," he stopped to say. I didn't realize that I was. "And it's beautiful."

I looked away and tucked my lips into my mouth, trying to force a stop to the blush breaking across my face. It was crazy to think that he'd achieved that. "The people could be a little more understanding," I said, using that thought to change my mood. My brows dropped thinking on the woman who just meant she wasn't going to waste time translating anything for me. I just knew she spoke English.

"Trust me. Some really do try to assist."

The walk in the town square was soothing. The statues on the opposite side of the street at the beginning of our stroll held my interest. I wanted to know the story there. I would certainly be back to examine them. I drew a breath. I just loved it. From the mimicked painting displayed on both sides of the street by different vendors, to the speeding bikers with two or even three passengers zooming by and honking their horns as if theirs was the only right of way that mattered.

It was crazy how what seemed like chaos to me was considered normal to those living here.

We walked through an area where most tourists gathered under the shade of trees. In silence, I admired the simplicity of it all. How it was humbling to see a man taking pride in shining another man's sneaker of all things. A smooth, warm melody floated from a musician's saxophone as he competed with another group a few steps down busy playing their accordions. The pigeons gathered at certain places on the square, waiting to be fed with the leftovers of those nibbling and enjoying a bite to eat with friends or loved ones warranted a photo.

Without warning, I was grabbed by the wrist and hauled into Trevor's arms right before a motorcyclist zoomed by inches from my body, my cape swooshing forward with the gust of wind as he did.

Tense and not wanting to part with the beauty of all I was taking in, I closed my eyes and then rested on his chest. My senses heightened. I stood listening to the evident quickened beating of his heart. I slowly opened my eyes, took a step back, then looked up to find him intently searching my face—his lips slightly parted, having questions to ask. Completely focused on him, I saw that his eyes had a tint of blue around the pupils, indicating to me that he was wearing lenses. I should've already concluded this, but never took the time to notice until now.

"I'm okay," I finally said, my chest heaving a bit. "You sure?" "Yes," I smiled, taking a moment to inhale his scent.
*Why did I just do that?*

I took another step back, swallowed hard while adjusting my stance, and straightened up.
As if hearing a whistle blow, he blinked and released me. "We're here. Let's go in, shall we?"


"I'm sorry this was a dead lead. I didn't mean to waste your time." "That's okay, at least I got to see a piece of Santo Domingo." My eyes briefly wandered away from my companion sitting across the table just to survey my surroundings. I was taken by his intense look when they returned to him. "What's wrong?" I queried, wondering if he was still on the motorbike thing.

He took a deep breath and exhaled through his mouth before saying, "Nothing."
His frown deepened.

"What? Just say it!" I was getting tense. He hesitated before speaking. "Ah," he groaned, passing both hands over his face before saying, "is it bad that I want you to be a little weak sometimes so I can step in and comfort you?" "Huh? Yes, it is," I said soberly.

I then remembered how it felt just moments ago, having found myself in his strong, firm arms. I relaxed and then allowed a smile to cross my face, which caused him to chuckle lightly. Once again, my eyes broke from his and started to wander around the

room. Dimly lit, yet full of life with expressive paintings. The restaurant set in an old-time building made of bricks was charming, to say the very least. Although the music was at a reasonable level, couples leaned into each other as though not able to hear one another. It was cute, watching as a woman encouraged her male companion with a smile, which he in turn reciprocated by lightly stroking her arm. Unconsciously, I passed my hands over my arms, remembering what that once felt like.

"Are you cold?" Trevor inquired. My attention raced back to him. His brows were dipped, indicating concern.

"No," I said before clearing my throat and fixing my slouched posture. I was a bit too relaxed, and Trevor's lingering gaze, although warming, sent a shiver of excitement through me, raising every hair on my body. I took another sip of my wine. I needed to redirect that energy with something that excited me in a different way—my kids.

"So, the 'Build a Child a Home Project' was a complete success. Did I tell you?" "Yes, you did." His voice was warm and unexpectedly arousing. I needed to try harder. "Those kids, they really enjoyed and are proud of being a part of something that will not only help them but others as well." "They should

135

be. They're amazing to be around." He took a sip of his wine. "You were also amazing to watch in action. That project showed me a different side of you." His eyes narrowed, and it made me nervous. What was he thinking? What side? And did he like it?

"Yeah, and what side was that? That I can be an even bigger bitch with power?" I chuckled, waiting for some sign that he was in agreement with the statement. He didn't crack a smile.

"That your passion takes hold of you like nothing else can. Once you love, there is nothing standing in your way of giving it your all." He took a sip of his wine before he continued. "That you devote yourself to that thing which you love. I'm jealous."

"Why?" I asked, totally entranced, his words doing so much to me. Had he never found a cause worthy of fighting for? "Because I want that too." "Want—" I was rightfully interrupted by the waiter bringing our meal. God knew I would have drawn something out of him that I probably wasn't ready for.

Trevor had ordered a steak while I settled on chicken breast with a mushroom sauce. The food looked delicious and so enticing, yet neither of us went for our cutlery. He was waiting for me to finish my line of questioning. I refocused and asked, "Why are you jealous?"
It's like the room fell completely still as I waited on his answer. Then, all of a sudden, he licked his lips and went for his knife and fork. He started cutting his steak. "Because finding something or someone you love that loves you back is rare," he said.

136

Sensing he wasn't quite finished, I didn't interject. "Because seeing you love something and knowing you can easily lose hours in it makes me believe in time well spent." He took a fork full of meat and started chewing vigorously before swallowing. "And because seeing how intense you get when you're focused on something makes me curious about experiencing that focus." His eyes were now on me, holding me in a cobra-like trance.

His last point brought a follow-up question to mind, but I shushed myself from asking it. I fluttered my eyelids and decided to dodge whatever he was setting me up for. "You'll find something that does it for you. Just be open to new things," I said, picking up my fork and knife. I then sliced through a stem of broccoli. "I just hope you don't bow under pressure and give up." He leaned in and sat his elbow on the table. He placed a finger to his lower lip. "I'm sure you see I don't give up on things that have my full attention."

My fork stopped close to my parted lips. The undertone of that sentence had me speechless.

"Trevor," I started, dropping my fork from my mouth. I took a quick pause and looked at my dish, thinking of something to switch to. "How did you get information on my dad possibly being here?" I stuck the broccoli into my mouth and waited on him to respond. He sat back, released a low chuckle, raised his eyebrows, took another sip of wine, and then sobered.

"You think you're the only one who has the resources and means to confidential intel? I had someone snoop a bit. I must say, information on you is very hard to find. You've done well at hiding what you don't want people to know about you." I smiled. Before, he'd only intrigued me to the point of thinking he was just a guard dog for Curtis. But now, my curiosity was in full bloom. I was definitely going to do some more digging on him.

"Now, there is something that has been on my mind." "What is it?"

"The woman at the party. Is she your lady?" He smiled and chose to answer with a question of his own. "What do you think?"

"I think the 'look at me, look at me, I'm pretty' type of woman suits you. But it doesn't matter what I think," I dared saying.

"Are you saying 'shallow' is what you think I'm into?" "No, more like you prefer not to chase too hard." "I actually prefer that over 'easy.'" "So you've never slept with her?" He went quiet, and I took that as a definite yes.

"Exactly my point."

"And what about you? Is there someone waiting for you to get back?"

"Most men find me difficult."

"They're either right or they aren't worth it. Their effort alone will determine that."

I looked at him and found his intent gaze on me, which made me look away. Might have been the wine or the setting that had him speaking earnestly, but I knew better than to continue along this path and get too relaxed with him. I still had to keep my guard up with Mr. Mathews. The rest of the evening was light. He'd even cajoled me into dancing with him. Oh, he was smooth and held his own, I must say.

# Trevor

I'd shocked myself tonight with my burst of boldness. Must have been the wine. She was so interesting to observe in different settings. When

comfortable, she would take the time to admire little details most people would see as insignificant. If overwhelmed, her intensity would be her stumbling block, allowing her frustration and insecurities to lead her emotions.

A mischievous grin raced across my face remembering what had transpired at the airport. If that lady only knew what I'd saved her from.

"I didn't take long, did I?" Bria said, taking her seat at the table. She had excused herself to go to the restroom. We were just about ready to end the night, which I was not too pleased about.

"No, not at all."

She was digging around in her purse. My eyes went up to her face, and I couldn't help but stop at her lips. She looked as if she had just reapplied her lipstick. *Am I expected to kiss her tonight?* was the thought that quickened my heartbeat.

I had gotten away with a dance and might have been feeling a bit too invincible. I would have better luck winning the lottery than walking away alive and unscathed from kissing her. But I would chance it. "How much do I owe you for my order?"

The question threw me. *Why would she even ask that?* I wondered, watching her pull money from her purse. "How much?" She looked at me.

"Don't insult me," I said harshly, not able to hide my sudden anger on what she was asking.

"Insult you? There is nothing wrong with

the question."

Honestly, her independence was adorable at times but in this instant, totally fucking annoying.
"I already took care of it. It was my treat. I asked you out." "Yes, but it wasn't a date."

What part of it wasn't? "Look, put your money away. It's been paid for, and I don't want to hear another word on it." "You don't want to hear another word on it." Her eyebrows raised and then dropped lower than I was prepared for.

"You listen to me. I am not the type of woman who grovels at your feet. I won't fetch your slippers while you retire into the study for a smoke. So you will not speak to me as though you are my superior," she stated.

"I didn't mean it like that," I said, feeling like I was about to be ripped to bits by a puma.

"Take me back to my hotel. Please!" she said, rising to her feet. What could I do but stand and allow her to lead us out of the restaurant?


## Bria

Was he serious? Goodness, men could be so full of themselves. I headed into the hotel and made a dash for my room in case he was following me. Plus, these pumps were killing me from all that damn walking and dancing. Thought he was Eddie Torres with his dance moves. Ha!

I stuck my key into the slot and whipped the door open. I swatted the light switch, and to no surprise, found it flickering mercilessly. This hotel was the worst. They so oversold it on the internet. And who exactly gave it a four-star rating? I mean, what room had they stayed in, and in which dimension?

Luckily, it was my last night here. I'd verbally committed to it beforehand in front of Trevor. He would have been smug if I had given in and switched. Alarmed by an obvious hand being placed over my mouth, my body stiffened. I was locked in place when the intruder looped his other hand around me. I started jumping, allowing my weight to take him with me to the floor. My muzzled cries did nothing to deter his actions. I swung my head back, landing a good shot on him based on his reaction of loosening his grip around me. His hand flew from my lips, giving me an opening to scream before being silenced again.

It seemed like an eternity before someone else had entered the room, yanking my assailant off of me. I heard a thud on the floor while I scrambled to the head of the bed, folding myself into a tight ball. There was a tussle before a darkened silhouette dashed through the door.

A hand latched on to me, scaring me. Trevor's voice then rang out. "Bria, it's me, Trevor. Are you okay?" His breathing was rushed.

My eyes shut, holding back the fear brought on by what had just happened. I clung to him, then found myself in his arms.

"Come on," he said, helping me to my feet and putting me on the edge of the bed. He quickly began collecting my things, going through the bathroom like a hurricane scooping up my belongings. My breathing intensified as I focused in on the shiny dagger-like shape next to my feet. I closed my eyes, finding flashes of the blade in action flickering

141

through my head. "Let's go!" Trevor said, taking my hand and pulling me to my weakened legs. Before long, we were out the door, not bothering to close it.

# Chapter 9
# **Setup**
**Bria**

He'd mentioned not being content leaving things how they ended at the restaurant, thus making his way to my room. I was more than relieved that he did. Trevor wanted me to make a report at the police station, but noticing that there weren't any cameras at the hotel and not being able to identify the intruder made me less convinced I should do that. I didn't want to spend the rest of my evening being translated.

I found myself in Trevor's hotel, standing next to him at the receptionist's desk. He intended to request a room change that would accommodate us both. He was handed a room keycard, and we made our way up in the elevator. We both got ready for bed, saying little, and slept fitfully through the night.

"So, did he make a move on you that night?" "Did you hear any other part of my story?" I said, exhausted with Mich. "And no, he was a perfect gentleman," I said, wondering why I had even bothered saying anything. Kayla was missing in action yet again. But on this day, her excuse was just plain unacceptable. I had called for a girl's get-together to bring them up to speed with what I was being confronted with, and I still had to apologize to Mich.

I had to admit, although we had our differences and were constantly getting on each other's nerves, she stuck with me. No matter how rude I was. And with Kayla barely making an appearance these days, Mich was turning out to be my most reliable friend. Maybe I was too harsh on Kayla. She probably wouldn't be able to handle things. Especially with the break-in she experienced months ago. Just because she wasn't speaking of it didn't mean it wasn't on her mind. It was frustrating having their roles in my life mixed up. I found myself hanging up the phone in Kayla's ear after hearing she wasn't going to make it. I felt bad doing so after the fact.

Mich, Jamila and I sat having breakfast in the lounging area at our favorite beach spot Dreams over on the French half of the island. It was extremely scenic there and looking out across the water usually brought calm to my soul—but it didn't today.

Someone had tried hurting me and left me paralyzed in fear that night. I felt it had something to do with what I was working on here, and I was going to get to the bottom of it. "I have a really bad feeling about this," Jamila voiced. "I mean, someone doesn't want you snooping around, and they knew you were leaving the island and had time enough to set a hit out on you."

"Or this could all be a coincidence. Maybe he was just trying to rob you?" Mich injected.

"Yet took nothing," Jamila replied.
We sat there in silence and welcomed the presence of the waiter as he brought us our meals. "So you think it's Curtis?" Jamila questioned.

I nodded. "Then none of us are safe. He might have a hit out on all of us." Jamila's paranoia was kicking in, and her facial expression told of a pending anxiety attack. I frowned.

"Okay, just stop it! Rest assured, no one is looking to kill you," I said, a bit agitated yet worried that it was possible and I would be to blame if anything happened to them.

"Girls," I exhaled, taking a moment to calm myself. "I'm sure it doesn't run that deep."

"Yeah, but what if it does?" Mich chimed in. "Then..." I shrugged my shoulders, not knowing what to say. Trouble seemed to be following me these days, and the thought did cross my mind how everyone around me might be at risk. But that was just a thought. I never considered it being a reality. My friends may have had valid reasons for their concern.

"What is that?" Jamila asked, pointing. I was glad for the change of topic. I turned my head, and Mich had just placed her bag on the table and was going through it. All eyes fell on the brand of the bag. "Now, I know there is no way you would go splurging on a bag like that with your nurse's salary," I commented with a frown. Mich kept quiet and continued shuffling through it. She then peered up from behind her shades and added a smack with her tongue. "An early Christmas present from your secret boo." Jamila's brows lifted, her lips pushed outward on her last word. "What can I say, I'm well taken care of. And this isn't from mister man."

I exhaled louder than I intended, and all eyes fell on me, but it should've been expected. I mean, she went from one guy to the next. I didn't even know she had ended things, yet she had already hooked her another one. She just wouldn't give herself time to recover and heal. Being single was unimaginable in her eyes. She couldn't do it long enough to find out how strong she was without a man. I didn't recognize this new Mich.

"I'm not really talking to him since the trip," she said, watching as if daring me to respond. "This one takes care of me just the same." "You find men who are highly motivated to take care of you. Wish I could." I just listened. It seemed as though neither of them understood the control being imposed through monetary assistance. "Hey, who am I to deny him the satisfaction of being a provider. If I don't take his money, I'm sure someone else gladly will."
This was just pure rubbish, and that wasn't even the worst part. Jamila was eating it up.

"I hope this one brings a bit more to the table than just a bag," I remarked with clear intentions of being heard.

"What was that?" Mich shot me a look. "I can't help it if men are drawn to me," Mich said, taking out her lipstick.

"Yes, drawn to you is one thing, but what about other things or having a deeper connection? It can't only be physical, Michelle," I retorted.

"Ladies, not today and not here," Jamila said, wide- eyed with her hands up, signaling to us to keep it down.

"What are you saying? Other things like what?" Mich's words oozed with attitude, disregarding Jamila's call for peace.
" Compatibility," I said, then exhaled through my nose. She released a gust of air. "What now? That can't be your answer for everything surrounding you not having a man," Mich stated, rolling her eyes before continuing to apply her

146

lipstick.

It was an obvious jab.

"Unlike some people, who settle for just material things," I stated, jabbing back, "I need someone who gives as much energy as he takes from me."

"He does that," Mich said smugly. "And more." I shook my head and continued.

"Not just in bed but in other areas of life," I shot back with a straight face.

"Hm-huh."

"Someone strong enough to pull me out of my own world just long enough to experience life as it happens," I said with my eyes closed. "Someone who understands how my insecurities as a woman have nothing to do with him."

"Like a *Waiting to Exhale* kinda moment," Jamila added. "You need a thump," Mich said. I fluttered my eyes open. Jamila's nod in agreement to what she said surprised me.

"You expect too much from men these days," Jamila stated.

"Dat dere...'" Mich said in her best Jamaican accent while pointing at me, "don't exist." I turned to Jamila hoping to find solace or empathy but found nothing of the sort. "She's right. Most guys give what they can physically because emotionally, they are unavailable," Jamila added. "Yeah, and I want to capture that which is unattainable or else he can stay where he is."

"I think I prefer stuck-up Bria over sentimental Bria any day," Mich murmured under her breath. I fidgeted, shocked at how silly I was being. I too had to admit that guys would quickly turn to the shallow means of expressing themselves through gift-giving and have their girl boast on what their man bought them than be caught expressing their true feelings. Sadly, that was a thing of the past. Nowadays, men barely understood the word 'affection'. Some were too busy loving themselves and illustrating peacock behavior instead of bringing something of actual value to the table. They were too busy trying to impress. They clearly had no idea what women wanted, and most of the time, they were completely unaware that real women weren't bothered with material things. Men were totally delusional in thinking we were keeping tabs on what they had instead of working on ourselves, or worst yet, that we weren't able to function in a man's world and give the same results or better than they could. This was sheer sexism.

The "New Woman," which was considered a feminist ideal, had a profound influence on the way women now functioned in this society. It was such a hard pill to swallow back then in the late nineteenth century when it all started. To this day, it is still a challenge for some men of high stature, or even less prominent ones, to accept our call for equal rights and our wish to not be subjected to double standards.

Women like Mich and even Jamila with her "just roll with it" attitude weren't doing anything to help combat the ideology that allowed men to think that they were better and that we always needed to run to them for support. They were what was wrong with the world today.

I sighed inwardly. This battle was not to be fought against these two. They were already

148

conditioned. I had to consider the fact that my way of seeing things could also be obscured. Nevertheless, there would be no winning this argument or even coming to an impasse. I took the final gulp of my orange juice and called for the check.


I needed a break or a distraction. Something that would take my mind off the fact that someone wanted me gone. Passing an hour or two at Pineapple Pete made an invitation from Jerome seem quite appealing. But after spending most of the night looking over my shoulders while being out with him, I knew that I would never rest again if I didn't get to the bottom of things.

"Your mind was so far tonight." He exhaled. "If I could only get to occupy half of the space, I would be satisfied." He cupped my face in his hands, forcing me to look at him.

"I know, it's just that… things are happening that I have no control over, and it scares me," I admitted. I then rested my hands on his arm. I was attempting to free myself. He willfully ignored the effort.

"Tell me what they are. Let me help."

"I can't," I said, pulling back, setting myself free. "I appreciate the offer though," I said, pulling out my keys while heading to the door. Standing on my landing, I felt a warmth on my neck. I dared to turn and found him leaned into me.

"We both know you would never accept my help, but maybe I can help you in another way," he whispered. His breath grazed my lips. He smelled of liquor. He continued to lean in. My eyes instinctively closed. My lips broke.

Gently, he rested his forehead against mine, nudging my head back. This was his signature move before going in for a kiss. My heart started racing. To be loved by this man again would open the door to so much I wasn't sure I had the energy to give. Yet, it was easy falling into old habits where he was concerned. Submitting to him would have me giving myself u p entirely. I was sure of it.

"I've missed you, Bri Bri." His hands gently gripped the sides of my neck. "Don't lie to me." I exhaled and pushed at the center of his chest. I shook my head, wondering if he knew whom he was feeding that line to. "Why would I lie to you?" He appeared agitated. "You're such an asshole," I said, going for the doorknob.

His hand gripped mine as I attempted to unlock the door. I redirected my gaze, which I was sure was his intended plan. "That's why I don't like telling you things. You always think I'm fuckin' with you."

"Not 'think,' I know," I said dryly.
He sucked his teeth. "I can assure you, there is only one way I want to mess with you."

His lips brushed mine, and my body quaked. I released a shallow breath and again shut my eyes. I stood waiting for him to touch me, but he didn't. I could only imagine what reaction that would've drawn from me. I need not open my eyes. I just knew he was observing me. It was part of his allure. The wait was making me want to submit to his every whim. He licked my top lip, and right then, I knew it was all over for me. I'd gone without a taste for too long. I went to my toes and leaned forward eagerly in search of his lips. I grabbed hold of his face, ready to take him. "Bria." Hearing my name called by a young, feminine voice shook me back to my senses. I drew back.

## Trevor

It had been days since I'd seen Bria up close and personal—but that didn't mean I wasn't keeping tabs on her.

The night in Santo Domingo had shaken me— thinking on what could've occurred if I hadn't swallowed my pride and gone behind her to apologize for being an ass. I should've just let her pay for the damn check. She would've probably ended up in my bed that night. But what kind of man would I be if I had? Aside from that, what had happened had me wondering if the lead that I had gotten concerning her father's whereabouts was solely to draw her out alone so she would be vulnerable—in another country, no less. It was clearly a set-up. Whoever was behind this had the money and the manpower to execute.

A chill ran down my spine. Bria was getting close to something. *Was she right about Mr. Bryson? What has she gotten herself into?* I thought, brushing a hand across my weary face.

I sat waiting in my car a few spaces down from her apartment, just watching. I'd reluctantly witnessed some of the exchange between her and her male friend. He must have been the boyfriend

151

mentioned in her file. I welcomed the interruption. I mean, who the fuck did that guy think he was, trying to kiss her? Why had it surprised me so much that someone else would find her worth engaging? She was difficult beyond a doubt, her tongue sharp—all the reasons why I wanted to silence it with a kiss myself. But now I wondered how I stacked up next to this guy. I blew a breath. How far was I trailing behind him?

I was surprised by a knock on my car window. It was someone from the neighborhood surveillance team—I was informed after rolling down my window a bit. He had blocked my view, which jolted me out of my heart-racing trance watching this guy move in on Bria. *These things actually worked?* I thought to myself, a bit irritated by the intrusion. However, I was then relieved, seeing Bria's date leave. Thought he was sleeping over, did he? Not a chance.

Not completely at ease with the explanation of who I was and why I was there, the surveyor then

requested a picture of me and my ID before moving along. *Tap-tap* sounded on my window moments after he left. I turned sharply and found two of the teenage girls from the foster home next door scrutinizing me. One smiling, the other, Mariska, who just hated me—this I gathered from my last uninvited visit. She stood glaring at me. Weren't they supposed to be in for the night?
I rolled the window down.
"Yes," I said as if nothing was wrong with the scene. "We told her you were out here," Mariska informed. "Oh," I said, now feeling like a stalker.
"Yeah, like for an hour now."

"Really." *You just had to add that, right?*

"She told us to tell you to come in," the other young lady said before both of them walked off. So, she knew I was out here. *Damn it!*

I took a moment, then quickly unbuckled my seatbelt, swung the door open, slammed it shut, and then locked it with the press of a button. With my head held high, I made the walk up to her apartment. "So what if she knew I was out here? I was just looking out for her," I mumbled under my breath. There was absolutely nothing shameful about me checking in on her.

I knocked on her door.

"It's open," she bellowed. My gut cringed.

I wasn't ready for this. She was sure to go in on me for trailing her and not being inconspicuous enough not to get caught. Carefully, I turned the knob. I pushed the door open and entered. She was nowhere in sight. The room was submerged in light, but I felt like I was stepping into what would soon become a crime scene. "I'm in," I said with caution. She rounded a bend and didn't come any closer. Her sober expression told me I'd better speak the truth.

"I see," she said, hands folded. "You're openly spying on me now." "I wasn't..." I cleared my throat after hearing my voice break. "I wasn't spying." "Sure," she said, making her way past me. I didn't move. I listened to her lock the door and waited for her to reenter the space I was occupying. She went past me into her kitchen. "And?"

"And what?" I dared to ask.

"Did you see anything worth reporting?"

I had to stop the anger building within me

153

from recalling the images replaying in my head of her with another man.

"Nope."

She came back with two bottles of beer. She handed me one. I then followed her over to the couch. She sat and patted the space next to her, beckoning me to sit. She rubbed at her eyes. "Must have been a day," I said, watching her as she freed her hair. I quickly fluttered my eyelids to regain focus.

"Oh, it was something," she said, taking a sip.

"I'd bet." Again in my feelings, I took a slug of my drink.

"How have you been? What have you been up to?" she asked. She nestled her hand in her hair. It was then captured by the curls. My palms itched, wanting to join in on the springy frenzy. "Well," I began, eyes still absorbed by her curls. "I went about my business for today, picked up my laundry from the dry cleaners, and ate a home-cooked meal, which I made myself."

"Hm-huh. You found time to cook?" she asked, amazed. I smiled.

"Let me finish." No words were spoken. She took a sip of her beer and then threw her hands up in surrender. "And then... I was caught stalking. That was my day," I said, rushing things off. "Really. What did your 'stalkee' do?"

"She invited me in for a drink."

"Interesting. At least you didn't see her lace it with poison," she said, slapping me twice on my knee before rising to her feet. I watched her bunch her hair back into a ponytail before leaving the room again. I wondered about my beer before smiling and taking another gulp. She rounded the corner with a bowl of nachos covered with cheese. She then placed the bowl on the center table before crashing into the couch again.

She flicked on the T.V. A cartoon popped up on the screen, and I could not help but smile, knowing that Aniah had full control of what was being viewed. "Have you thought about what happened in Santo Domingo? I mean, what made them come for me there? It can't just be a coincidence." I stared at her. She didn't flinch. Her eyes never left the television screen. I took a moment to relive what had happened. My heart weighed heavy in my chest.

"Why do you think... they came?" she asked again, this time, turning and directing her attention to me. I fell into her worried eyes.

"I don't know. I can't imagine why someone would want to hurt you."

She chuckled. "I can think of a few reasons." She went to her feet. My gaze followed her. A thought crossed my mind, and I decided to voice it.

"Maybe you should hold off. Someone doesn't appreciate you digging," I said uneasily. She looked at me, and from the crinkles on her forehead, I suspected she thought I should have known her by now. She wasn't going to stop anything.

"I think I'm getting close to the truth."

"Bria," I started. The deepened scowl on her face halted me, as if knowing what I was going to say. She didn't seem too pleased.

"And then what, hide? No," she answered my unspoken request. I stood and headed over to her. "They are not going to stop," I said, standing directly

155

in front of her, blocking her path.

"Good, and then I'll have more reasons to dig." She pushed past me. I followed her.

"Are you even listening to me?"

"Not really." Her voice was pitching at the end. I exhaled. "This is serious..." I was getting agitated by how casually she was going about it.

Phone in hand, she asked at her bar table, "Should I order Chinese?"

"Bria—"

"You're right! Pizza will be better," she said, heading over to her fridge. She then took the flyer of a pizza menu from where it hung under a magnet.

"Bria! Someone wants you dead!" My words landed an imaginary blow that caused her to gasp. Her eyelids fluttered. The place felt drafty.

Phone cradled at the center of her chest, she closed her eyes. I went to her and held her. She was noticeably scared, I gathered from her trembling torso in my arms. She started whimpering. The laughter of a sitcom playing on the television screen didn't match up to our reality.

"I know. I saw the knife on the floor. He was gonna kill me," she said, her voice barely audible at the end. An unsettling feeling took me.

"I promise, I won't let anyone hurt you on my watch." I held her until she had settled herself and pulled away. I immediately missed her warmth. "Okay. I'm good," she said, not giving me eye contact. She then began wiping her tears from my shirt.

"Sure?"

"Yep."

She looked up. An attempt at reassuring me that she

156

was okay, I guess. "I'm starting to make leaning on you a habit."

"I'm starting to reconsider my choice of shirts when coming near you," I said jokingly. She released a giggle and then patted me on my chest, giving me a little shove on the last. I stepped back, retracting from her personal space.
"Oh, there is something I wanted to show you. Come with me."
She led the way down the corridor and opened a door, switching on a light upon entry that illuminated the room red.
"Okay," I said, flabbergasted. "What?"
"I didn't think people still did things like this."
I was amazed by how she'd turned what I figured was to be a bedroom space into a darkroom for developing the film. These days, everything was digital. This was unique. A smile broke across my face. She caught it. "What now?"
"Nothing, it's just not what I expected. I thought I would find some man imprisoned, hoping for freedom," I joked. She chuckled while shaking her head.
What else did I not know about a woman I was studying for months now? She called me over to one of the baths she was soaking the film in. With focused precision, she took film paper out and hung it up to dry. Her movement was careful. I watched her, observing the subtle expanding of her chest as she took soft breaths, careful not to stir and distort anything. She then pulled out a microscope.
"Come look at this." She took down one of the pictures that was dried. I floated over to her.

157

"While taking pictures in Santo Domingo, someone kept popping up. Him." She pointed at the picture of a man sitting at a bar, then moved over to another frame. "Here he is again." The man w a s now at another location, gazing in the direction of the camera.

"Is it pure coincidence?" I hoped.

"I thought so, but then…" she said, heading over and picking up a set of pictures. "Here he is on the yacht." It was no coincidence. We were indeed being watched and followed.

"Do you think he was in my room that night?" Intently, she looked at me. I nodded at her question.
"I'm telling you, only Curtis would have reason to hire a hit on me. He doesn't agree with the whole freedom of speech. And me constantly putting him in the spotlight…"

I stood in silence, listening to her. Everything was undeniably pointing toward the man I called my boss. He'd done some questionable things lately, but I didn't think he would resort to killing those that opposed him. And Bria, there was no way in hell I would let him hurt her. Me spying on her for him was done and over with. I would be handing in my resignation as of tomorrow, right after I'd confronted him.

"I need you to do something for me," she said. Her voice was trembling as she tried to control her breathing.

"What?" I said, a bit tense. That gave her the wrong impression.

"You're upset with me because your boss

158

might be behind my attack?" Her eyes scanned the room, seemingly suspicious of me now and quite possibly looking for a means of defending herself if needed. "No, that's not... I want to get to the bottom of this too." That didn't assure her.

"So you can prove him innocent. God!" She walked over to the table. Her hands were bracing the rest of her as she looked into the distance. I found myself next to her.

"No, Bria. Just like you, I want to know why."

I'd been somewhat of a shadow these last few months, so it must have crossed her mind how I might have had some part in all this. She was struggling to trust me. "Tell me what you need me to do," I stated, determined to prove myself.

I observed her as she softened a bit.

"I need you to check his computer. There must be something there that connects him to Santo. You have to play things cool—so he doesn't suspect." Her plan was clear. I was now a double agent. Crazy. My years of studying were preparing me to go defective. I had some issues with this, but now was not the time to voice that.

"Okay, I'll do it," I said, swallowing hard. "Good."

She continued to develop the other frames. Soaking them and then hanging them. I began to settle, watching how each picture told a story that came to life whether muted or with explicit sound. "It's different in here, I know." "How do you mean?" I asked, wondering if her other talents involved telepathy. She smiled.

"How even though we were there, just by watching these pictures, we can make our own stories and change the ending." I grinned; she had a way with words. "Yeah, that."

She'd been able to capture beauty on paper the way a painter would. "That's why I enjoy writing as well." She released a breath. "Anyway, it's getting late, and I'm sure you've had a full day of spying on me."

"I see we're back at that again."

"Yes." She smirked. "I just can't believe you did it."

"I only did that because... I thought it would serve a purpose."

"Hm-huh." Her lower lip folded in. She then held it there by biting into it. My eyes shifted quickly to her expanding chest as she took breaths. My craving was starting to act up, and by the edginess I was feeling, I knew there was a great chance of me getting addicted to her. *Focus, Trevor.*

"And so tell me, did you really ever see anything worth reporting? I'm asking again."

"I did." But did I dare to say what I'd seen? Or how tonight might have brought out a few uncertainties in me?

"Tell me then."

I paused, thinking about how this was my opportunity to find out just how much of a threat the guy this evening was.

"I saw how very devoted you are to what you do," I said, treading carefully. "And that you care immensely for the people around you, and..." I hesitated, pondering how she would take the rest. *To hell with it!* "I saw how people gravitate to you, wanting to love you."

I felt warm inside just thinking about our last encounter, and then the thought of her with someone

160

else also flooded my mind, making me a bit agitated. She wasn't mine, yet I felt territorial. No one had the right to her but me. "I'm sure there is no gravitational pull to me," she said lightly.

"Bria, a guy isn't going to take the risk of getting rejected by leaning into you to kiss you if he doesn't have feelings for you." My jaw clenched.

I'd verbally expressed my jealousy and now stood waiting on her to dismiss it or challenge what I'd witnessed on her porch. "You did, that New Year's morning, and you didn't even care to know my name," she responded. I flinched from the blow her words dealt me.

"That's different."

"No, it isn't."

I exhaled. "My intentions were different then." I started looking dead into her eyes, finally spilling my truth on that evening. We stood in silence. My heart was galloping like a racehorse.

It was wrong for me to be here. Wrong for me to think of her lips pressed against mine. Yet, I couldn't help myself. I stood fascinated, wanting to play with the cluster of her hair that never made it into the bunch. The light buzz of alcohol in my system and the red light basking on her face all aided in placing me in a trance. My eyes walked the length of her, and my hands wanted to do the same.

She made a move to leave, and I found myself grabbing hold of her arm. Stunned,

I took a breath to catch myself before going in search of her eyes again. Our gazes connected, and I slowly began to pull her in. This was not the moment to rush things. But there was a hunger inside of me that needed to be fed that only wanted her.

I was drawing her to me. I placed her hand on my chest. My fingers played with her earlobe and then her hair, all the while she never took her eyes off me. She stepped closer, and I took the time to take in the slight hint of vanilla emerging from her pores. I ran a finger down her cheekbone and felt my body react with desire from observing her gasp at my touch. I wet my lips and swallowed, a grin twitched on my face. I was getting excited by her subtle responses to me.

I was stumped when she held and stopped my fingers from sliding down her neck. This couldn't be over. I'd barely started. My nerves got a dose of anesthesia when she took my arms and wrapped them around her waist. She arched into me, and I went for her neck. My mouth was tasting her skin before finding her lips. I felt a moan rumble out of her that only made me go deeper.

Her gasp made me break free, thinking I was carnivorous. But that was when she turned the tables, forcing my shirt upwards and off of me. She wanted me just as bad.

I followed suit and quickly started to unbutton her blouse. Her torso exposed and blouse now on the floor, there was nothing but a purple lace bra keeping me from taking her nipples into my mouth. *Why did women insist on wearing such a contraption?* My hands made their way around her and up to the center of her back. I took hold of the ponytail I'd been eyeing all night. The dent at the base of her throat was calling my name, and I was eager to answer. I went in on it, taking my tongue and running it down the middle of her body.

"Oh, Trevor." Her words sent heat throughout

me. Her hands grabbing lightly on my arms found time in- between to stroke them. I wasn't sure if she'd felt the relief of her bra as I unhooked it, but I wasn't about to let her fill out a questionnaire on the matter. She was no longer contained, and her body was at my discretion—at least the upper part. It was time to change that.

I started to unbuckle and tug at her belt. To my surprise, she did the same with mine. She'd set my waist free, allowing my pants to sag slightly. My briefs were exposed. Her hand then slid into them and started rubbing and pumping at my already engorged manhood. The sensation was adding to my wanting to break free inside of her.

At the thought of being emancipated, I groaned while in the middle of nibbling on her ear. I hastily shoved my hand into her pants, forcing it downward. That harsh movement forced her back against the table, making something rattle. I had no intention of destroying anything in here. I only wanted to break her off tonight.

My hand then crept slowly up, following the curve of her buttocks. My palm rested at the arch of her lower back. It was time for her panties to find their place on the floor. I bent through my knees, sending my hands momentarily upwards to caress her body. On their way back down, my hands fixed themselves between her skin and her panties, sliding them down. I was on my knees when I threw one of her legs on my shoulders. I then took hold of the flesh, helping to hide the swollen plum,
which I knew waited eagerly on my touch.

I tilted my head into her and found her

extremely wet. I would feast tonight and drink plentifully. Moans that were so erotic started to erupt from her, and the feel of her gripping firmly to my head only stimulated me, encouraging me to go the distance.

My hard-on was becoming impatient by the wait, and I surprised myself when I took her down to the cold floor in order to satisfy my own hunger. In seconds, I found myself inside, wrapped in her warmth and thrusting like a maniac while gyrating my hips. Her legs and arms held me captive. Her moans started to increase, which inspired me to stop holding back on my grunts. This was a mouthwatering pleasure. Euphoric in every sense.

My build-up was nearing its rapturous end, but I wouldn't allow that until she'd climaxed. It didn't take much before I felt her tense. Her ecstasy-filled cry gave me the green light to release into her—my sporadic movements only ending after the last drop of me was taken.

This woman…

She wielded such power over me. She could bring me to my knees to find pleasure from every part of her. And no matter how she chased me away, I kept coming back. She was more than I'd bargained for that day she found me waiting for her in her office— not to mention the first time I'd tasted her that New Year's night.

"You need to get off of me." Her voice was strained.

"Can't we just lay here?" I replied, completely weak.

"No. You're squashing me."

With what little strength I had, I began to roll from her. She made a few sounds of discomfort while I was doing so. I then searched for a bathroom.

I drained whatever was left of me, then flopped onto the seat, more so to catch myself. Well, 'satisfied' would be the correct term to use. I was jolted by the thought of w o n d e r i n g if I'd pleased her. The apartment was fully lit, and yet I stumbled like a drunk on my way back to her. I heard the jingling of a belt buckle and assumed she was busy clothing herself. I wasn't ready to leave yet. Besides, why was I the only one left weak?

My mouth fell open, finding her with my pants and wallet in her hand. "What the hell are you doing?" I said flatly, frightening her. I wondered if this was all part of her plan to get information out of me. Would she go to this extent for a headline? I grew enraged by the thought.

"It's not what you think," she stammered. I stormed over to her, jerking my pants from her grip. "I went for my jeans and your wallet fell out of yours. I was just putting it back in," she explained and then shook her head. I just watched as her face went from being scared to what I believed was infuriation.

"Okay, tomorrow I have a full day ahead of me. So, you should probably leave," she said, hands folded. This was overly embarrassing. I wasn't expecting for her to be kicking me out of her house right after sex. How did I end up being the one at fault here? Before I knew it, I was being escorted out. I mean, didn't I work hard enough to at least get

a cup of coffee? "Don't hesitate—"

"To call you," I said, sounding way too desperate. "Yes, when you find something out." Her expression was firm.

165

That was nothing near close to what I thought she was going to say. "Goodnight," she said, then closed the door.

*What the hell just happened here?* I wondered, standing there facing a shut door. Either I was doing something completely wrong, or I didn't know anything at all. I silenced the thought of me not being adequate enough in pleasing her. *That couldn't be it, right?* I turned and started back down her driveway.

On my way to my car, I ran through what had transpired this evening, and doubt started to creep in. I mean, she was moaning and reacting to everything I did. But was it all staged? Was her climax faked so she could be done with it?

I was extremely exasperated thinking about it by the time I'd gotten home. Now showered and laid up in my bed, Bria kicking me out was still haunting me. It was eating at me how I wasn't welcomed to spend the night in her bed, and it had already been proven that I couldn't keep her in mine. What woman didn't want a man to sleep over? It wasn't as if we didn't know each other. And tonight, despite being with her again after so long, the feel and taste of her were like nothing I'd ever experienced. I couldn't blame her for seeing me as an asshole after being that engulfed by her. *With the event at the helm of my thoughts, it was going to be impossible to get some decent shuteye,* I thought, punching at my pillow and lying sprawled out on my bed.

# Chapter 10
# **Unethical**
## **Bria**

For the last few days, I was totally distracted by what had happened in my apartment. I had yet again had sex with Trevor and had acted as though it was all business by immediately throwing him out afterwards. He actually thought I was using my body like a prostitute for information. What was wrong with me?

"Oh, god," I said, repeatedly banging my head on my desk, hoping to knock my head hard enough to suffer amnesia.

It was boxing day, and here I was, alone at my job in my office, trying to smother myself in paperwork before heading over to the foster home to see if the children were still enjoying the gifts I'd collected on a toy run. Other than that, I'd tried everything to forget Trevor, who hadn't even called since our last rendezvous. I fought the urge to think on all the things that happened that night. From the feeling of his body entangled with mine to the way he held my gaze. His deep breathing and sex-filled eyes kept me enthralled—his mouth plastered against mine and the way he held me while I rode him. My core tightened. It was easy to get carried away enjoying the ride I was on. And his scent, god, like I'd never smelled a man before.

He was surely out doing his rounds, undoubtedly enjoying the holiday season of giving. And boy, did he give good—

"No. Stop that!" I said aloud. I shoved my chair back and rose to my feet. I went over to the window and opened it, allowing the fresh air to engulf me. The sound of quiet was the opposite of what I'd experienced in the streets of Santo.

My mind was instantly filled with the memory of honking horns, yelling street vendors, and the fear of being ran over by a driver not caring if I was on the pedestrian crossing or not.

Trevor hadn't bothered to bring me up to speed on his progress or whether or not he had discovered anything. That had me worried a bit. I couldn't help but wonder if he'd had any plans on even searching. What had I expected? He was working for the guy. My attention was drawn to the ringing of my phone.

It was Mich, calling me for the umpteenth time, obviously to complain about the new guy she was messing around with. *Today would be no different,* I thought, and after him not showing up yesterday for some of the Christmas turkey prepared by her mother, an explosion was probably next on the menu.

I had ignored her long enough, and anything more would lead to her unfriending me on Facebook. Which didn't seem like a loss now as I thought about it.

My phone rested on the envelope I had once again tried having Jamila deliver. The to-be recipient just wouldn't cooperate and take the damn thing. And now he was insisting I deliver it personally, but there was no chance of that. Peaceful measures weren't working. It was time to involve my lawyer. Frustrated, I picked up the phone.

"Yes, Mich," I answered and was stunned by her words. "Shot?! By whom? Is Kayla alright?" I was horrified thinking my friends were being targeted. Having her on speaker, I listened to Mich relay the story of what had happened, all the while packing my laptop into my bag before making my move out of the building.

This was insane. A robbery at a hardware store. Of all the places to go in search of money on boxing day. Why not a grocery store? It made no sense how criminals thought these days. And Kayla, where the hell was she? I'd tried numerous times to reach her to no avail. Having her not answer her phone was making me very restless.

After checking on Bryan in the hospital, I was put at ease hearing from Mich on how Kayla had finally picked up and was on her way. I could breathe normally again but would certainly be addressing her behavior. I now sat in the waiting room collecting my thoughts. With all that had happened in the past few months, I just wanted to reset the clock and start afresh in the coming year. I was glad to have the end in sight.

"So, you're gonna stand there and act dumb. Ask him!" Mich's raised voice drew me back to the present day.

"That's an outlandish accusation," a male voice barked back. What was going on now?
Seeking and finding balance would be the first thing on my New Year's resolution list. I rubbed my neck and made my way in the direction of the ruckus. I found Mich at the center of the commotion with her chest heaving as though she'd been in a fight.

"Mich, what's going on?" I asked, now standing at her side. "This asshole is trying to show himself because I caught him with his pants down in front of—"

"Just get her out of here! She's talking nonsense, yuh hear," the man quickly insisted, making me wonder who he was and why Mich was wasting her time quarreling with him. "Talking nonsense! You have no right to send me home. None!"

"Mich, let's go." I started tugging her past her gathered audience. Even in the parking lot, she still hadn't silenced herself. And from what I'd gathered, he—her boss' husband—was the man she was knowingly having an affair with. He was also cheating on Mich.

I said nothing, understanding that now was not the time to be voicing my opinion on the matter. We rode in silence back to her place where I dropped her off and then left upon her request. She needed time to herself to process everything. I got that.

About three hours later, there was a knock on my door. I opened it and found Kayla standing with a bag, which I assumed had goodies in it knowing she liked to bake, holding it up like a peace

offering. I stepped aside to allow her entry.

"Are you ready to tell me what's been keeping you from us lately?"

She stood and made her way over to a picture hanging on the wall. She reached her hand out and slowly traced its frame. "I was cheating on Bryan," Kayla said, not turning to look at me.

"What?" I exclaimed in total shock. "Mich said you suspected that."

"No, she's been hinting at it. I... never took it on," I said, drifting off in the end. Of course Mich had seen the signs. She was involved in an affair of her own.

"Does Bryan know?" I asked, wondering if that was the reason he found himself in harm's way. He just didn't care anymore.

"No, I've only told you," she said, most likely because no secret was safe with Mich. I nodded in understanding.

"You said 'was,' does that mean that it's over?" She responded with a 'yes,' but the sadness in the tone of her voice made me think it was not of her choosing. I had so many questions to ask. The most important one being, how could a woman who seemed to have all her ducks lined up still be left wanting? She was the most put together of us all. Observing her lost like this was disconcerting. "Mich told me about your doctor's report.

Sorry I wasn't there when you needed me most." "Oh, yes, the report." I'd almost forgotten about my shortcomings as a woman. I stood and took the bag containing a bowl filled with the Christmas meal Kayla had brought. "Nothing is certain yet," I murmured, shoving the bowl into the refrigerator. I then went over to the table.

"Bria, you have options," she said, coming to stand next to me. She then turned me to face her and held me by my elbows.

"Like what?" "Like adoption."
I pulled away from her. "I want my own," I whined like a spoiled child wanting a toy all to myself. She took me into her arms, and I rested there. It was just unfair. I'd cared for so many children only to be told

171

how I might not be blessed with a child of my own. The universe was shitting on me with every turn I made.

I stood there in silence, allowing her to cradle me. However, I needed to move past this.

I broke free of her embrace. I was not going to let this beat me. "Don't worry about me. I've got this," I said before releasing a quick exhale. "If I could hold my own up against moody teenaged girls, not forgetting a five-year-old, I most certainly can handle this." My statement caused us to laugh. She reached out and wiped a tear lingering under my eye.

"I know you can. It's who you are."


Again, I was made to wait for someone claiming to be running late with a meeting. The establishment was already on lockdown, but employees hustled like bees in a hive trying to get

their work done before retiring to their homes for the day. I stood out as the oddball sitting in the hallway. I was summoned, so my presence was expected. The grant committee chairperson had requested I meet with him to discuss my progress concerning submitting documents. I must admit, I was running behind on the whole thing. It was contradictory to what I'd heard from civilians seeking help from government institutions, particularly at the end of the week. The stories were usually of workers breaking for way too long or not coming in at all. The weekend of those who worked in this office assuredly only started when their desks were cleared. And their level of courtesy was unlike anything I'd experienced. There was really no reason to complain here, I just hated waiting.

"Mr. Mathews will see you now," I was informed by a young man. The name shocked me. I honestly never took the time to find out who was part of the board. I quietly followed behind him as he led me up a flight of stairs. There were quite a few offices to the top of the landing with walls made of hazed glass, I observed. I was ushered into an office where Trevor sat on the phone. He held up a finger to me indicating that he was almost done. I did a quick perusal of his office, walking around the room inspecting the few paintings hanging on the wall.

"Sorry about that. I had to wrap things up with a client," he said, going to his feet.

"It's okay," I said, walking back over to his desk. I then took a seat expecting him to take his. He didn't. Instead, he headed over to a cappuccino machine and fixed himself a cup. He offered me one, which I graciously refused.

"I must say, you run a tight ship here."

"What do you mean?" He frowned, seeming genuinely unable to follow.

"Everyone is so… orderly. That's good."
His eyes softened as he accepted the compliment. I smiled. He must have thought I was being sarcastic. "How many offices do you have?" His lips curled at both ends.

"I invited you here to discuss your application," he said, ignoring the question and going straight into business mode. "The deadline is quickly approaching, and I look forward to personally speaking to all those involved," he said. "You should know that I had no say in the selection process."

I was relieved hearing that. The last thing I wanted was my conscience beating me on how I'd gotten selected over a much more deserving foundation because I'd slept with the guy in charge.

"Okay, what do you want to know?" I adjusted myself on the seat, crossed one leg over the other, and rested my hands in my lap.

"Ms. Pantophlet—"

"I think it's okay for you to call me Bria now, you know, since... yeah," I said, feeling my face go warm. A gasp of air escaped him as he simultaneously blushed and licked his lips.

"Bria..." My name was said softly and warmly, surprisingly stirring me. I swallowed and shifted, hoping to stop the sensation that ignited between my thighs. *Okay, that was... unexpected,*
With a nod, I encouraged him to continue.

"There is still something pending from your submission. One of the requests was to have the finalist submit a thirty-second video on their group. Why is this important? Basically, so organizations and potential sponsors will be keen on donating and will continue to contribute after the fact."

I understood perfectly what he was getting at. I just didn't have the time, and my usual go- to guy was M.I.A. This was unbecoming of me, especially when it came to my kids.

"I know you've been busy, so I've asked someone to assist you with this with no cost to you," he said earnestly, completely taking me by surprise. I needed a moment.

"Thank you," I muttered, all choked up.

The room kept its silence for a moment longer before I abruptly stood. "I told him to get in contact with you today. Here is his number," he said, handing me a business card. "Call him if he doesn't by noon. He's pretty good at what he does, and it can consume him at times. But he's ready to work with you."

"Again, thank you."

Overwhelmed by the gesture, I took a breath to compose myself. I looked at him and found him staring at me. I fidgeted.

"Is that all?"

"Yes," he simply said.

I then stood and headed to the door. I heard him exhale before ticking at the keys on his keyboard. Outside his office, I saw Curtis closing a door before making his way down the stairs with someone. I didn't recognize his features. I also wasn't aware of Curtis having an office space here. I guess there were still a few secrets he held. I walked cautiously over to the door he'd just exited. I was pleasantly surprised finding he hadn't locked it. I made certain I was clear to enter undetected.

I headed straight to his desk, not at all sure of what I would find. I started rummaging, but there was nothing there. Frustrated, I exhaled and stood, scanning the room, taking the time to think.

"If I had something I didn't want anyone to find, where would I hide it?" I muttered, observing as silhouettes of cleaners walked past the room. I started casing the place with my eyes, which rested on a painting on the wall to the back of me. It appeared to be jutting outwards. I took hold of it and found that it swung open towards me, revealing a secret compartment. A safe, I now understood, watching the metal casing that hid behind it. I got extremely excited.

"Password, what could that be? Think, think, think."

I tried his date of birth, which didn't work, and then I tried his license plate number, which also came up empty. I assumed I had one more chance to get it right, yet had no idea what to punch in.

Oh, my god! I had followed the rainbow, but the pot of gold was still out of reach. Just then, the door flew open, making me scatter behind the desk. "Come out, Bria."

## Trevor

I watched as she rose from behind the desk with a sheepish grin on her face. She was utterly maddening with this obsession she had with Mr. Bryson. "I think I'm gonna have a tracker placed on you."

"Shh," she said, waving me over. "You have impeccable timing. Now come help me with this," she insisted, to my surprise, not bothering to even play the part anymore of someone embarrassed by being caught snooping. She would be a second-time offender in the eyes of the law, but jail time didn't even faze her.

"Bria, what are you doing?" I said, coming around to meet her. "You're gonna get us both in trouble." "Just come," she exclaimed, hushed. "And don't worry, I'll keep your name out of this. You'll have full deniability." She tugged me to her side. "I can't figure out this code."

I scratched at my eyebrow, then exhaled. I watched as she mused over the code. "You're really not going to stop with this, are you?" She shook her head, her index finger clenched between her teeth. "Alright then."

I stepped forward and entered the code. The safe unlocked and I stepped back, giving her room to search freely, which she did with way too much enthusiasm. She slowly pulled out a stack of papers and started to examine them. Her mouth opened and her breathing became deep and audible. She stood frozen, skimming through the documents. "What is it? What did you find?" My question went unanswered. She started to turn and then rested her findings on the table, her eyes meeting mine.

"What didn't I find?"

She went back into the safe while I continued to decipher what was on his desk. "Building permits, receipts of illegal purchases. It's crazy, these things date back so long ago. Is that his signature, and why does he have these?" she asked, pointing, not waiting for me to respond to anything. "This is exactly what I suspected. It reeks of bribery and embezzlement. I have to check all of this. Wow, he even has ties in the labor office," she concluded.

"Something doesn't feel right," I said, also being handed a stack of newspaper articles written by Shane on his millions of suspected transgressions and instances of dubious behavior. I'd checked the safe a few days ago, and none of this was in it.

"You would think as the minister of infrastructure, he would be less obvious and more

177

discreet with his corruption."

"Why would he put this here?" I murmured. "He knew I had access to the safe."

It seemed overly suspicious and premeditated. "Why wouldn't he? He trusts you, right?! Plus, you're his legal advisor. Sorry, but even if you did find out, you're paid to hold his secrets," she said, taking hold of the papers again. "This is going to make headlines." A smile beamed across her face. "If this is all true, then—" I yanked the papers from her hand. "Hey," she protested, her voice low.

"The truth will die here." My breathing was deep. "He's an influential man, Bria. Do you know what that means?"

"Yes, his fall will be heard around the region, and that will set an example. Then people would know I wasn't just targeting him." My mind was racing, thinking on all the things she'd already been through because of me keeping him posted on her whereabouts. He was having her followed every step of the way, constantly throwing obstacles at her and enjoying it. The police warning her to stay out of trouble—the delivered documents concerning her father that sent her racing to Santo, which almost got her killed—the setbacks with her foundation. That was all him. I couldn't allow her to put herself in harm's way again.

"No, Bria, none of this is getting out," I stated, eyes wide. She stared at me dead on, challenging me. "Look, the minute he decided to misuse his authority, he placed himself in a position to be scrutinized. Someone needs to take him down," she declared soberly, pulling out a miniature camera. She wasn't getting what I was trying to say.

A man who had tasted power for so many years and had gotten away with it was not about to be willingly dethroned. He was clearly capable of anything to stay on top. I grabbed her by her arms, forcing her to look at me.

"Do I have to say it!? He's not gonna just let you come out with this. You would be putting your life in danger. He can really hurt you," I emphasized, shaking her a bit while staring directly into her eyes. She held my gaze. Her eyes scanned my face.

"Okay, I hear you," she said calmly, then looked down at my hand. I did a rapid blink and released my grip.

"Let's go."

In silence, I took her back to where she had parked her car. I didn't feel safe letting her walk there—no matter how short the distance. I then followed behind her in my car as she made her way home. She had to realize that she was in over her head and that no good would come to her if she revealed any of the information she had found today. I wasn't sure that I'd truly convinced her to stay off it. I pulled into a space next to her car knowing that I had to play this one cool. With the door opened and me hanging on it, I proceeded.

"Why is it that I always catch you snooping?" I said after she stepped out of her car.

"I don't know. Why is it that you're always around where I am?" she said, looking my way while locking her vehicle.

"I guess we are sort of the same." "How do you figure that?"

"You spy. I snoop." Her face lit up with a smile. I silently agreed.

"I shouldn't have to say this again, but Bria, you need to let this go. Promise me you'll let this go," I reiterated soberly. She nodded, then searched for her house keys. A nauseating feeling took me. I knew better than to believe she would do as asked. I had to find a way to get through to her. My stomach rumbled, and I took it as a sign. "I can do with something to eat, what about you? You must have worked up an appetite," I teased. She gazed around. "Okay, you want to meet up later?"

"No! I don't want to give you a moment to change your mind or for something else to distract you. Let's go." Leaving her alone tonight in her excited state would be catastrophic. Within a blink of an eye, she would have an article ready for print tomorrow. She looked down at her clothing, and I found it cute how she brushed at a smudge on her shirt. Gazing up at me with worry in her eyes, she frowned, and that simple gesture took my breath away. *This woman has me hooked*, I admitted to myself. I would do anything to protect her.
"It will be fine."

"Let's go then," she said, coming over to my car and jumping in. Grinning, I thought how easy that was—finally!
I decided to take her to my favorite spot.


"I should probably warn you about the time I

wrote as a restaurant food critic. I'm not exactly welcomed everywhere. T h e drive-thru would be the safest bet right now." I chuckled.

"Tell me, exactly whose skin have you not gotten under?" I asked, taking my eyes briefly off the road to look at her.

"Huh." She shrugged and placed her gaze outside the window. Having her in the car with no way of running, I decided to seize the moment. I cleared my throat.

"So, it's no secret. You know I've been keeping tabs on you."

"Yep."

"Yet I don't know what your favorite color is." "And you never will. That's too personal," she joked, allowing a smile to take over her face. "What about this restaurant?" I asked, pulling over. "Nope, bad review." I was back on the road again before I knew it, driving at a slow pace. "Okay... this one." "Too crowded," she commented before I could turn off the road. I quickly switched off my indicator.

"Will we be able to eat today?" I asked.

"I doubt it, but we can try," she replied, sitting up. "We're running out of options here." She chuckled. "Maybe we should give up." "Not a chance," I said, determined for the opportunity to feed her again. I had a stroke of genius. She probably wasn't welcomed on the Dutch side of the island, but that surely wasn't the case on the French, I gathered. I sped up and headed toward the quaintest spot I'd ever eaten at—Yvette's Kitchen.

# Chapter 11
# **Conflict of Interest**
**Trevor**

"Hey, take it easy, it's okay. It's probably best for me not to go there."
"I didn't agree," I said.
"You didn't dispute it either."

She was utterly exhausting at times and thrived on being right. Oddly enough, we weren't at each other's throats but debating whether bellbottoms would make its return in this century. She was against, and I was secretly on the same page but chose to oppose her just for the fun of it. "No, you spoke, I sat quietly and listened and had a difference in opinion. That's how conversations work sometimes."

"Okay, if you say so," she said, yet her tone indicated otherwise.
"You remind me of my mother. My father never won with her either," I said with a smile on my face.
She adjusted her posture in her seat.

"You can't blame me for being skeptical. For all I know, you're a poser. I can hardly picture you in high heels," she said, smiling her signature smile, which I found beautiful.
I gasped, hand at my chest, pretending to be insulted. She then cracked up. Her bubbly laughter spurred a reaction from me, which made me shift to contain my excitement.

Finished with our meals, we allowed the waiter to take our plates. We had requested dessert, and although full, I was looking forward to enjoying some ice cream.

With all the giggling that was going on, I was confident we would be asked to keep it down or leave. But that never happened.

I reached for my goblet and bumped into my water glass, making it spill over. Luckily, I'd been sipping on it all evening, so it was fairly empty. She dabbed at the spot with a napkin.

"You know, you are very clumsy for such a well- put-together guy. Why is that?"

"I guess you have a way of rattling my nerves. I don't function the way I should around you. I feel like I can expect a punch from you at any moment."

That caught her attention, making her look me in the eyes. She released a gust of air through her nostrils. "How did you know I would enjoy eating here?" she asked lightly, moving the conversation into a more casual direction. "Because I can tell you appreciate the simple things in life." I took a sip of wine and then added, "And I was praying you had never found this place. I ran out of options on the Dutch side. I was beginning to think I would never be able to enjoy a dinner date with you."

"Who said anything about this being a date?" I looked on intently and took another sip of my wine. I wasn't getting into that again. "Oh, I heard about your friend's opening. Congrats to her." "Thank you." I saw her staring me down and fidgeted, knowing something was up.

"So, tell me. What's your story? Why are you so closed off?" I gulped at her candor, needing a moment to stabilize myself.

"I would hardly say I'm closed off with you.

183

More cautious if anything," I admitted out loud. "That's not what I'm referring to."

Our eyes locked. I knew exactly what she was on, I just thought to play coy.

"Maybe I'll leave that story for another time," I said, watching the movement of me resting my glass on the table.

"Your 'Gabby Listens' column, tell me about that," I said, clearly changing the subject. "Well, it's not all fun. I did study psychology. I take the opportunity presented there to enlighten and empower women, mostly."

"I see, but how can you write about something you haven't experienced?"

"That question again," she said under her breath. It made me wonder if I'd asked her that before. She winced and took a sip of water.

"But I have for the most part," she replied, then took a spoon of her dessert. "Certain things play out very similarly in other people's lives. The characters are the only ones that are interchangeable. People rarely stand still or know others are experiencing the same fate."

I understood that all too well. Nothing surprised me anymore, especially when it came to humans. Not to be cynical, but many in the world were self-absorbed or self-serving. It all came down to satisfying one's own need at the present moment— regardless of the pain one might inflict on others.

I became curious about her beginning statement, though. But I wasn't sure I really wanted to know what she meant. I wondered if her response would have an effect on the way I felt toward her. I wondered, so I asked, although fearing the answer.

"In what way can you relate?" She held out for a moment.

"Well, some women weren't strong enough to walk away from a cheating man while others walked right into one. One of my friends, for instance. I know she's stronger than that." So she related through a friend. I was relieved to know that.

Looking down into her bowl of rum raisin ice cream, she took a tiny spoonful of it and seized the moment to indulge in allowing her taste buds to play at it before I visibly noticed her swallow.
I couldn't tear my eyes away from her.

Her gaze then found mine. She fluttered her eyes and then exhaled through her nostrils, as if defeated. "I was kinda both at some point," she stated, stunning me. "I'm ashamed to admit it, but maybe that's why I'm hard on her."

I knew she wasn't a saint, but I wasn't expecting that blunt admission outside of a confessional booth.

"You were someone's mistress?"
She closed her eyes and rubbed at her neck and face. "Yes." I was angry, as if I had the right to be. Some asshole had placed her in a situation and probably had her thinking it was love.

"Was that the guy?" I probed.

"What guy?" she asked, her voice low, apparently confused.

"The one who kissed you on your porch the night the girls told you I was out there." She paused before saying, "Yes and no. He didn't kiss me. I was about to kiss him, and she's not an ex but his present lover." Her words took me on another ride. The emotions that were running through me all at once made me shift uneasily in my seat. There was a lot I didn't know about this woman, and now there were things about her I would never forget. I sat in judgment of her—looking on in silence as she confessed her sins.

"I didn't understand why I was fighting so hard to keep it, because although I envied what she had with him from time to time, I honestly didn't want it. I would never be able to trust him entirely." "So, you ended it?" I asked while the thought of recently seeing them together occupied my mind.

She looked away, and I felt a zing of jealousy run through me. "We have an 'on again-off again' kinda relationship." "Why?" The words escaped from me without much consideration. I wanted to know yet didn't want to understand why she of all people would portray such arbitrary behavior.

She released a breath. "I guess because I wanted to fill a void. And something familiar might be safer to do it with." She shrugged. "I sound way too casual about sex, I know." "You need to end it!" I commanded angrily, making her wince. I refused to believe she was still sleeping with him.

"You think I haven't tried?" Her expression hardened. "I even went to the extreme of forcing him to break up with me, pushing buttons and saying things all men hated in order to chase him away, which it did. It just took me by surprise how heartless he went about it. But he had to be the one to do it because I kept going back." She dropped her head. "He never called back, and I didn't reach out to him. I just dove right into my work and my passions— fooling myself that I could breathe freely, yet now

186

and again…" She raised her head and met my eyes. "I crave him. And I am tempted to—"

"Check, please," I said, not wanting to hear the rest. I was totally enraged by the conversation I had initiated. Not waiting for the waiter to bring it to the table, I shoved my chair back and headed over to settle the bill. I found myself in battle sitting in my car as she exited. Frustrated, I threw my head back and cracked my knuckles. I was punishing her with my silence and felt shitty about it.

Knowing I was being a jerk and should walk her to her door, I swiftly jumped out of my car. I slammed the door and started behind her. Her house and porch were in darkness, and she struggled to find her keys. She turned after inserting it into her front door slot.

"Look, I make mistakes, sometimes fully aware of them, and I know what I said tonight probably made you dislike me again, but—" I grabbed her and found myself kissing her passionately. I took her in as if wanting to devour her. I tasted the rum raisin ice cream she had indulged in. I wasn't a fan of the flavor up until now. She clung to me, wrapping her hands around my neck before pulling me into her. She melted in my arms.

She would forget all about him tonight. I would make sure of it. I found myself pecking her, placing kisses around her lips and seeking more of her. I wrestled against wanting to taste her in different places, which made me question who this woman really was that wielded the power to make me do things I wouldn't normally do, yet that thought enticed me further.

My hand objected to leaving her body, but I

needed to get her inside. Otherwise, I was sure of taking her here on the porch. I broke from her lips, trying to narrow in on the knob. She continued kissing me on my neck. The moisture of her lips against my skin triggered a flash of electricity through me. I swore I forgot how to open a door.

At last I'd been able to unlock the door and steered her inside urgently. I fought to get my jacket off. She took hold of my shirt and ripped at it, showing no regard for the buttons as she sent them flying. I cupped her face in my hands and continued to shower her with kisses. She loosened my belt buckle and tugged me in the direction of her bedroom. Her fingers played along the waistband of my underwear. She broke free of my lips before she harshly yanked my pants to the floor. Without a break in my stride, I stepped out of my trousers which took my shoes along with it.

She had yet to be undressed while I stood in socks and boxers. Now in her bedroom, she flipped the light switch before continuing with me toward the bed. She applied a shove to my chest, and I willingly gave in to a backwards freefall. I felt each finger touch my skin before gripping my boxers. She then tugged them past my buttocks and off of me.

She straddled me, her eyes imprisoning me. Her skirt rolled up her legs, exposing the smooth texture of her skin. She slowly began unbuttoning her blouse. My hands rested on her hips as I laid enjoying the show. I knew she could feel me pressing hard against her, waiting for the moment to be let in. I patiently watched and gave my lips a lick in anticipation.

The last time we'd connected like this, she'd

taken full control. This time would be different. Tonight, she would be submitting to me.

## Bria

My blouse undone, he slowly slid his hands up my torso, making my body curve in the excitement of feeling him. I pushed them off, denying him the feel of my skin at his fingertips, hoping to keep control.

My bottom lip folded between my teeth. I leaned forward, giving him a lick on his ear. This seemed to have surprised and turned him on. He flinched before taking hold of me once more. I assisted with wrapping his hands around me. He held on to my bra straps and undid them. With a snap, my breasts were now free and eager to be taken by him. His mouth fell open, and I knew he wanted nothing else but to take them into his warmth. Just the thought of him playing with them made the tender points of them tighten.

He began rising, but I pushed at his chest, stopping the action. He must have thought he was going to take control. A smile cracked across my face, and a light giggle followed. This game would not be won by the swift. I could see the frustration on his face at me insisting he follow my lead. I was certain to be building his primal instinct of taking what he wanted without asking, but nothing of the sort would happen. He would be obedient and wait. I started swaying to the rhythm in my head.

My eyes closed, and I began to grind on him. He laid there, completely accepting. I felt his aroused shaft growing harder.

He took hold of me, and my eyes fell to the man who was giving me immense pleasure. He ran his hands slowly up my torso and began to fondle my breasts. He then drew me down to him and gave me a soft kiss while I was still riding him. His mouth open, I observed the slight quiver of his lips. His breathing was telling of his enjoyment.

I felt him flex within me, and that triggered a feeling I thought was long forgotten. I wanted him deeper than he already was. I wanted to feel every ripple of his penetrating shaft. It was pure magic, and I groaned in total satisfaction. I watched his expression as he pumped into me, his focus unwavering from my face. He wanted to make sure I was being fulfilled. Our rhythm remained steady and uninterrupted. I began a slow circulation, which was countered by a moan from him. We both picked up the pace.

"Speak to me," I said in a low, sensuous voice. He frowned. "I don't know how to do that," he replied before wetting his lips.
His response was a bit disappointing. Was he that innocent? A smile curved my lips, and I adjusted myself before continuing with whirling my hips.

Surprisingly, I felt close to the edge, and my moans were a dead giveaway. I felt him flex again, and that triggered a shockwave that ran through me. My pace quickened. The sensation of his hands running along my body was becoming too much.

Without stopping, he shifted into a seated position. His hands at my waist started pulling me down repeatedly to meet him, grinding my body back and forth. His pumps into me were deliberate.

He wanted me to come hard.

I tilted my head back in total ecstasy just waiting on the explosion that was due any moment. This man, whom I'd constantly been at war with, was he going to blow my fuse like no one ever had? I ran my tongue along the outer lining of his throat. "Bria." My name quaked from him. I felt myself close to the edge and thought on fighting one last time to hold on. I didn't want to give in to that euphoric feeling. "Trevor," I moaned, feeling the rise and release that made me latch on to him. I squeezed and held my breath with what little power I had as a faint sound flowed from me before ending my climax.

"Christ," he said, followed by him sucking air through his teeth. His release was evident by the groan that proceeded. I felt him jerk and shift, knowing he was breaking within me.

"Shit..." he said as though it wasn't a profane word. Our breaths heavy, I felt his body release. He rested his head against my chest. My grip loosened, making my hands slide down a little. I fell into his embrace before I drifted into an unconscious state.

"So, this isn't what I meant by 'therapy'," Mich said, shaking us both from our slumber. Trevor rolled from the bed, falling with a thump to the floor. "But it's a surefire way of relieving tension." She chuckled into her hand. "Mich! How did you get in here?" I screeched, pulling the sheet up over my chest.

"Honey bunny, you left your front door unlocked. But I can understand why with the trail of clothes that I found on the floor. You were in a rush." "You saw clothes on the floor and still barged into my bedroom!"

"I wasn't sure what to think. Would you believe I feared for your life?" Her sly grin told me otherwise. "Just the other day, you were having a deep moment that involved searching for compatibility. Today, you're wrapped up in bed with lover boy here." She threw him his trousers. "I didn't know you found it so soon. Wait, is that...?" She laughed. "Priceless!"

Trevor was visibly shaken, caught off guard by Mich's intrusion. Bumping into things, he scrambled around in search of something. "Looking for that, sweetie?" Mich said, pointing at the boxers crumpled at the foot of the bed.

"Yes, thank you," he replied, his breathing rushed. "You're welcome," she responded with a grin.

Trying to exit and fighting for balance, Trevor tried pulling up his pants. He almost fell doing so, putting on one hell of a show for his spectator. "Oh, my..." Mich said, then bit into her bottom lip. "What are you doing here?" I said, embarrassed and completely over the intrusion.

"I think I'd prefer to discuss the naked man trying to get out of your house."

"Mich!"

"Okay, okay, I came over thinking we should talk," she said, plopping onto my bed.

"I'll call you later, Bria," Trevor said before reaching for the doorknob. "Wait!" Mich said, stopping Trevor. "Your name?"

"Trevor Mathews," he said, extending his hand while still holding his boxers. Mouth open, Mich sneered, watching it as though it was filthy.

"Trevor Mathews, I'm sure you'll understand if I don't shake that." Trevor nodded in understanding. "Bye," Mich said, her head tilted to the side as she watched him leave. "Wait, is that the guy you won't shut up about?"
Her gaze met my angry glare, but she didn't care to acknowledge it.

"Nice to have finally met you!" she bellowed.
"Why are you here?" I yelled, out of patience.
I wrapped my sheet around me. I headed towards the bathroom. I had a bad habit of turning on the faucet before even being ready to brush my teeth. "Shouldn't you be off somewhere jet-setting?" "I ended it, okay!" she bellowed.

"Ended what?" I said, foaming from my mouth. I spat and then continued the vigorous assault on my teeth. "You were right," I heard her say. This made me turn off the water. Slowly, I reentered the room. "Come again?" I said, needing to make sure I had heard her correctly.

She exhaled in defeat. "It was a bad idea to go with him on that so-called business trip," she said, looking down to the floor. "His woman kept calling him like she knew something was up, and I just couldn't take it anymore." "I think you kinda knew that would happen."
She sighed.

"Why was I trying to convince myself that I was different?" She shrugged, her mouth pinched on both sides. I knew she would never have been satisfied with what little time and how that time would be spent with him. Deep down, she wasn't the type. But like so many, she wanted love and would settle for anything, fooling herself that she had it.

Some guys thought it was fine to substitute love with money. Some women were okay with that. I'm glad she figured out she wasn't one of them.

"I ended it before the boss lady's husband came into the picture. And as you know, being with him was also a disaster. My Two- for-Tuesdays break-up story." Sadness engulfed her.

"You know, I actually found out about the first one using me as his midlife crisis affair when he got hurt at work and she was at his bedside in the hospital. I was working and decided to sneak off to see him. Imagine my surprise stepping into the room during visitation hours and finding his woman there. I just pretended I was there to take his vitals. Ridiculous, how simple I am."

"Sweetie, you're not." I started searching for words. I sat next to her on the bed.

"It's just... men are pigs," I said, forcing a laugh from her. "I mean literally. They don't mind rolling around in dirt all day and calling it work." She laughed longer this time, causing me to join in. I was relieved to see she could actually laugh about it. She wasn't that much disappointed in the outcome. Her coming here was a testament to that.

"Look at me, shedding tears over somebody else's man," she said, wiping a drop from her eye. A pitiful laugh followed. "Borrowing other people's problems." I held her hand in mine.

"I must be an asshole magnet," she said, gazing at me. "No, you're not! It's just the last two guys were major dickheads," I stated

She tilted her head back and said, "God, please

194

do me a favor and steer all the other dickheads in someone else's direction." She then exhaled. The room kept its silence for a smidge longer. "So, what now?" she finally asked. I looked into her earnest eyes. "Now, you relax and enjoy being free. Take your time to find someone who will be satisfied with only you. You deserve to have that." I went in for a hug.

"Yeah, and I'm sorry I got on you the last time." "It's okay. I'm sorry I was a bitch about it." "You mean 'super bitch'."

"Don't start," I warned sternly, then lightened up, giving her a break just this once.
"A Galactic Bitch," she added with glee. "Out!" I said, pointing to the door.

With her tongue out and a shake of her head, she stood and headed to the door. I must admit, our friendship wasn't the easiest, but it was direct. I was still getting used to her.

# Chapter 12
# Taking Casualties

We were all poised for the press conference that was called by Curtis. News anchors, reporters, and a large group of his followers all lined the community center hall, waiting for him to address the latest accusations thrown at him. He would most definitely also use the opportunity to slam his opposition on promises that had not yet materialized. He was certain to have every news platform telling his truth to the public.

"Are you ready?" Ricardo asked, all smiles while placing the camera on its tripod. "Oh, I'm so ready for this," I responded. I was leaning up against the wall going over some questions I'd prepared for the occasion. The only thing that had me a bit worried was if they would give me the opportunity to ask. If he did allow me to ask questions, it would certainly have to do with him anticipating me coming, and I could only guess of one person who would make sure Curtis had the upper hand.

*I have to be able to ask that one question that would start the avalanche that would overtake him*, I thought. I watched on as his team entered, taking their seats behind the tables stacked next to each other in a row. Trevor took the seat on Curtis' right, making me consider the significance of his choice. His eyes found mine looking at him, and he held his stare until it was broken by Curtis turning to whisper something into his ear.

The meeting was called to order by a member of his cabinet. Curtis followed with his usual nonsense, and everyone listened attentively with a few people murmuring here and there. Then the floor was opened for questions, which were easily answered by him, and I gathered by the end of this charade, he was sure to have a new set of followers. He just knew what to say to those who already loved him and undecided voters listening out there. He was quite adept in convincing people of his feigned sincerity. He would be ready for the upcoming election cycle.

"Hey, aren't you going to ask a question?" Ricardo nudged.

It was indeed time for me to speak. I raised my hand thinking that there was no way Trevor, who was leading the question and answer segment of this conference, would ever allow me the floor. He skipped over me a few times and then finally, to my surprise, called me by my first name, making almost everyone turn to see who he was referring to. It was clearly a slip on his part, I noted, seeing his quick reaction to correct himself by using my last name.

He then looked at Curtis, who was staring at him. He himself probably didn't understand Trevor's reason for selecting me. "Give it to him," Ricardo encouraged under his breath, knowing I had no plans on going easy.

"I just have two questions for you, Mr. Bryson," I said, coming off from against the wall.

"That would be a first," he said, laughing. Those present joined in on the cackle. I allowed the crowd to settle. "Do you like children?" I asked, making him narrow his eyes. He was surely perplexed, wondering what I was up to.

"I would have to say yes seeing that I'm

loaded with nieces and nephews. I don't want to get into trouble," he said, smiling. I looked over to Trevor, who I thought was maybe holding his breath. He was motionless. "Great!" I paused. My lips curved at the corners, hearing his expected answer. "So why do you insist on selling their inheritance to the highest buyer?"
The room went quiet.

"What do you mean?" His aggravation was instantly showing on his face. He would have done himself a favor if he didn't ask that.

"I mean, I have documents implicating you in the illegal sale of land, which was previously announced to be used as a recreational park, now having your signature on a purchase agreement to an offshore company for the development of a casino, who," I paused to catch my breath and build anticipation, "in return would invest heavily in your political campaign trail," I said, producing a stack of papers in my hand. I saw the beads of sweat forming on his forehead.

"And while we are on the topic of fraudulent activities on your end, let's connect some dots, shall we?" I said in case those present needed more convincing. "Why do I have footage of you eating with a Mr. Binder—the offshore investor mentioned in this document?" I said, waving the paper around.

"That's outrageous! You're clearly trying to defame me. I was simply having lunch with a friend," he insisted, slamming his palm on the table. I flinched, but I wasn't frazzled by it. I was more amused that I'd gotten that kind of reaction out of him.

"How so? Your reputation hardly paints you

as a saint. It's not the first time you've been accused of bribery or the illegal sale of land, not forgetting vote buying and human trafficking. The list goes on. Yet you're here singing a swan song about how I'm gunning for you regardless of all the scandals you've been tied to. So how can you stand there and tell us to take you for your word?" I fired back.

I'd awakened a dormant volcano as those in the room started throwing their own sets of questions at him.

With my breathing heavy, I stared on, holding his focus as he glared at me. I had finally gotten my hands on the paperwork, which corroborated my stories. I'd secured them that day in his office before Trevor had gotten the chance to reclaim them.

Curtis pushed at his chair and headed for the exit. This was him realizing that his career as a politician had come to an end. My eyes followed him out and then went to Trevor, standing in place. He gulped, wetting his throat, and after adjourning the meeting, he too left.

## Trevor

She'd blatantly disregarded my warning on confronting him with evidence of his involvement in corruption, ultimately making herself a target. I'd basically begged her not to go through with it for her own safety. Yet, she did. She was subsequently holding no regard for her own life. Why was I surprised? This was Bria. I should have known she

199

would do the opposite of what I'd asked of her. If she'd sat quietly, they would have compared her to a thunder cloud with no rain. I sat in the hall as if waiting to see the principal who was preparing to hand me my punishment. I could only imagine what the conversation with Mr. Bryson was going to be like.

"Trevor, get in here!" Mr. Bryson ordered me into his office. Curtis had high-tailed it out of the meeting and was unreachable for the remainder of the evening. The conference last night was a complete disaster, having the opposite effect we were going for. I stood and adjusted my tie. I then headed into his office.

"Hold on a second," he said, his head holding his cellphone locked between his shoulder and his ear. I didn't bother to sit and found my hands sweating within my pants pockets.

Still busy with his phone conversation, he dug into his desk and withdrew a brown envelope. He flung it onto the table, making it slide to the edge of the desk.

"What is it?"

"Let me call you back," he said to the person on the other end. "That," he stressed, "is something I should've shown you a long time ago. Go on and open it," he said, clasping his hands and interlocking his fingers. His glare locked in on me.

Hesitantly, I went for it. I was taken aback by the first image extracted from the envelope. Wide-eyed, I continued to skim through the pictures, trying extremely hard to control the rage that was building.

The photos showed images of Bria and me in

every setting possible—even during our intimate moments. I froze on a picture of our recent night together. She lay next to me in her bed with one of her legs and her back exposed. The photographer had crossed the line when he intruded into her home and took pictures of us as we slept.

"I must say, I don't know why I was surprised last night. She had inside help." He stood and headed over to his window, giving me his back.

"Where did you get these?" I questioned through my teeth, already knowing the answer. I found myself not only swallowing hard but trying to contain the thoughts that told me to kill him myself. "Please, you can't be surprised," he said, turning to face me. "I would be crazy not to keep an eye on those around me."
I continued scanning through the pictures.

There were a few taken of her from outside her living room window, wearing only a bra and panties. I could just kill whoever was in her bushes, taking her at her most vulnerable when she thought no one was watching. "I thought you would be different, but I guess all men, no matter their ambition, fall prey to a pretty woman in heels," he stated while his secretary entered the room with his morning glass of whiskey. She rested it on his table.

"You wouldn't be the first to be distracted from your purpose here." His brows dropped. "I too enjoy a wet pussy from time to time." His gaze fell on his secretary as she made her way back out. My breathing deepened; m y nostrils flared. I still couldn't believe what was happening here. "I'm sure she was most enjoyable. I hope you don't mind me keeping a few."

My eyes shot to his. I was outraged by his comment. "You fucking repulsive pervert. You've no right to—" "No right to what?" He snapped, losing his calculated composure for a second. "After last night's meeting where you allowed her to gore me, it is *you* who has no right. You can't possibly think you have a foot to stand on," he snarled. How could I retort? I myself saw how ludicrous it was allowing her to ask her questions. I had basically sealed his fate. But then again, these were two separate cases we were dealing with. "Your judgment has been questionable since you insisted on going with her on that little lover's trip of hers. Certainly, you understand why I began to doubt your loyalty."

I made a move towards him with the intention of shutting him up. He'd said his piece and was now due for a hell of a beatdown. A sudden rap on the door made both of us direct our attention to it. It flew open and in stormed men in uniforms wearing masks. They were from the Kingdom Criminal Taskforce, one of them announced while handing me the warrant to search Mr. Bryson's office and arrested him. I stepped back, completely taken by the scene. It was all happening so fast. "Get me a good defense lawyer," Curtis said, clearly understanding that I wouldn't be representing him any further.

There was no trace of Bria for days, and all my efforts to contact her had come up short. She wasn't sleeping at home. I didn't know what to think and feared the worst. Her friends finally told me she was in the care of the Kingdom Witness

202

Protection Division and would be kept under close watch until all those connected in the wrongdoings of my previous boss were either cleared or in custody. This I should've figured after being held for questioning myself.

The island was buzzing with the news of selected members holding high-level positions being ripped from their homes and hauled off in the middle of the night. The country was divided regarding bringing down those that lived in our community. Some had been extremely charitable in the past and had basically worked on building a reputation based on misplaced loyalty. People just didn't feel right about locking up those that had been at the helm of our island's infrastructure. It was a valid topic of discussion, and some were enjoying the political scandal, but I wasn't about to go into it. I had one thing on my mind, and that was making sure Bria came out of this unharmed. I
needed to see her.

I'd heard about sightings of her but had yet to make contact. I wasn't sure she wanted me to.
It was strange bumping into her weeks later while she shopped for something to wear for the planned gala that was being organized in honor of the foundations vying for the special grant. She and her friends were laughing and giggling after coming out of a store. Her smile slowly faded when her eyes fell on me. I didn't know what to think. "You guys go ahead. I'll catch up," she instructed. They waved goodbye and continued on their way.

"Hi," I managed.

"Hi. I meant to call you."

"Why didn't you?" The question asked a hundred and

one times in my head.

"I was afraid of what you would say. If you would even pick up." I shrugged. I felt the same. Being irrelevant to her was seemingly one of my worst fears. "So, politics…" I said, not wanting to waste time on the past, yet figuring I should choose a topic she would never tire of.

"Yes, look, I'm sorry I stayed away. I just didn't want to damage your image with potential clients. I didn't want them to think their secrets weren't safe with you," she burst out.

"Full deniability," I remarked, remembering her words. "Yes, that." So her staying away from me was her way of trying to protect me. Bullshit!
"I see." I looked away, not wanting her to see my disappointment with her trying to feed me that lie.

"Let me make it up to you," she said, gripping my wrist. Her touch stilled the anger in me. "Okay," I managed.

"Tonight. Dinner. I mean, it's the least I can do for making you lose your job." That was the last thing on my mind, but it was so true. I smiled, and she smiled back.

"I'll meet you at—"

"I'll pick you up," I said, wanting to be absolutely sure she'd be there. She exhaled and relaxed. "It's a date then. I better go catch those ladies. 7:30?" she bellowed, looking back while on the move. I nodded in agreement. My eyes followed her until she disappeared in the distance.

With my legs clipped together and hands where they could see them, I sat, strangely enough, extremely nervous in the presence of Aniah, Mariska, and two others in Bria's living quarters, waiting for her to emerge from her bedroom. It was such a scene found in many movies. I never thought it actually happened. The young ladies, although staring at me, kept quiet while soberly scrutinizing me. Bria entered the room, and I instantly found my feet. She was gorgeous, d r e s s e d in a black off- the- shoulders cocktail dress with a double row of pearls strung around her neck. I couldn't take my eyes off her.

"It was well worth the wait," I said.

"You make sure she's back by bedtime. That's eight," Aniah commanded, making me gaze down at her. It was seven forty- two according to the clock up on the wall. I flashed a smile at the pint-sized adorable bunny who didn't smile back. Before heading on our way, we walked the girls back to the foster home. Aniah questioned why she wasn't invited and seeing the time it was taking to convince her that it was something grownups needed to do from time to time, Bria came to a compromise to take her out on a separate occasion. *Tenacious young lady*, I thought. But she gave me an ingenious idea, which I would be proposing to the committee. "All of that was going on with your friend Kayla?" "Yeah, we never imagined him being the bad guy."

"Crazy." I took a moment to catch myself, doing so by skimming my surroundings. Dimmed lights lit the outside terrace where Bria had reserved for us to dine. Soft jazz helped to set the ambience of relaxation and tranquility, which I now focused on enjoying with her. The day's humidity was replaced

205

by a light breeze that tapped along my skin. I'd asked the waitress to bring us a bottle of their best and was immensely gratified savoring the smooth, light burn of the liquor as it trailed down my throat. But all this paled in comparison to the woman I had sitting opposite me. I was impressed by her choice of dining to say the least. She had put effort into this gesture. The choice of what to order was hard, and I ended up flipping through the menu at least three times before deciding.

I found myself staring at her glossed lips as they captured the fork between them before allowing its unhurried freedom. My eyes danced down the length of her neck, where I'd enjoyed planting delicate kisses. I watched as she playfully passed her finger along her collarbone while tilting her head back to thank the waitress for filling her water glass. My mind hitting the replay button gladly reminded me of the opportunity I was given on a few occasions to serve her in a different way. I caught myself just in time to focus on the questions being asked by her. It was a good thing we were sitting. My arousal would have caused quite a stir.

"Yes, I forgive you for costing me my job," I said, answering her question. "It actually freed me up to a higher purpose." "Ah, how are the plans going for the event?"

"Great, actually. It was a bit heavy in the beginning, but I must say the team is really making sure things move along. They're on top of things."

"It's an awesome initiative."

"There is much more in store. You inspire me, Bria," I said, raising my glass. She smiled and raised her glass for the toast before taking a sip. "So, just a bit of politics, and I'm done." I knew she was coming with it.

"I was informed that the prosecutor is building a case against Curtis." "Yes, he's been held for questioning, claiming his innocence and demanding whatever charges brought against him be dropped. He's gonna fight this with all he has."

"I'd like to see him get out of this one." I swallowed hard and braced myself before saying, "he's claiming the evidence to be circumstantial."

"What!" she screeched. I expected such a reaction. "He's joking, right? I mean, everything proves his guilt. I can't believe this." She looked away. Her body language then changed, and I got a glimpse of slight worry on her face. "What's wrong?"

She shook her head. "I just thought things would be settled by now and it would be over." She exhaled through her nostrils. She must be concerned being expected to testify against him.

"They are going to request an extension on his detainment so they can collect all the evidence that proves his guilt. No loopholes, Bria," I said, hoping that would be enough just to ease a little bit of the unsteady feelings she was clearly going through. " And hey, I promise, I won't let anything happen to you." Her eyes clung to mine before moving along over to the next table. There, an older lady was being serenaded by the staff and her company. It was her birthday, and she was greatly surprised by the attention.

My eyes found Bria's expression softening as she looked on. I wondered what was going through her head. "I'm gonna ask to take her picture," she said, rising to her feet.

207

She pulled out a camera, which shouldn't have surprised me, but it did. I watched as she was given the okay to document someone else's occasion for what I was sure would be for her personal collage. She came back and bent next to me in order to take a selfie of us. I found myself focused on her smile. I then waited for her to take her seat again. "There, the conclusion of our quest together documented." Those words left a dent in my stomach.

It had indeed been one for the books. Our adventure together started the night I first tasted her at a crowded New Year's party. Not recognizing her in her office was shameful on my end. Thinking on it now, it was also extremely presumptuous of me to think I could keep her under control, especially since I couldn't even keep her in my bed. *Hopefully, I'll be given another chance to at least spoon her*, I thought. "What are you smiling about?"
I caught myself and replied, "Nothing, just a silly thought." I took a breath. "So, let me mention that I'm starting my own law firm."

"That's wonderful. Congratulations. Wow." She was all smiles and it felt so right sharing it with her. "But before you move on to the next chapter in your life, you have to fill me in on your backstory."
"What do you mean?"

"How is it exactly that a man like you found himself working for Curtis?" I sat back. "Right! My story," I said, my hands clasped in my lap. "Where to begin…"

"Start from before me."

"I don't want to bore you." "Please."

I knew what she was asking and understood that it was time she heard what caused our paths to cross. "Okay, well... we were both ambitious, equally matched defense attorneys who worked for the same company. Compatible, some would say, yet sometimes, I wondered."

Bria sat and listened attentively as I told her how I could barely recall ever speaking about children with Nicole. I had justified it by saying I wasn't sure if it was because she thought I didn't want any or if it was just assumed we wouldn't have time. Whatever the reason, I had already convinced myself that I was satisfied. But everything changed

the day I had to defend a man accused of molesting a little girl. He had told me straight out that he'd done it and my job demanded that I cleared him. He didn't want a lecture, and I was in no position to give one. I had a job to do.

"Let's just say my ex-boss and I had a difference in opinion." I was sure Nicole would support me, but when I was met with vitriol, I found myself questioning our relationship.

"That must have been hard."

"It was," I said, looking into my wine glass while swirling it.

" 'Being a criminal defense attorney is where all the money is' were the words that stood out to me during our argument—we'd studied for it and knew that we could be confronted with atrocious human beings. Because of that, unfortunately, I didn't want it anymore. That choice caused me to resign, which inevitably sent her into the arms of someone else at the firm. Curtis took one look at my resume and hired me as his legal advisor." Ingenious, don't you think? Who better to keep him out of trouble than a criminal lawyer with regrets?

"Now you're caught up." "So I am. And Nicole?" I shrugged, not wanting to go there.

"I'm asking because it just seems like something that could break a guy. I'm wondering how you survived." Her eyes were soft, hoping I would reveal my soul to her.

"I stayed away from love songs and anything that could potentially make me vulnerable. I guess I'm just another messy heart," I said with a chuckle, hoping to make light of things. It didn't appear to work. The waitress returned, placing our meals on the table. During that time, I wondered if there was any significant other in her life. We'd been intimate but never was it suggested that we were to be an item. I felt the urgency to determine where I placed. She had mentioned having casual sex, but I wasn't playing by the same rules any longer.

"And you?"

"What about me? My life isn't exactly a secret."

"The guy at your home that night. Is he…" I swallowed the remaining words. It was hard to finish, mostly because I'd seen how passionate she could be with him. I couldn't stomach it and didn't want to be told how I couldn't compare. "I've been meaning to ask you to finish telling me about him," I said soberly, my jaw clenched and my fist balled, thinking on the last bit of information she'd told me. I was fighting to control my disdain for a man I saw myself punching out.

In silence, she started playing with her food in what was already an awkward moment. "Jerome was a distraction that happened a year ago and lasted way past his expiration date. I met him after being broken by a man I thought was my destiny. My initial intention was just to have someone to talk to. At some point, my wires got crossed, and... I wasn't sure if it was him I wanted, but I wanted something, and... he found me." She looked down into her plate. "I only then realized that there were never any real feelings there." Her eyes came back to meet mine.

"The night you saw him at my home, I was having an extremely shitty week. If I could go back and erase his entry into my life, I would." Her words finally gave me a sense of reassurance. He meant nothing to her. That asshole just kept creeping in to take advantage during her weak moments. "And as for my past, like I hinted, he turned out to be a jerk." She stuck her fork into a sprout and sliced it. "He hurt me so bad, I fought to breathe in the end. Luckily, my girls caught me before...it got any worse." She lifted the fork to her mouth, examining it. "I'm not allowed another breakdown. One of the girls are due first," she stated with a forced smile.

She popped the piece into her mouth and started chewing. Although she tried to keep her face from giving anything away, I could see she was still having trouble with it. Whoever he was had left a scar that still itched, resulting in her being extremely guarded. "I guess I do have a type."

Her eyes narrowed on me. Speechless, I disagreed with a shake of my head. She was mistaken if she was honestly comparing me to them.

I pressed the dial, and the tuner sped along in search of a station on the car radio, landing on the following preset: 94.7 FM. The old R&B song playing was from the group New Edition, and Bobby Brown was just doing his thing. I heard her humming along to the tune and saw that as an opening. We hadn't quite relaxed since the conversation at dinner.

"What you know about this song?" I said jokingly. She started dancing and belting out the next few lines before she broke into laughter. I started laughing as well. "It's rare that I get to see the silly side of you." "Yeah, well, don't get used to it," she replied, still smiling. "Do you say everything that pops into your head?"

"Only to people I couldn't care less about," she jested, then stuck her tongue out. "Wait, I forgot we're sworn enemies. But I thought you liked me." "I don't even like you a little bit."

I played into it, clicking the unlock button for the doors. "Ah well, tuck and roll." She swatted at my chest and threw her head back in laughter. I was completely taken by it. "Oh, wow, this… this is my song," she said, referring to a slow jam by Kevon Edmonds, which happened to be one of my all-time favorites as well.

"This *is* your song," I said, raising the volume. I then decided to pull over.

At daytime, the view would have been the neighboring islands, but I settled for the consolation prize of having the heavens lit with diamonds in the sky, which was just as magnificent. I adjusted the audio before stepping out of the car. I then made my way around and reached out to her.

"What are you doing?"

"Come dance with me."

212

"What? Here? Are you crazy? People will see us. No," she said, folding her arms on her chest. I wasn't about to back down and took hold of her, guiding her to her feet. She was reluctant yet complied. "Just relax. I want to enjoy and share this with you."

I started to dance and eventually, she swayed, albeit a bit off beat, but I didn't mind. Her being pressed against me with no space between us sent my senses wild. From the smell of her hair to her hand being cupped by mine. Nothing was better than this moment. Nothing else mattered.

"I am not very good at this," she admitted after knocking my knee again, which made me flinch.

"What are you talking about? Your motion is very fluid," I said, trying not to focus on the striking pain growing in that one spot. She giggled. I pressed her even closer to me, my hand gliding down to the small of her back.

"I meant being spontaneous in this way. I already know I'm a horrible dancer." A warm feeling spread through me after she rested her head on my chest, getting comfortable with me.

"Ha-ha. That I can tell," I whispered, knowing my voice would have probably done some weird crackly thing and given away my excitement. It did.

"Don't laugh at me. I know I am." Her voice w a s just as soft. I shifted my head and found myself rubbing my lips against her hair before pecking it. My breathing was so heavy it drowned out the noise of passing vehicles. I drew her even closer and felt her submit to the pull.

"Yes, but I love you—" I jolted, hearing my words, feeling her stiffen. She pulled away. "—for still trying," I quickly added, but it was too late.
Her sober gaze told me I'd made a huge mistake. She pushed at my chest, freeing herself completely from my grasp. "I know exactly what you're doing. This stops right now," she said, totally confusing me.
"I don't understand," I said, a bit panicked.

"A kiss or sex with you isn't going to turn me stupid if that's what you think. You underestimate my willingness to survive over having a man in my life. I know this game. I warn women every day about guys like you." "What are you talking about? What did I do—"

"Mind games!" she erupted. "You think I don't know when I'm being worked over?" Now I understood. She was boxing me in with the men of her past. "Look, I'm not here trying to get you in bed with me," I said, shaking my head.

"You're not?" I wasn't, but that didn't mean I wouldn't love to end the night with her in my arms on a cozy bed. "Then tell me, why is it that just a couple of months ago, you saw me as a nuisance and wanted nothing more than to have me locked away, and now you're here professing your love for me. Bullshit!"

That stung, and the pain resonated from my chest out to my limbs. Seeing myself through her eyes for the first time was painful, and it was absurd for her to still see me as the enemy trying to rattle her. I knew men played recklessly with women's hearts, but I wasn't one of them. "Bria, look at me. People change," I pleaded, knowing she just needed to see I was sincere.

"Take me home," she said, not budging on her position, leaving me standing there with my hand reaching out. I clenched my jaw and swallowed hard to flush the taste of rejection building in my throat. I then headed back to my side of the car.


"You told her you love her, and she bolted. Damn, your game is weak!" Devon, one of my soon-to-be ex-coworkers said after I was forced by Veda to get another man's perspective on the matter. I blamed everything on the music. Veda had dropped in offering lunch while I packed what little I had brought into my office into a storage box. It was weird coming into work today, seeing as my boss was probably about to be locked away for good.

My colleagues had organized a farewell party for me and were stepping in one by one to say their goodbyes. Although looking forward to a new adventure, I felt an overpowering need to fling my desk chair out the window. But with my luck, it would probably only land on my car. Instead of finding my way off the premises, I spent most of the morning staring out the window, daydreaming about my intimate times spent with Bria. What was it about this woman that had me telling myself to keep it together? I was no Mr. Suave when she came around, that's for certain.

"It's about time you realized you have strong feelings for her." Veda's eyes held mine.

"What gave me away?"

I swallowed hard, wondering if it was that obvious to everyone. "The tone your voice takes when you simply say her name. From the moment you started obsessing about her, I knew it was bound to happen. I'm surprised you're only now figuring that out, Professor."

That gave me a weird feeling in my chest, knowing she wanted nothing to do with it.

"You need to reevaluate the situation and see if this chick is worth it." Devon continued with his unsolicited advice. I would settle for throwing *him* out the window. I rubbed at my face remembering last night. We'd struggled in the middle with our confessions, but after that part of the night was over, we were flowing. I just had to spoil things with the whole "I love you" slip. What the hell had possessed me to say that?

I'd had flowers delivered to her office but was still ignored. I sat staring at my WhatsApp, wondering if I would catch her online—if she was missing me and if I'd made it into her thoughts. Waking up with her on my mind had become customary, but it's not like I could just call her when I felt the need to. I'd finally given in and called her job only to be told she wasn't even in. A frown broke across my face wondering what sort of mischievous adventure she was getting herself into and who her victim was this time around.

Whoever it was, they were getting more attention than I was. Veda now held my phone so I'd stop coming across as an obsessed stalker. I knew better. "You need a plan 'cause women like Bria aren't gonna take just any bullshitter's word." Thrown by Veda's statement, I looked at her. Her hands went up in defense. "I'm not saying you're a bullshitter."

"What she meant to say was that that

girlfriend of yours can see you bullshitting her from a mile away," Devon said.

"How is that any different from what she just said?" I retorted, already exhausted with the conversation. "Look, don't get on us. We're just trying to help." "Well, I wish you would stop," I said, going over to my window. Looking out, I observed how the road catered to one direction for traffic. Kind of like my thoughts. She had consumed them. I couldn't help but wonder what she might be getting into next seeing that her nemesis was most likely going to be locked away for a while. What would now be her focus, and would I be part of it?

"You need to be just as intense to get through to her." "No, that could be explosive. What he needs to do is be the calm in her life," Veda advised. "Don't try to lock her down, she won't let you. Just let it go. You're a good-looking guy with all your hair. There will be other girls."

I sighed. I had listened to the both of them. They both had points. Seeing her pattern, Bria had the tendency to run, yet could stand and fight when challenged. She was intense either way. Although she opened up about her past, she didn't allow anyone the opportunity to get too close. There was still distance. However, there was a pull to her. It was strange, but I felt a connection with her, and it didn't only have to do with sex. At some point, following her around became less of a chore and more of a necessity. I wanted to be where she was.

I saw her change from a woman out to conquer the world with little regard of how she would do it into a woman who placed those she loved before herself, making sure they were protected.

Thinking on it now, that's who she always was. The activist in her seemed less extreme once I realized what her cause truly was. She wanted to safeguard a legacy for the future generation, that I knew, but something was missing in regards to how she functioned. It was impossible that I hadn't broken through to her yet.

"So what's it going to be? Run or die trying?" Devon's statement was right on the money. I couldn't have phrased it better myself. While rubbing a finger repeatedly over my bottom lip, I closed my eyes just for a moment to think. The answer was overpowering, and I just had to accept it. Tilting my head back, I released a sort of acknowledgement into the universe.

"How do I get her to fall in love with me?" The words felt extremely right and absolute. They made my body finally relax. My being was already on board. It was just waiting for my heart to get with it and uncage itself. Veda cheered and clapped.

"Love. You should work on getting her to like you first," Devon said, making both me and Veda sneer at him. She shook her head. "The event you're planning. Go hard. She'll love you for it." I must admit I'd thought about using that angle. But what kind of man would I be if I played at her heart strings like that just to gain leverage? I shook the thought for the millionth time from my head.

"No, there must be another way."

"After what happened last night, for you to still want to make her your woman, you must be crazy," Devon strongly voiced. "Glad to see you're not running." Veda beamed.

Running. How could I run from a source having such a gravitational pull? The only thing I could do was surrender to it.

# Chapter 13
# Pick Me

## Bria

Ma was busy in the kitchen preparing a light snack for Dad. I was seated at the kitchen island sorting out some footage of the foster children collecting trash on the beach. It wasn't a planned event, but after going there to enjoy ourselves and seeing the spot where we usually assembled sprinkled with garbage, Aniah suggested we clean up. She immediately started putting garbage into her toy beach bucket. The older girls grumbled a bit but eventually joined in.

"I think I'm gonna try to adopt her," I said, feeling a twinge of anxiety. "Do you think I'll make a good mom?" "I think if that's your first question, you'll do just fine," Ma replied after coming back from giving my grandfather his sandwich. She then came over to give me a squeeze. I held on to her, thanking God for having both my grandparents present in my life. Because of them, I'd had opportunities to pursue all my dreams and now it would be my turn to pass on the blessing to Aniah. "I was wondering what took you so long."

I never saw myself adopting someone else's child, mostly because there was a fear in me of having the parent begging at my doorstep to return the kid they'd left behind. That would be heartbreaking but having someone else take the child I'd admittedly come to see as my own would

be devastating. She wasn't mine, but I hoped she

would want to make me hers. Unlike the other kids whose parents came to visit and even took them for a weekend when possible, Aniah was more orphan than foster child. Her biological parents were presumed dead according to her only living relative—her aunt. She was sort of a drunk and never made any attempt to claim legal guardianship, but there was always the possibility of her turning her life around and vowing to take up the responsibility to care for Aniah.

It was silly and ignorant of me to have shunned the idea of adopting—vehemently stressing how I wanted a child from my own womb. I didn't realize how perfect Aniah was. She didn't need me, but I needed her. I was becoming a better person because of her; I cared for others and didn't just think on the things I wanted for a change. I wanted that feeling to stay.

"I want memories like this between us," I said, showing my grandmother a few frames still saved in my camera of a mother and daughter shoot I was hired for recently.

"And you will. Are you ready to read?" she asked, placing the last of her washed dishes on the rack. She dried her hands and came to sit next to me. She then picked up the Bible, which she'd rested on the table earlier. It was something we'd done every Monday since I could remember. "Our guidebook through life," she called it. I felt as though we'd read the entire thing at least a hundred times or even more. She began thumbing through it in search of a chapter as though she would find a story we had never read.

I grinned. I just loved having these moments with her—seeing her insist I take time for her even though she never really had to. I wanted to be here. After returning from my studies, I was the one who'd insisted we started it up again. Seeing her smile when I handed her the Bible that day was so rewarding.

This would be something I would definitely do with Aniah. I planned on creating our own tradition along the way, something we would enjoy for years to come.

My grandmother's pick of reading the story of Job was my favorite. How his faith in God never wavered, although all was taken from him including his family, resonated within me. I'd been tested through life. I was even close to ending it, but somehow, either through a voice I'd heard in my darkest hour, my friends and family, or through someone showing up at the right moment, I found the strength to fight back and push. My mantra was "I got this." But it was only recently I realized that I never did. God had it all this time. He kept me safe and had never left me. He did that for someone who barely made the effort to get to church on time. That said a lot.

We read the first four chapters and would be picking up where we left off the following Monday. "Bria, what happened to the man you said was helping you find your father?" I wasn't ready to answer her, especially since I was the cause of the distance between us. I was simply refusing to be loved by him, that I knew, if it was even love he was after. I mean, I'd already slept with him, what else did he want? I couldn't bring myself to apologize and had just stayed away completely.

Gazing up at the clock, I saw that I was

running late for an event. I carefully fixed my camera back into my bag, then gave my grandmother a quick squeeze and a kiss on her cheek before I headed for the door.

"We'll talk later, Ma."


## Trevor

By advertising on the radio and in the newspaper, I had gained some traction and had a few consultations scheduled for the week. I was accumulating some notable clients, which made me extremely optimistic about my future. It was midday, and I was looking forward to some time spent in the gym. Making time to decompress would be an important part of my process and was something I had promised to keep as routine. I still had to change out of my work clothes, but first I had an assigned task to take care of. "Thanks for coming to get me." "No problem," I said, knowing Veda was going to owe me big time for this one. She'd asked me to collect a guy she was messaging over the internet who lived in Anguilla. They were to meet today, but first I had to make sure he was harmless. As much as I'd argued not being able to make that out within our short trip back, she tastelessly joked how if anything, I would know what her murderer looked like if he was placed in a line-up.

I had to hand it to her. She was a risk taker who lived by trying everything at least once before passing judgment. Minutes away from the border, my eyes bumped into a person attempting to climb up onto a brick wall having a fence that ran along it as an extra barrier. It didn't take long for me to realize it was Bria.

"What the… Bria." I pulled over abruptly, the blare of a horn cursing me out for not indicating my sudden need to turn. My curiosity piqued, I wondered what she was getting herself into now. We hadn't spoken since the night I was ordered to take her home, and I was still trying to figure out my next move in getting her to at least admit she held feelings for me. I was using being too busy as a cover for not moving the ball along.

"What's that woman doing there?" my passenger asked.

"Be right back," I stated while getting out of the car. "Bria," I said, announcing my presence, making her flinch.

"Oh, shit, you frightened me," she said, holding her chest. She then turned and continued to pry open the gash found in the fence. I approached, my brows dipped. Clearly, she was trying to sneak onto private property. In hindsight, I should have known she would never stop snooping. She was simply an inquisitive being.

"Come help me get through," she said, beckoning me.

"Bria—" I protested. I fought with what I knew was wrong, yet I found myself stripping off my jacket and rolling up my sleeves. I hiked myself up the wall, ignoring the fact that we probably looked like two foolish criminals trespassing in plain sight. She instructed me to pull at the fence where the split was in order for her to slip through. I complied and watched as she slid her bag through and then herself. "Should I come too?" Veda's internet buddy bellowed.

"Just wait in the car," I replied before finding myself through, feeling like I needed hiking gear to scale the slight slope leading up to someone's home. I worried about the welcome an uninvited guest would receive. "Did you ever consider there might be dogs?" I said, catching up to her. "And why are we here?" I asked while losing my footing.

I slid a bit and almost found myself feeling the shaved lawn against my face. I stood and was frustrated seeing I was the only one struggling. "There are no dogs. A wedding is happening. I'm here to take pictures," she responded while trying to control her breathing.

"Oh, so why didn't you use the entrance?" I dared asking. She stopped, and I knew it was so she could catch her breath.

"Because without an invitation, they aren't letting you in." She looked away. "I forgot mine, and I'm already late," she mumbled, continuing up the slope.


Now at the top, we headed around the back of the house where the kitchen staff prepared for the reception. She pulled out her camera and connected an interchangeable lens to it. I waited while she took a few pictures before actually moving further. I figured we would go in search of the bride, so it threw me when she told me to follow her quietly. By her actions, I came to terms that we were sneaking around. This woman had once again involved me in something questionable. She had most certainly not been hired to capture this wedding.

"Bria," I called, seeing her take cover behind a pillar, face pressed against the camera with one eye squeezed shut. She then stepped out and focused in on one of the windows on the second level of the house, turning the barrel on her camera as if to get a clearer view of the person somewhat visible through the blinds. "Bria!" I was growing angrier by the second.

"Shh," she responded while pressing the capture button on the camera. I didn't see the purpose of this venture and voiced it to her. She completely ignored me and just continued snapping and moving along the outside walls of the house, trying to be as discreet as possible.

At some point, I stopped complaining and found myself following her around, waiting for her to finish up. We eventually got closer to the ceremony where she stood in silence watching the proceedings. It was an intimate gathering. Flowers on pillars lined the aisles with five rows of chairs on either side. The gazebo where the bride and groom stood exchanging their vows was replicated on the top of a six- tier wedding cake nearby.

I was shocked when I realized exactly whom the ceremony was for when the groom turned after the couple had been pronounced husband and wife. It was the guy on her porch that night. Her "now and again" lover had just gotten married to someone else. His bride was the total opposite of Bria, I concluded, solely on her physical appearance. He'd chosen, and it wasn't Bria.

I looked over, observing Bria. She was

motionless. I was guessing she'd come here for confirmation. Maybe even closure. The calm movement of her chest and batting of her eyelids were the only signs of life. I wondered if the event was even registering within her. "Hey, what are you two doing there?" a man called out, jolting her from her daze. "We should go," she said, then instantly took off running. I followed, struggling to stay on my feet as we headed back the way we'd came. Damn, she was fast!

I helped her onto the wall, and she again squeezed her way through the gash in the fence before I did. On the other side as cars raced by, we sat panting, presumably safe from harm. As if she'd lost her damn mind, she started laughing. I looked on in disbelief. "I'm so sorry, that was so crazy." She placed her hand over her mouth, trying to contain herself. "Yeah, it kinda was. Did you hear the dogs?" I asked, still trying to catch my breath. She shrugged while completely beside herself with laughter. I found myself joining in.

"I just thought you would try to talk me out of it. It already took me a hell of a while to go through with it." "So, you've graduated to stalking now?"

"I guess I have." She tried to collect herself.

"And what, did you do some kind of ninja training? Goodness, you *flew* through that fence. *Whoosh,*" I said, adding a hand gesture. "Look, my shirt is ripped!" The laughter continued. She waved her hand, indicating that she'd had enough. Tears ran down her cheeks. I was a natural comedian. "Promise me that in the future, you'll put up a bit more of a fight when things seem strange. Because getting you to help me was too easy."

227

I slowed my laughter and seized the opportunity to lock with her gaze. I swallowed, understanding that it meant she expected me to stick around. In what capacity, I didn't know. Whether as a friend or lover, I would gladly assume the part. "I promise I'll try to sense when you're absolutely out of your mind and about to get us both incarcerated."

"Look what I confiscated." In her hand, there was one of the thank you tokens.

"God, the list of charges I will have brought against me in court keeps building the more I hang with you. Now I have to add theft?" She simply giggled, her mischievous nature shining through.
I was glad that she could laugh about it—that she wasn't brought to tears having seen her lover marry another woman.

"I hadn't heard from him in weeks, but there were rumors. I had to see for myself," she said, eyes to the pavement. " I guess I needed to let go of my past in order to fully embrace what was next for me." Her eyes met mine. "I understand." My heart skipped a beat. There wasn't much else I could say. I saw that she needed closure, and I hoped this would sever all ties from this guy. I fell into her eyes and wanted nothing more than to be included in what was next for her.

"Sorry, but we goin' or what?" my forgotten passenger bellowed from outside my car, making us both look up in his direction. I was sure he would have left without me. "Let's get out of here before they come looking and *really* release the dogs," she said, standing. She then extended a hand to help me to my feet, which I accepted.

"So, it's all happening tonight, huh?" "Yeah, the moment of truth."

"I'm anxious to see how many friends you *actually* have," she said, making me laugh. The tone of our acquaintance had changed. Her being openly glad to see me was a good feeling—a feeling I wanted to last. "Should I bring my camera?"

"No, tonight is only about fun. I want you to laugh and eat to your heart's content," I said, passing my index finger along my bottom lip. I couldn't wait to see her in a sleek, elegant dress that made all eyes gravitate to her like Cinderella. I'd be the only one to dance with her.

Just then, there was a quick knock at the door, drawing her attention away from me. Without waiting for approval, in rushed Cindy, my secretary. Things were progressing well with my business, and Bria had stopped in with a card and office plant as a congratulatory gesture.

"Sorry, but this needs your signature," she said as she hurried towards me. Accepting the file from her, I took a split second to check it out. I looked up briefly to find Bria surveying my office. Her eyes seemed to stop on a picture of me standing next to the then Princess Maxima and the soon-to-be king, Prince Willem-Alexander.

"I have a few surprises set for this evening that I know you are going to love," I said, looking up after signing the document. I nodded at Cindy, letting her know that it was okay for her to leave with it. Smiling, Bria then looked at me with curiosity. My attention was once again fully hers. She broke the stare, taking her gaze to the floor as she rubbed at the back of her neck, then passed her fingers down her collarbone. Ah, her collarbone—how I could gaze forever at it, watching as it came together at the distinct hollow at the base of her throat. I swallowed hard as my fantasy took me much further than gazing. I wanted to run my tongue over it. "I wanted to ask you something," she said, helping my mind out of the gutter.

"What's that?"

Looking a bit frustrated, as if whatever she wanted to say wasn't easy, she first exhaled, then continued with her question. "I wanted to ask you if…" She closed her eyes and swallowed hard. "If you would be my date for tonight?" she asked hesitantly. It must have delighted her to ask because she was smiling and twiddling with her fingers. She kept her eyes briefly closed, and her brows dipped slightly. I accepted the fact that I was truly taken by her and couldn't resist her, but then again, I didn't want to. "I wasn't expecting that," I said, completely surprised. After all these months of her ripping at me at every chance she got and it taking time for her to bury the hatchet and let me into her circle of trusted friends, I was finally convinced that we were truly there. I was feeling jubilant, to say the very least, but that was before reality kicked in. "However, I can't."

That made her stop altogether, and she seemed to hold her breath. "Not that I don't want to. It's just that I have to be there early to make sure everything is going accordingly," I said, which made her finally exhale. "And… I'm already escorting someone." I felt agitated. The last thing I wanted was for her to show up with a date of her own tonight, and I hoped that wasn't her plan B.

"Oh," was all she said, and I needed to break the awkward tension that was building.

"She's special to me. I was actually going to introduce you to her tonight," I said, certain that it didn't make matters any better.

"Well, I'm happy for you. I am looking forward to meeting her," she said in an unconvincing tone. I contemplated telling her exactly who my date was, but before I could get a word in, her attention was drawn by the buzzing of her phone. "That's the girls. I have to go."

"Okay, thanks for coming in," I said, watching her as she used just her thumb to text. She made a noise of agreement before vanishing behind the door as it swung shut. For some reason, I thought that maybe I shouldn't have been so secretive about who I was bringing, but all would be revealed tonight, and she would surely see me in a different light.

Night had finally arrived, and I was excited and nervous, to say the least. I knew I would be judged on all aspects, and I wanted Bria to see that I took everything I did seriously. There were to be no mistakes. It was an elegant event, for which the ladies wore long, glittery gowns with sparkling accessories, and the men looked sharp with their suits pressed to perfection.

*The venue is magnificent.* I observed the beauty of it all. Crystal chandeliers hung from the ceiling while white drapery ran down the walls. People sipped on the finest wine, as I refused to cheapen this event with anything that wasn't the best. The tables were staged to perfection by Artemia, the only event planners on the island I thought

231

capable of pulling off such a grand spectacle. I had to show Bria that I was more than what she thought of me—that I too cared for others but had a different approach to things. This Feed Our Children Now fundraiser was already generating a substantial amount of money based on ticket sales alone, and this was just the first of a planned four-day run.

I watched as the invited guests streamed in. Everything was on track and going smoothly, I observed, as a group of entertainers began singing their prepared piece, allowing those who ventured onto the dance floor to swing their hips to the master work of a well-known band on the island. This was utter perfection, yet something was off. I was beginning to get a bit antsy, mostly because I had tried calling her phone but had been diverted to voicemail.

Time was slipping away, and everyone was expected to take their seats in the next fifteen minutes. I'd reserved a place for her and her friends at my table, positioned at the front, where she would be able to witness everything without having to squint. It made me smile to think of how someone so vibrant refused to wear her glasses when necessary because she didn't care for any insults. Yet her glasses, which she probably saw as an accessory that highlighted an imperfection, made her more attractive to me. As a matter of fact, whenever I was blessed enough to see her up close, my eyes would dare to look closer in search of the almost invisible scar hiding in the cleft of the bottom of her right eyebrow. I was longing to hear the story of how she'd gotten it.

Now I was outside, anxiously waiting for her

to drive up the slope and make an entrance in a dress that would make heads turn. I geared up, hoping to make a better impression on her two friends, to whom I'd had to make my own introduction. That hadn't fazed me; I knew exactly that it would happen. As if my thoughts had conjured my reality, here was the limo I'd tasked with getting the ladies here. My heart skipped a beat. How silly was that? Unable to see inside, with my hands pushed deep into my pockets, I watched as the vehicle came to a complete stop. I swallowed hard. The chauffeur got out and made his way to open the passenger door. I took a deep breath, straightened my posture, and then exhaled, feeling somewhat relieved that, although she was late, she hadn't missed the scheduled presentation I was to make. I felt sweat building in my armpits.

"Keep it together. Cool and collected." I released a rapid breath. As I'd expected, her friends appeared first, allowing the build-up that was typical of these types of scenes. My nerves started to show themselves; I felt my palms dampen. My lips curved upwards as I politely nodded and greeted the women who had, no doubt, ensured Bria's presence. The driver then pushed the door shut, which immediately caught my attention. Open-mouthed, I made a gesture to him, my palms up. Shaking his head, he indicated the one thing that I didn't have under control: Bria's assured attendance.

"Where the hell is she?" I said with obvious frustration, passing my hand over my mouth, adding a deep, slow exhale. "Sir, we are ready to start," my secretary announced.

I was designated to say the opening words for the

evening along with my date—which was Aniah. She looked so beautiful in her long, blue princess gown.

It wasn't just her I invited here tonight. We had sent an invitation to all the organization, inviting ten of their children, both boys and girls, making sure to take care of their attire. I'd sent a special request asking for Aniah to be my co-host. This was kept a secret from Bria. I thought it would bring her to tears. Why did I follow Veda's advice to not tell her? With her hand interlocked with mine, Aniah, with a tiara and gloves, accompanied me onto the stage. Those present applauded. I bowed to her, and she took her place at my side.

I looked into the audience at the table Bria was to be seated at and fought back the agitation of her not having the decency to show. I found it hard to focus on the teleprompter and was nudged by Aniah to read. I took a breath. I then recited the lines displayed on the screen, welcoming everyone and telling them about the planned events. Before long and not a minute too soon, my task was completed, and I was off to pay one of my mandatory guests a visit.


## Bria

I lay curled on my couch. A documentary on the African diamond trade caught my attention while I flipped aimlessly through the channels. I was doing my best to keep myself occupied. It was getting to me that I'd decided at the last possible minute not to go to the fundraiser. What had me

234

reeling was that my decision revolved around him.

Kayla and Mich had left about two hours ago after trying to convince me that I was being irrational about the whole thing. They told me that they couldn't believe this guy had gotten the best of me and made me miss out on representing my own foundation.

The funds collected from the event were to be split between two chosen organizations already selected and known to the directors, but they would be announced to the public tonight at the end, after the award ceremony. It was also being televised in order to encourage those watching at home to call in and pledge their donations. Trevor had definitely worked hard on it, and it was a proven success ahead of time. The selected organization was certain to receive enough funding to last them an entire year. This Christmas was going to be special for more than a handful of kids, and it was all because of him.

"What a dick!" I said, now at the refrigerator, peering in as my thoughts diverted back to the organizer of the event. "Right now, I could be drinking wine, laughing at someone with my girls, eating tiny and overpriced but delicious food, and having a great time, but no, I'm stuck here waiting on pizza," I said, completely agitated. I slammed the refrigerator door shut.

With much hunger and anticipation, I was waiting and sure that the delivery guy would soon be honking his horn, beckoning me to come collect my pizza. *And if he knew what was good for him, he'd better have made damn sure it wasn't cold*, I thought, with a malt in hand, making my way back to the couch.

"Bria, control your temper. Don't let this guy get to you," I said to myself, taking a deep breath before fixing my hair in a bunch. Sitting with my legs crossed in my white with black stripes pajama pants and red top, I first nestled my drink between my legs before stretching my hands over to the side table to retrieve my crossword-puzzle book and pencil. I then picked up my glasses that were resting to the side of me and fixed them onto my face. I was comfortable now and determined not to let my frustration consume me.

Of course, that was when the deliverer of my late-night meal would choose to arrive, knocking as if I'd kept him waiting. I observed that the time was ten forty-five, two minutes after the time he was scheduled to be here. I then took a breath to spare the poor, unsuspecting delivery guy my fury because he was late.

Calmly, I placed the book and pencil on the couch and then bent, placing the malt on the floor. Again, there was harsh knocking at the door, and that was when I decided that he was not to be spared the greeting he was about to receive. Hell would freeze over first before he got a tip out of me.

Unlocking the door and then swinging it open, I was ready to rip into him. "Why the hell didn't you come tonight?" Trevor asked after the brief pause he took to take me in. He looked a bit wild with his tie pulled loose, his sleeves rolled up, and his shirttails out of his pants.

"Well, you're certainly not the pizza guy," I said, turning and making my way back to my living room. "I changed my mind. I had other things I wanted to do." "That's a lie, and you know it! I

236

heard you with your friends. You were excited."
"Hmm."

"Bria, do you know how much effort went into tonight? I made sure every single thing was perfect," he said, following me, I gathered, after hearing the door slam shut and his heavy footsteps on my tiled floor. "Then congratulations to you. That is what giving back feels like," I said, picking up the book and placing the pencil in my mouth before taking my seat.

"Everything is a joke to you, right?" he said. It was as though he struggled to find his words. His question was followed by a sudden knock at my door. "Oh, that must be the pizza guy," I said, taking the pencil from my mouth. Again, I placed my book aside, but this time, I was fighting a smile as I witnessed the extreme frustration on Trevor's face. He then raised his hand, stopping me from going to the door. He continued, "This was something you suggested me doing for a change. And now that I have, you decide to mock me by not showing up." He opened the door, took out his wallet, and handed the guy money without saying one word to him. He then took the pizza out of his hands and slammed the door shut.

"Hey, that wasn't nice," I said, ironically displeased with his behavior towards the delivery guy. "Yeah, whatever. Tell me—what happened between noon today and now? Because you were completely geared up and ready to come."
"Nothing happened. I just changed my mind," I said nonchalantly, lying. Why would I have gone when he was bragging about bringing someone special, completely humiliating me with his rejection of being

my date?

"You expect me to believe that you just changed your mind? Just like that?" He set the pizza down on my kitchen counter. "That's bullshit!" he roared, coming toward me. "Then that's what it is," I said, diving back into my book. "No. No, it isn't!" He yanked the book from my hands.

"Hey," I said, going to my feet. Matching fury with fury, I was up in his face, not at all intimidated by the height he had over me.

I listened as he tried to control his breathing. My eyes narrowed, watching him searching my face. I noted how his lips broke apart partially before he wet them with his tongue, swallowing hard.

Whatever he was thinking, he would surely be mistaken. Moments passed as he took the time to settle himself. His eyes went to my chest, staying there, observing me as it rose and fell. I felt his hand brush and carefully take hold of mine, and I looked on as his head started descending. My frown deepened. Was he serious? *Is he... going to kiss me?* I thought, standing there, perplexed. He was definitely in for a surprise if he thought this was to be a "take me" kind of moment; he would only be finding out just how " ghetto black" I was, according to the prissy woman he was into.

He dared leaning in further and started a kiss that took my breath away. *He had the audacity...* The thought dwindled. I fought to hold on to m y power, searching for the strength to kick this asshole out of my home. With what little strength left in me, I forced myself to let go, breaking the link our tongues had made.

"Get out!" I yelled, my voice shaking.

"No, not until you tell me the truth!" he roared back, puffing like he was about to breathe fire.

"You want the truth? Here is my truth," I said, and without thinking, started to spill it. "I was hiding. That was evident through me finding a place on the highest hill there was on this little island. Over time, I felt safe. I even started to feel comfortable and began involving myself in things that made me feel alive again. But I wasn't prepared for you." I swallowed hard, realizing I'd revealed a weakness.

I got angry and added, "You know *nothing* about me. About my life. You assume everything you heard about me was true." "Assume? Bria, before, I would do that, yes, I'll admit. But now..." His voice dipped into a whisper. "I can say what I know to be true."

"And what's that exactly?"

"That you keep people you truly care about at a distance. But just close enough to look out for them. That you will give everything to make sure they have a fighting chance. I see that with the kids—with Aniah," he said, coming closer.
He clasped my hand in his and then continued. "I just want to get close enough to love you."

I gasped.

Ignoring the flutter in my stomach, I screeched, "You would want nothing more than to break me, wouldn't you? You would love to get me under control," I stressed, pulling away from him. "No, Bria, only a fool would try to control you, and I don't want to break you. I won't do anything that you won't allow. I wouldn't be able to." He released a breath. "What I want is to do what possibly only a few lucky enough to get close to you have tried yet failed to do. I just want to be with you."

Taking me by my chin, I watched while he stared intently into my eyes. I couldn't read his expression. Was it sadness or pity? I wasn't having it, and I wasn't about to be taken by his sweet lies. That was the last thing happening here tonight. His brows dipped, and I knew it had to do with the fact that I was clenching my jaw. He knew what was coming.

"Get out!" I said sternly, tilting my head up and out of his grasp. "No, not this time," he said, gripping me by the hips, regaining his hold on me. He barely got the chance to say the words, which were but a murmur on my lips. The kiss made every hair on my body rise. My fingers found themselves hooked in his. Yet, they weren't stopping him. They then released and found themselves moving across his cheekbone until subtly resting around his thick neck.

*Gain some control, Bria, or you'll regret this,* my inner voice warned, which I ignored. I had an undeniable thirst for this man that even reason couldn't talk me out of. One of my legs curved around him, and I found myself trying to mount him. Our lips broke, and that was when the words forming in my head verbalized. "I want you," I surprised myself by saying.

"I want you more," he said, taking me by my pajama pants and pulling me closer, which seemed impossible. There was just no space left between us. My tongue made a break for his Adam's apple, licking at it like I was possessed. I started scratching at his shirt impatiently in search of the buttons. It stunned me having him grip me by both my wrists, then gently draw me from him. In his hold, eyes locked, I stood fighting to control my breathing, waiting to hear what the hold-up was, certain that the word "confused" was stamped on my forehead.

"I want to take my time with you. Okay?" His words struggled for composure. "Okay," I replied impatiently. My eyes then searched frantically for my next targeted spot. "No rushing, Bria. Keep still," he ordered gruffly with a little shake. He released my wrists, then stepped back.

I took a deep breath and observed his slow approach. He started kissing me slowly and softly on different places of my face, and I closed my eyes and followed his command. I was enjoying the feel of his lips as they touched my skin. The one long smooch planted on my nose made me giggle like a schoolgirl. He then moved down my neck and I subtly held on to the side of his face. A hand glided down my body, unlocking a moan from me. I stood there awaiting his next move. I gasped feeling him take my top shirt off, and the chill in the air hardened my nipples. I bit into my bottom lip, drugged on anticipation.

Ever so softly, his fingers tapped against my abdomen. He then took hold of one of my breasts, rolling the peak of it under his palm. I gently cupped his face and leaned forward, eager to taste him. My mouth opened, wanting him to enter. Welcoming the slant of his lips over mine, he engulfed my lips and secured his control of the kiss. He was just as needy as I was but acted with more restraint. One of his hands curved at my neck, pulling me to him. I couldn't fight it any longer and held him with no intention of ever letting go.

241

One of my hands glided over his biceps hidden behind his shirt, his subtle grip reminding me he had a pace he wanted me to adhere to. His body pressed into me. Our lips broke with a smack. "How wet are you right now?" Was he seriously asking that? I was fucking juicy. "Extremely."

"Good." His hands cupped my buttocks, and he hiked me from my feet. I felt a hardness against me. My pelvis leaned into it. He placed me on the couch, which I thought an uncomfortable spot to have sex but didn't object to his choice over the bedroom. While my sleeping garments were being removed, he continued feeling on my body, adding kisses. I then waited for him to get rid of his. He knelt between my legs and one of his hands slowly moved up the length of my thigh. His other hand felt at the warmth of my center before rubbing against the plump flesh within my valley, lubricating me with my own sap. I moaned, gyrating my hips, yearning to feel him within me and claim him once more.

He rose to meet my lips, and I gripped his swollen member riddled with pumped veins and stroked it, wanting to milk him.

"Trevor," I whispered, my eyes on his. "Yes, Bria," he said my name hoarsely.

"Love me," I begged.

"I plan to."

His words brushed across my lips. "I just want to pleasure you," he responded. He was teasing me, making me want him, and it was working. He descended again and kissed the inner part of my thighs, and I shuddered in delight. He drew circles around my navel, and I gripped his head, feeling the sudden movement of his lips on my tummy. He kissed my abdomen, and I clenched my eyes tightly, wondering where he would kiss next. Pleased by him coming atop me, I spread to allow him clear passage.

He settled between my legs and like I'd never felt him before, my being quivered when he dipped into me. I felt completely overjoyed by his penetration. I clung to his firm glutes, refusing any such notion of him pulling out. My walls acted as the gatekeeper, denying his escape. He felt so delicious within me. It was mouthwatering.

His thrusting was methodical. The soft and caring expression on his face painted the picture of a man truly considering his lover's pleasure above his. My body swayed to the rhythm of him, and I enjoyed his motion, grooving with every contraction and flex of his body as he dove in and out of me. It was simply incredible. The sensation of him gliding along my walls enraptured me. Looking past the dark color of his eyes, I saw something that made me think how this wasn't just sex for him anymore, and for the first time, I'd finally seen him unmasked.

I whimpered, feeling the surge of raw emotions mix with a wave of pleasure unlike anything I'd ever felt. Moans rapidly building, I held onto him like my life depended on it. He picked up his pace and I held on, hoping to delight in his lovemaking a bit longer. My toes curled, and I contracted my walls in a last attempt at savoring the feeling. They then uncurled, spreading like a bird soaring on through a cloudless sky, feeling the freedom and indulging in a ride I never wanted to come down from.

My grip was unyielding as I held him tight in

my embrace. I was weak, but nothing would get me to break the connection. He held me, allowing me to stay where I felt safe. I'd given myself to him entirely and completely without compromise. This I knew was certain. He'd captured me, and for some reason, that scared me. I budged as if to free myself, but he was unwavering and chuckled into my neck.

"You should get off." He grunted. "You're not going anywhere," he said in a raspy after-sex voice. "I love feeling you beneath me." He then buried his head in my neck. The heat of his skin acting like a warm blanket was easily becoming my favorite thing.

"Did you…?"

"Nope, this was all about you," he commented, my unfinished question concerning his climax answered without delay.

I couldn't believe how weak his lovemaking had left me, which had him now carrying me into the bedroom. It was so simple, yet getting here was energy consuming. He sat me down onto the bed and scooted under the sheets next to me. He then scooped me into his arms.

My hair in a frizzed fluff covered my face. I laid captive in my lover's arms while entangled in my sheets wearing his dress shirt, as though I didn't have a closet full of clothing. He brushed at a tress, causing me to look up into a face where a very tiny mole interrupted the growth of hair in one of his eyebrows. My gaze then dropped into eyes that entranced me.

The feeling was familiar, yet I was uncertain. I looked away. This could easily become an addiction, which I wasn't r e a d y for but saw no problem getting used to. Resting on Trevor's delicious body while his hand rubbed my buttocks was simply amazing. My head rested on his chest. I listened to the sound of him taking breaths over the relaxed beating of his heart. The air conditioning's cold air—amplified by the spinning ventilator—ensured that I kept my naked body under the sheets. My eyes flickered open and what had seemed like a minute of recuperation turned out to be more than an hour of rest.

I gazed around and found him enjoying one of the many films found on my portable hard drive, the images projected onto my bedroom wall. Like a cat loving the comfort of being stroked, I moaned, making my contentment and consciousness known. He planted a kiss on the top of my head and squeezed my shoulders lightly when he did. He then began rubbing his hand on me. I had to admit I felt safe, free, and a sense of belonging all at once. I had no need to go running anywhere.

He planted a few more kisses before tilting my head back to taste my lips. The kiss came soft and luscious. He was awakening that feeling within me again, and by the feel of his hardening member growing and jamming into my lower back, so was the sexual beast within him. Surrendering to his grasp as he held my head in place, cupping it in his hand while his lips grazed against my neck had me fighting to contain my eagerness to be filled again. The brush of his lips over my eyelashes tickled me.

Now I could admit how this man had the ability to unlock different parts of me with a mere touch. Was it wrong for me to want to capture him between my walls again and enjoy feeling him give his strength over to me while he released, his grunting and jerking signs of my victory? A smile parted my lips, thinking it sure wasn't. He without a doubt wanted me to.

"What amuses you?" he asked, quiet and medieval-like, his eyes burning with desire.

"Nothing," I managed between kisses. "But that guy dies," I pestered without looking, giving away the end of the movie. "Not that I care," were the words that came with warmth against my skin.

"I thought you should know," I mocked.

He squeezed me tighter. "So that you know, I haven't been paying any attention to this movie. I'm too busy thinking about my chances of spending the night here and what that would entitle me to." I looked up at him.

"You're not spending any night until you tell me how bad your breath is in the morning. I don't have a spare toothbrush to defend myself if it's horrible," I teased. "You're not kicking me out, woman!" he said, turning over onto me.

"Trevor!" I yelped while being flattened.

He unbuttoned the shirt and plunged my nipple into his mouth. The cold of his tongue then warmth stretched them, making them willing participants. I held onto his ears, reveling in the sensation of them being toyed with in his mouth. "I'll bring it tomorrow," he said, stopping to my dismay. "But I'm not leaving tonight." He then came and laid next to me.

A muffled buzz coming from his pants caused us to look over at it where it rested on the floor. "You need to get that. Your phone has been vibrating like crazy." He exhaled and continued to ignore it, keeping his gaze to the ceiling. "Trevor, it

246

could be important." His head fell to the side, eyes filled with mischief. "No more important than this. Let me taste you a bit." "No you won't, you freak!" He ignored my protest and scooted down, lifting the shirt up.

My brain went to mush when I felt his tongue between my walls. My eyes closed, and my lips parted. I slowly took breaths, all the while allowing my mind to illustrate what I believed was going on down there.

I gasped and shamelessly moaned his name. I held tight to the sheets. The buzzing faded into space, and as the drums of the final scene in the movie indicated its climax, so did I. My quick release I blamed on being too sensitive to his touch. Nestled between my legs, he laid stroking my thigh. I sent my fingers down to touch his head. His phone began to buzz and instead of the circular movement I was planning on initiating, I began tapping him lightly.

"You need to check that," I insisted reluctantly, not wanting it to be any news that would take him from me. He sighed, and the warmth of his breath on my thigh felt so good. Frustration was written all over his face as he looked up at me. His overexaggerated, irritated actions on his way to retrieve his phone made me chuckle. I pulled the covers up, trying to secure the warmth left by his body.

"What's going on?" I asked, seeing his wary expression. "It's the secretary, nothing big." His eyes focused on his phone.

"But I'm guessing you're needed," I said, sitting up straight, observing how comfortable he was stark naked. "Well, I prefer filling another kind of

247

need." He looked at me, his eyes dangerous. "But I have to do something at the gala," he said while he climbed back into bed. He then took me into his lap. "I have to get back. It would look bad if I didn't. I kinda said I was going for ice."

"Really?" I mused. "No one in their right mind would believe that." He shrugged. "Worse yet, all the shops are probably closed. I have no way to account for my disappearance." We both started laughing, and I found myself leaning into his chest. "So, your date..." I fidgeted. "She won't be too happy," I said, remembering the reason I'd stayed my ass home tonight.

"No, she won't, and I'm sure she'll scold me on it." I tensed, wanting to leave, hating myself for feeling jealous.

"Bria, Aniah was my date."
I gazed around, unable to follow his direction. "It was to be a surprise. The children were the guests of honor at the event. You should have seen how thrilled she was jumping out of the limo." "Oh, wow, I missed that." It was a moment in Aniah's life that I would never get to witness, and it was all because of my stubbornness. I felt horrible. "She's still there. You can still show up for her," he said as if understanding what I was feeling.

"I don't have enough time to doll myself up to look the part. It would take me forever to get ready," I said, patting at my face and lips—roughly an hour on hair and makeup alone. "You look perfect," he stated, making me blush. *If the theme is 'wrapped in sheets' maybe, yes, but my nudity needs covering up.*

"I can't go like this," I said, springing from the

bed and turning to face him. He rose and stood completely naked in front of me. "Then I'll make us look like a pair." A smile broke across my face. "Just come," he begged.

I took a moment, then nodded.

His gaze drifted from my face to my chest. One of his brows rose, and his eyelids fluttered. He licked his lips.

"What's wrong?"

"Your..." he trailed off, deciding it better for me to guess while he played charades. Briefly, I looked down and found my breasts on the outer side of the shirt. "You got to be kidding me. You just had a mouthful of them, now you're blushing." I sucked at my teeth, hiked the shirt up, and fastened the loose button. He looked flustered, gawking like a pimple-faced fifteen-year-old who'd just seen real breasts for the first time that wasn't displayed in a magazine stashed in his mattress. "Let's go, you doofus." "There you go with the name calling again." "Just get ready."

The lather was thick, and bubbles seemed to have taken over my body. I don't know if the extra time I was taking in the bathroom had to do with knowing someone was probably timing me, or if I was trying to erase all signs of just being pleasured immensely before heading out. Knowing Mich, she would be able to detect that as I entered the room.

Whatever the reason, I was taking way too long and had to speed up the process. Having sprayed my hair with water and adding shampoo, I tilted my head back to rinse. Most of the soapy liquid ran in the opposite direction, avoiding my eyes, but a trail was finding its way down my face. I wiped at it.

While rinsing, feeling the suds as they skied down my body, it was impossible not to think of what it would be like showering with him. Opening my eyes, I screeched, completely surprised by Trevor's naked body making an appearance in my bathroom. "You scared me. What do you think this is, some kind of movie? You don't do that," I said, throwing suds at him, then hiding my nakedness. I guess it was to be expected. I hadn't locked the door. He turned his head, preventing getting some in his eyes.

"I figured I could do with a quick one."
I looked down and right away understood what he meant. "Get out! We don't have time for that."

"I'm making time," he said, stepping into the shower. "I don't like that you caught me off guard just now." He stepped in regardless, and I caved, adjusting the nozzle so the both of us would be sprayed with water. His hands slid up my body in a circular motion, taking time to stop at my breasts before continuing upward to wash the soapsuds found at my neck. I turned, giving him my back to take care of while I continued with my front. I felt him hard against me. He held on to me and started to rock slowly. "I could so get used to this."

"No one is stopping you," he said, kissing me on my back, making me quake with expectancy. My legs felt like mush beneath me. I was falling and needed to be caught. I needed to snap out of this. I bent going for my soap, wanting to lather him up quickly in order to get out of here. I squeezed the bottle above his collar, and guessing from his reaction, some got in his eye.

Scooping water, his hand then flew to his face, hoping to soothe the burn and kill the flame that was turning his eye blood red. I dropped the bottle. "I'm so sorry. I was just..." I watched as he frantically tried to ease his pain.

"Whose idea was this again?" His voice strained, giving away his agony. "Yours," I quickly said, trying to hold back on laughing.

"Was it? We should get out."

"We should, yes," I said, stepping out and grabbing my towel, then taking his hand to lead him out. It had always been a fantasy of mine to have sex in the shower, but maybe we needed practice. God knew how T.V. made everything sexy and never had anyone burning their eyes attempting it.

# Chapter 14
# **Puppets**
Trevor

*Am I so unlucky to have that happen and
spoil a moment that could've been epic?* I thought,
looking at myself in the mirror—my eye stinging,
bloodshot, and way smaller than the other.

"What a doofus indeed." But I was going for suave.
She had given me a moment to recollect myself after
the event that nearly cost me an organ, and now I
couldn't bring myself to face her looking like I had
the pink eye. "Are you okay?" she inquired, her
hands clasped, expression solemn, coming to stand
next to me while I watched my reflection in the
mirror.

I dropped my head, embarrassed at what had
taken place. "So that you know, I'm quite capable
in the shower. I usually get through bathing with all
my limbs intact," I said, trying to lighten up and
make her laugh. I pulled her into me and got excited
seeing she was the perfect fit. I kissed her hard on
her forehead.

"Really, 'cause that was crazy awkward."

"I guess we have that crazy-awkward-
uncoordinated kind of love thing going on where we
bump heads and so on when trying to be sexy."

"We haven't bumped heads though."

"Not yet—something to look forward to." I
grinned sheepishly, then winked with my good eye.
"Come on, get dressed. We need to go like now," she
said laughing, pushing free from my arms.

She then made her way out to dress herself.
The water from her hair dangling on her shoulders in

small curls wetting her blouse made me hesitate. She was such a rare beauty. All natural, nothing artificial or enhanced. She was the essence of a Nubian queen. I watched as she went to get her ringing phone, knowing that this woman had surely spelled me, and there was nothing I could or wanted to do about it.

"Kayla, calm down. I'm on my way," she said, and from the troubled look in her eyes, I could only assume her friend needed her right away.

"I'll drive."

We hurried to the venue in search of her friends. From what I understood on our ride over, it was Mich who needed help. Kayla had communicated to us that she had locked herself in the toilet stall, refusing to speak to anyone.
The artist performing delighted the guests with a melodious original piece, the chatter in the venue just low enough so you could hear her clearly.

Every eye that had found Bria took note of her jeans and pinned- up blouse, and their mouths didn't hold back from snickering or scoffing. But she didn't care. All that mattered was getting to her friend. "Trevor?" My name being called and an added hand resting on my shoulder alerted me, causing me to stop. From Bria's facial expression, it wasn't someone she liked. I turned and found Jasmine standing at my side.

"Jasmine," I said, feeling a cold sweat building. I hadn't seen her in forever, and usually when we *did* hook up, she would offer herself as dessert. I didn't have time for whatever show she wanted to put on and to no avail, tried to escape her grasp. Tensed, I hoped she would recognize I wasn't up for her games—especially at the cost of Bria's emotional state. She wasn't satisfied with a handshake and pulled me in for a kiss on the lips. I dared not look at Bria. "I see someone didn't get the dress code," she said, giving Bria a once-over. She then added, "Baby, will I see you later? We need to talk about something important."

"I really don't have the time for this," I said, trying to get her arms from around my neck.

"Are you really brushing me off for 'Ms. Simple' here?" Bria's mouth opened to say something which I could only imagine would be followed by a hair- pulling brawl. "She's anything but simple," I said, halting all movement and ending further discussion. With that said, Bria relaxed while Jasmine's eyes narrowed on her. "I'm gonna go ahead and find Mich," Bria said, giving Jasmine a look that spoke of her irrelevance.

## Bria

I rushed into the restroom and found Kayla at one of the stalls, trying to coax Mich into coming out. "What is she doing? What happened?" I asked Kayla, seeing Mich's feet poke out from beneath the door. Kayla shrugged. "She got a call. Excused herself from the table. And after she failed to return, I went looking for her and found her here. Speak to her," Kayla insisted before heading out, throwing her hands up, completely over it.

"Mich, what's wrong?" Head pressed against the stall door, I waited for a response.
"I told him I didn't want to be his number two and started to walk away. That's when he grabbed me, and then..." Mich trailed off before the door swung open to reveal her sitting and hanging on to the toilet like a drunk. She looked up, and the anger of seeing dried blood on her face made me want to kill the guy that did that to her.

The thrill of the affair was only heightened when both women knew. It also served to boost the male's ego as they watched while their women competed. Not playing along was against the rules. Mich had learned that the hard way. I stood angry, holding her accountable as well for allowing this to happen. "Would you get up? That's nasty," I said, trying to grab one of her flailing arms. She fought me, refusing to let go. She then started pouting again, making me wonder on the champagne that was being served. Already a mess, her makeup tracing black lines down her cheeks didn't help her appearance. She was also embracing the role of a battered woman.

"God, I must be a total mess," she shrieked all dramatically. "Girl, get the hell up!" I said, tugging at her arm. I just wanted to pour hot coffee down her throat or stick her head in a bucket of water filled with ice. Theatrical Mich was one character I couldn't stomach right now.

"I'm totally worthless, right?" she pouted.

I saw her broken-hearted and realized I was being too hard on her. I knew she was trying to show the strength I told her was in her, but a trampled heart could only take so much. And now he was beating on her body.

I was frightened while forcing her to her feet and discovering a thick, red substance where she was sitting. "Mich…" I said, alarmed, releasing her arm. I then pointed down at the red substance she was slushing around in that had stained her dress.

"Oh, no," was all she could muster.

"Kayla, call the ambulance!" I ordered, then redirected my attention to Mich.

"What's going on with you?"

"Clearly, that stupid test lied. I'm pregnant, Bria," she barked at me, sending me into a different dimension. "At least, I *was*. I'm not sure now."

This was a slap in the face. Of course Mich would be pregnant. She was perfectly healthy. I, on the other hand… My eyes started to sting with the build-up of tears. My throat dried.

"Why didn't you test twice?" It was just like Mich to accept something she preferred hearing over finding out the actual facts. I mean, how hard was it for her to take the test again or even visit her doctor? Instead, she was in here poisoning an innocent child with alcohol.

"I don't know!" I couldn't take it and tried barreling out of the room. Kayla stopped my escape at the door. I froze in disbelief—hating Mich for my own incapability and inadequacy to bear children of my own.

I felt myself breaking, crumbling to pieces while a stream of warm, salty tears scurried down my face. I couldn't hide it anymore. This was my last straw. Everyone was making babies around me and celebrating births while I was only granted the title of godmother. The blessing of carrying my own child to term would always elude me, and it was not because I chose. *I never had the choice.*

"I'm sure you have plenty to say about this. Especially since the father will probably want me to get rid of it!" Her words made me whimper. My body quaked. I pushed past Kayla and made my exit. "Bria, don't leave me!" were Mich's words just before the door closed.
I couldn't breathe and needed to get some air.

Blurred vision, spilling a drink or two, I bumped into island icons in a crowded room. I found myself outside. Trying to gain control of my emotions, I lifted my head and took a deep breath before blinking the tears away. I needed to compose myself and find refuge. I had to realize that this wasn't about me.

I gasped, afraid to take another breath that might ignite the pain that had me now bent over. I was trying to override the aching pulsation in my pelvic area. The pain ended just as the sirens approaching the building did. I watched as the ambulance personnel jumped out of their vehicle and made ready to enter.

"This is definitely not my year," I struggled to say as it slowly subsided.

"Was it ever?" a voice said, startling me. I adjusted my posture as best as I could.

"So much drama, right? But I guess it feeds your writing," Jasmine said, coming to stand at arm's length next to me. "Look, I can't do this right now. I need to get to my friends. I'm not gonna make an even bigger scene for your amusement."

I tried to make my way back in with the

emergency medical team but was stopped by Jasmine grabbing my wrist. I pulled away. She grinned. "I'm not feeling all too well myself. Must be all that frolicking with Trevor. Tell me, do you think he'll be happy as a father?" she said while resting her hand on her abdomen. I felt cold and misplaced. Yet, with composure, I managed to remove myself from the scene and continue on with the stretcher that was to haul my friend out of here.

Mich and Kayla rode off in the ambulance. I would follow behind them in my car. I still hadn't gotten the chance to fully catch myself. From Trevor to Mich then back to Trevor again. Now, my phone was ringing with the caller ID indicating it was someone from the foster home. It was all just too much right now. I answered the call. It was one of the mentors at the home telling me to brace myself for some heavy news. I thought nothing could top what had just happened. But my heart stopped after hearing that someone had called in claiming to be a legal guardian of Aniah, saying they would be seeking full custody. My heart couldn't take it, and I went weak, allowing the phone to hit the ground.

It was then that I saw Jerome and his wife. I panicked and found myself ducking behind some pruned, low-cut shrubbery.

I hung back, hoping the night would be sufficient enough at hiding me. I dared not make a sound and waited, praying to God that I wasn't spotted and that those that saw me would not bring his attention to me. "Bria." My name was whispered. But it wasn't Jerome. I peered up from behind the bushes and saw that he was heading back to his car. His wife entered the venue without him.

Completely forgetting about the person calling my name, trying to get my attention, I stepped through the bush and tried to make a break for it. I needed to make a quick getaway. "Wait! Your father! Don't you want to meet him? I know he's *dying* to meet you," the man said, which caught my attention. With that came a vision of me having a tea party with my stuffed animals and a faceless man as my guest of honor.

"Curtis told me you would love to—even die for the chance. And oh, did I forget to mention that little fluffy-haired girl? She's such a sweet, little lamb. She's there too."

My whole being was on high alert. This man was lying, and I felt my life was in danger, but the urge to make sure Aniah was alright was stronger. "How did he get out?" I asked, referring to Curtis. "Bail, sweetie. He was released on a 23.000— guilder bond." "No, that's not right."

My limbs went cold wondering how they could let such a monster roam free. I knew I had to go to him in order to ensure him not hurting anyone I love.

"Bria, are you alright? What's going on?" "Trevor!" I said, reaching out for him, then realized I didn't need him to save me. I retracted my hands. He would be having his own drama to work through. "Bria, what is going on?" he reiterated sternly, looking intensely from me to the driver and then back again. He stepped closer to me, taking hold of me by my shoulders. I fought myself free of him. I had no time to explain and really didn't care to. I needed

259

to get to Aniah. Nothing else mattered

"Look, *we* won't work," I started. I knew what I needed to do so he'd let go, like ripping off a Band-aid. "Where is this coming from?" I ignored his question and continued, "I want a guy that's worth it." "And you don't think I'm that guy?"

"No, I don't."

"Bullshit! I'm not gonna stand here and let you think you just need to push some imaginary button for me to run. I ain't going no- damn- where." I shook my head vigorously. This approach would take up too much time, so I had to make it count.

"There is no button. Just listen. I want somebody who's not gonna make a fool out of me. I don't want to have to leave my expectations of what a relationship should be like so he can feel like he's the Alpha Male. And I definitely don't want to share him."

"You won't with me."

"Yeah, how about you fine- tune that bit with Jasmine first?" I said, looking away from him. "What does Jasmine have to do with us?" he asked, frustrated, trying to regain eye contact.

I wasn't about to entertain a lover who was only available during work hours, reserving weekends for his family, making him unavailable for calls when night came. I never cared for the concept of timeshare in real estate—much less in a relationship. My guy, whoever he was, needed to understand that he would be expected to put in an equal amount of energy as I did. So, dividing himself between multiple women was a no-no. He wouldn't have the strength to keep up with me, and nothing would convince me otherwise.

"Baby girl, if you want to know, you need to come now, sweetheart," the driver stressed impatiently. "Never mind," I said to Trevor while jumping into the man's car.

## Trevor

Who was that man, and where were they heading? Her eyes being flooded with tears I was sure didn't happen solely by touching base with her friends. Something didn't feel right. Now I was filled with agitation, wanting to know what or who had upset her to that extent. It couldn't have been me. She was clearly letting off steam. The night wasn't supposed to progress this way. It had simply gone in the wrong direction starting from the moment I persuaded her to get dressed in order for me to show myself. All of this came out of me wanting to prove to her I could impact her life in a positive way. Show her that unlike the men in her past, I would fit well with her.

I needed to find out what had happened. "Mr. Mathews, please, we need you inside." I was reminded of my duties by Ferdinand, the foundation's secretary, while attempting to enter my car to find her. "I have something to take care of first." I tried excusing myself.

"Mr. Mathews, your presence is needed after the closing speech." He asserted himself, getting on my nerves.

"You can handle it!" I said, starting the car and closing my door. My engine roared as I applied gas, signifying to him that he should step away or be ran over. He slammed a hand against my chest, causing me to look at him in anger.

"Huh, no. I actually can't. Your signature is required as authorization on behalf of the foundation. You need to prioritize this first."

My jaw clenched. I was fuming for reasons I couldn't voice. I knew it was my responsibility yet questioned why I had this fellow following me around that was deeming himself useless at this point. Gripping the wheel as if expecting water to drip from it, I fought for the composure needed, but how could I gather myself completely when all my being was telling me that my priority was not at this function?

"I'll do it when I get back!" I growled, my foot on the gas pedal. I pulled out my phone and pressed the speed dial button. It rang out before going to voicemail. "Bria, where the fuck is he taking you?" I was so tense and worried at this point. I pulled out the device I'd first felt shame when buying. But now it would serve its purpose. I switched it on and was relieved seeing it was working. She would kill me if she ever found out I had this done. I placed the device in my hands-free holder and stepped on the gas, following in the direction the tracker indicated she was heading in.

## Bria

My eyes connected with that of the driver's in the rearview mirror. While a million and two things were going through my mind, we were on our way off the compound when the driver stopped. I was surprised when Jerome got into the car and sat next to me. What was he doing here? "Looks like the boss wants to see us both," Jerome said, answering the question written on my forehead. The brief illumination of the car on his face gave away his annoyance of having to be here.

"How are you connected to all of this?" I asked, tension building within me. My eyes searched for the white of his in what little light there was. "You'll find out soon enough, little mama," the driver responded for him. We sat in silence, my heart picking up the pace now and again in expectancy, wondering what would become of me. I felt off, like I was being served up like a lamb for slaughter. Why had I jumped into this car? Why had Curtis been released? It just didn't make sense. According to his pretrial ruling, he was not to be let go under any circumstances, not even if he made bail. So why was I in this mess?

"Aniah," I mumbled. I needed to be certain she was okay, and if it came down to me or her, I would exchange my life for hers. That was the decision I would gladly make. I exhaled, releasing the energy into the air. Accepting the choice, I adjusted my defeated stance. I would go out strong and fighting to the end. Curtis would face-off with all of me, and he would just have to deal with that. "Where exactly is the little girl? I thought you were to grab her too," Jerome asked, making me even more alert. "I tried, but as I started to get close to her, that little Chia pet began yelling 'stranger danger' and wouldn't shut up, drawing attention to me, so I split." *So, they don't have her*, I thought, more

263

relieved that she wasn't in this mess.

"Before I forget," the driver said, gaining my attention. He peered at me through his rearview mirror and nodded. "Do the thing."

"Oh, right," Jerome responded, apparently aware of what the driver was referring to. I watched suspiciously as Jerome retrieved a little box from under the passenger seat. He opened it and produced a bottle. He then dug into his pocket.

When I saw what he had retrieved, I instantly knew what was to happen.

"No!" I yelped, going for the handle on the door. His hand covered my nose with the rag he was holding, and for as long as I could hold my breath, I struggled against him as he tried to subdue me. The door swung open, and I forced my head back, connecting with his face. Without thinking, I made a leap out of the still moving car. I landed on my side, giving a bit of a roll before stopping. My mouth was filling up with blood.

"Go get her!" I heard and knew I had to shake off whatever it was trying to take hold of me. Strength was leaving me. I saw a bar in the distance and gathered all I could muster, ignoring the pain in my ribs and face. I started to stagger, doing the best I could to make it over to those laughing and enjoying their night out.

I was getting closer, but the music seemed to be coming to an end. "Look, over there!" one of my kidnappers exclaimed, making me hobble as fast as I could, trying to manage the pain that was ripping through my core. I gave a faint cry, hoping it would still be heard before collapsing. My vision became

264

blurred. Darkness then took over what little light was left.

# Chapter 15
# **Lamb Amongst Wolves**

"Aniah," I groaned, waking up to her jumping on my bed. I rolled over, completely exhausted and beaten, bruises covering my skin. "Hey, you're awake." I rolled over onto my back to connect the face to the voice and found Trevor holding a plate and glass of water. I had difficulty as I tried to sit up straight.

"Be careful," he said, resting the items on the night table next to the bed. He then raced over to meet me, putting me to lean against the bedpost. "How long was I out?" I said, fighting with    the simple question, feeling as though I was hit by a bus. "A few days," he said, slapping the sleep out of me. "You've been in and out."

"What happened?"

He exhaled. "Aniah, can you go get the glass of juice I left on the counter?" h    e    requested, waiting for her to leave the room. She did so without hesitation. He then looked into my eyes as if reading something there. His gaze was strong, making me wonder what I'd been through.

"Well, according to what you told the police, you were being abducted, but you got away and those people at the bar you called out to helped you." "Curtis…" I trailed off, wondering if I'd mentioned who was behind everything to the police. "Yes, he was arrested and so were the other two. You're safe now," he said, giving a faint smile before sobering. "I blame myself. If I had only stopped you from jumping into that car, none of this would have happened."

With a heavy hand, I reached out to touch his face. "It was me. I shouldn't have acted the way I did," I admitted. "I just needed you to let me go. I thought Aniah was in danger, and I wanted to do it all by myself." I removed my hand from his face, using it to brace my body. "And then there was mention of my father... I just had to be certain."

"You never have to do anything alone again," he said, taking me into his arms. I relaxed, feeling sure of his words. I was relieved that my ranting hadn't chased him away. He was the strength that I needed, the man of my dreams.

"I have something for you," he said, going into his pocket. He withdrew a small box, resting it in my lap. My heart sped up. I looked at him, seeing the smile build on his face. "Bria, you drive me crazy the way you talk to me, but when you completely abstain, it's even worse. These last few days waiting for you to catch yourself so I can look into those beautiful eyes of yours have been something else. I knew then that I would want to look at them for the rest of my life. Will you marry me?" he said after a deep exhale. He softened, seeming scared, waiting for me to answer.

"Yes, yes, yes," I said, going for his neck. I groaned in pain but chuckled at how crazy everything was. It was all moving so fast now, and I was okay with it. My life was finally going the way I only dreamed it would. We held each other a bit longer before Aniah reappeared into the room.

"She said yes, little lamb. We are going to be a family," Trevor said to Aniah, who looked like she was about to explode. She ran out of the room and before any time had passed, she came back with a paper in her hand. "Ma, come look what I drew," Aniah said, showing me a drawing of three stick figures holding hands in front of a house. We were all smiling, and I couldn't wait to put it up on my refrigerator.

"It's only appropriate that we make it official."

I was so happy. Trevor had professed his love for me without me having to compromise, which was my biggest fear of being with him, and Aniah was mine…

"Wait, 'Ma'? When did I adopt her?" I said, looking at Trevor, my brain trying to find the memory of that happening.

"You tell me. This is your dream," Trevor said.

The reality of his words took its time before registering. "I'm so sorry about your father, by the way. I guess we all make sacrifices," he said, which came like a slap. His voice and image w e r e losing form before me. The sting of harsh tapping on my cheek made me fight to bring a hand to my face.
I wasn't sure what was going on.

I started to make out the person sitting next to me. Soberly, Jerome was knocking at my face, bringing me back to my present predicament. I went for his hand to stop him from hitting me. "That's better. Come back." "I jumped. I was safe, people saw me escape." Groggy, I mumbled, confused as to how I'd ended up here.

"Bae, you never made it out of the car," he taunted before leaving me to sit alone. I was more than likely still heavily under the influence of the substance used to subdue me. I tried focusing on the silhouettes before me. My limbs were heavy, making my initial plan to fight hard to carry out.

"It's a shame, but what else—" The man I was yet to make out broke off.

"You getting up or what, baby girl?" The man came over to me, bending in front of me, making his face clear up from the haze I was seeing him in. It was the driver. He then went back over to the two. I was extremely weak, watching the group standing in a huddle before me. My sight was taking its time to return, and I had to focus hard to make out the third man.

"Curtis?" My eyes squinted, trying to positively identify him. "Why are you doing this... to me...?" I managed. My vision was returning, but I was now dealing with a pounding headache, which was utterly in need of a painkiller.

"Me, no, I had nothing to do with this. I see you've managed to get the attention of the devil," he stated and made his way to the door. "Fortunately for me, you won't be getting out of this one," he said, then left the room. "What are we going to do in the meantime?" the driver asked. His full frame made out, I then recognized him to be the security guy I saw getting shot at the boatyard.

Jerome made his way over and sat next to me. He then started to unhook my buttons. I looked up at him, watching in disbelief, unable to do anything else. "What else is there to do?" he replied. The other man looked like he was about to object but didn't make a move to stop him. Instead, he grunted. Taking his eyes off me for a second, Jerome looked over at the man. "Please, some privacy," Jerome added to my astonishment. Without protest, the man made his way through the door.

Jerome continued to slowly unbutton my blouse, never once looking me in the eyes. I just wanted to knock the smirk off of his face. As if cued, the door swung open and there was Trevor. He took a moment to survey the room before storming towards us. Jerome quickly stood.

"Get the fuck away from her!" he said, pushing at Jerome. He then swung at him, connecting a hard fist to his jaw, knocking him over the couch I was on. "I've been wanting to do that from day one." I watched him dare Jerome to get up and fight back, which he didn't. He just chuckled.

"You wouldn't know what to do with her energy," he sassed while attempting to get to his feet.

"And you..." His rage was directed at me now, his eyes smoldering. "Button your fucking shirt back up!" he growled. "The fucking lengths you would go to for a story," he huffed, yanking me by the hand to follow behind him. I couldn't believe that was what he thought was going on.

"No," I managed, trying to gather myself. Was he seriously thinking that? "I have everything under control," I said with difficulty staying on my feet. "What's wrong with you?" he asked after having me collapse in his arms. Tension was increasing on his face as he observed me. "Did he drug you?" Trevor wheeled his head around, likely ready to drum a bit more on Jerome's face.

"Not a thing is wrong with me, and by the way, Jasmine is pregnant." His brows dipped.

"What?! Not by me if that's what you're insinuating!" He looked around the space before lifting me from my feet. "Let's get out of here."

I had no strength to fight and clung to him as he held

me in his arms and carried me to the door.

"Oh, I didn't know we were expecting company," a man said as he stood on the other side of the door, accompanied by someone else. He was blocking our path and started in, forcing Trevor to step back inside. "Please take a seat." That's when his accomplice leaned over and whispered something in his ear.

I didn't know who he was but something about the other guy felt familiar to me. "Aw, Ms. Pantophlet," he began. "First, let me introduce you to your father, Bernard," he said, gesturing for the man next to him to step forward.

I looked over to the man staring with a softened expression at me and started to scrutinize everything about his appearance in search of telltale signs of myself in him.
His nose I could see was similar to that of mine and his brows, although slightly thicker, curved the way mine did.

I swallowed and tapped against Trevor's chest, suggesting to him to put me down. Intrigued, I slowly made my way over to him to get a closer look. He stepped towards me as if shy before taking my outreached hand in his. I stood there for a second, staring into eyes that reminded me of mine. Tears welling up, I was taken into his embrace. I needed no other form of confirmation. My head resting in the nook of his neck, I felt a calm take me. A peace that was completely new. All the hate that I thought would have manifested if I'd ever laid eyes on him had never even shown up. The silence was now filled with a light whimper coming from me.

"This is so touching. It almost makes me want to cry along with you," the man who'd introduced my father said while faking sobs. I drew from my father. I still didn't know who this other man was, but I had a feeling he wasn't here just so he could reunite me with my dad.

I gradually loosened the hold I had on my father and stepped back. Trevor was looking on in silence, keeping an eye on Jerome, and I now realized there were more people to consider as Curtis and the driver entered the room. "And you are?" I asked, wanting to know who the man was that had everyone's attention.

"That isn't important. What is, is how I plan on fixing the mess created by everyone in this room."
On those words, I instinctively glanced around.

"Let me apologize for drugging you to get you here. I honestly didn't think it necessary. Your curiosity I'm sure would have been enough," he said, looking over to the two responsible for my intoxicated state. "I'm still not sure why Danny would suggest it," he said, giving away the driver's name. The man headed behind a little bar and poured himself a shot of Hennessy. I then realized that I hadn't taken in my surroundings, which was so unlike me.

The room was lined with windows and cast under a red glow of light, having a desk and two grey, cushioned chairs in front of it a n d had the appearance of a mob boss' office. There stood two thick columns on one side of the room, evidently keeping the ceiling from caving in. Plants were positioned in front of them, which were trying their best yet failed miserably at giving the space a welcoming feeling.

The bar where the boss man stood had four bottles mounted upside down on the wall, and to the side of that rested the L- shaped brown couch where I was almost sexually assaulted.

"Now that all the necessary salutations are out of the way, tell me, Ms. Pantophlet," he said before taking a sip, his face contorting. "Why even with so much information placed at your feet, you just aren't satisfied? I mean, I basically hand-fed you."

My eyes narrowed. My mind needed no time to decrypt what he was saying. "You set Curtis up, didn't you?" "Wow, she's fast!" he said with a huge smile that exposed his teeth. "Sweetie, I knew you wouldn't stop digging, so I had to do something. The files were planted in the safe, yes." "You son of a bitch! They are going to lock me up for that!" "You're lucky you're not dead yet," he retorted, shutting him up. His eyes were cold and calculating, overpowering the stare thrown his way by Curtis. I didn't know this man. I understood now that he probably had a connection to Curtis, but in what way was still a mystery to me.

"Let's just say, it's in my best interest to keep things hidden, but something told me you wouldn't stop at Curtis. Now—" he clasped his palms together, "—this is what's going to happen."

"Wait, what about him?" I said, gesturing with my head to the one person in the room I thought had no cause being here.

"This girl just doesn't stop with the questions, now does she?" He chuckled in amusement. "You're referring to Jerome?" We all looked at him. "Curtis did that, thinking he would distract you and keep you from sniffing in his direction. But you are tenacious." Solemnly, I turned to the man identified as my father.

"Were you really trying to make contact, or was this all part of Curtis' plan to have me killed overseas?" I said, my tone of voice having a hint of disappointment. Why did the possibility of my father not trying to contact me bother me that much?

I couldn't bring myself to ask if he didn't intend for his whereabouts to be known. I couldn't bear the thought of him preferring to stay hidden and not needing to know me. I waited anxiously, feeling like an orphaned child all over again, for him to chase all doubt from my mind and openly reclaim me.

"I was trying to keep you from getting hurt... and I wanted to see if you would want to know me. I've been following you for quite a while. Your work is amazing," he said earnestly. I felt a sense of pride regardless of the circumstances that brought me here. "You tried having her killed?" my father asked in a dry tone of voice, looking at Curtis.

"I saw an opportunity to fix all my problems," Curtis said nonchalantly.

"You fucking bastard," Trevor interjected, making a move to him. Curtis shifted behind Danny.
I grabbed at Trevor's arm, making him look at me. His jaw clenching, I held his gaze, hoping he understood that I needed him to stay calm. Tensions were already high, and I couldn't afford him getting hurt because of me. An escalation of this situation with a fight was the last thing needing to happen right now.

"So, everything Bria said about you illegally

selling land, all the paperwork found in your office connecting you to crimes, not forgetting you sending someone to the Dominican Republic in order to have her killed was true?" Trevor probed, daring him to fess up.

"Yes. It was all me."

It surprised me even more having Curtis own up to all that he'd done, basically incriminating himself in almost every allegation brought against him in the past few years.

"You lying coward!" I cursed, adding a few more explicit words to my vent.

"Let's all just settle down," my father murmured, voice deep. Indeed, we needed to relax. I was looking at Trevor, wondering why he'd asked questions he already knew the answers to. "Now, if there are no more questions," the man who still hadn't revealed his name or identity or even his connection through all of this said, "it's time to clean things up!" I froze hearing those words. My heart started pounding out of control. Nervousness exploded into outright fear.

We were about to be wiped out.

With a hand placed on my side, Trevor maneuvered me behind him. The man gestured to my father, who then drew a gun with a silencer. He pointed it at Curtis. This was not how I'd envisioned our reunion going. The last thing I needed was seeing my dad murder somebody—no matter how I felt about that person. "Wait, Dad! No!" I pleaded, coming from behind Trevor.

"Sugar, your father works for me now. He does what I tell him to do. You get to walk out of here alive in return. Isn't that quite fatherly of him and generous of me?"

I stood there, speechless. Unlike all the things a child wanted from their parents, like a pony or a power wheel, my father's gift to me was trading his soul for my life. I watched him, his eyes dead, his facial expression blank. I couldn't let him do this. Taking someone's life should never be negotiable. "Kill him."

With that and without further consideration of my own safety, I sprung over to my father, wrapping my arms around his neck.

"Don't, please, just be there for me. I promise I won't go snooping. I just need you to not hurt anyone. Please." My eyes blurred with tears. This was worse than never meeting him. How would I live knowing my father had killed for me? This was just too much of a sacrifice. I held him, feeling him wrap an arm around me. Having him walk out of here with me and Trevor would be the only gift I needed. I couldn't lose him this way. "Baby girl, I have to. You'll never be safe if I don't." He started forcing me out of his path.

"There must be another way." "Shoot him!"

"That's quite enough," Danny said, pulling out a gun of his own and pointing it at me. "Put your hands in the air where I can see them, or I'll shoot."

He then pushed at Curtis and Jerome's backs, shoving them over to stand with us. He was clearly about saving his own skin. "Take the gun from him, darling, place it on the floor, and you walk slowly over to me." It was clear, I was to become his hostage and possible ticket out of here.

"Let's go," Danny said, hurrying me along.

Before I could make a move, a shot rang out, making me hit the floor. My ear pierced from the sound. Eyes closed in fright, I laid curled in a ball, covering my ears. A few more shots rattled off as the back and forth continued. A body slammed down onto me, and I tried pushing the person off. "Stay down. I got you," Trevor said, breathing heavy. He then reached for the gun.

"Come with me," he instructed.

On my elbows, I quickly crawled alongside him. We made it behind the columns and pressed our backs against them. Trevor lifted the gun and said, "Stay here." "What? No!" That was the craziest thing I'd ever heard him say. Was he seriously thinking about joining in on the gunfight? This wasn't some video game. I latched onto him, refusing to let him go. My eyes pleaded with his to stay.

Then, my heart stopped, looking up and finding Curtis over us. He was holding his abdomen, clearly applying pressure to the spot where blood was leaking from.

He raised his gun and pointed it. I'd destroyed his world with my openness, and I was to pay for all that had happened to him. The thought of a life for a life came to mind. A shot fired that made him buckle, sending him to the ground reeling in pain. I locked onto eyes filled with loathing as the man who intended on taking my life cursed with profanity. My breathing was out of control. I was overwhelmingly certain I would not be making it out of here alive. A second round of shots cracked into the space, forcing me to close my eyes again. I latched on to Trevor, not wanting him out there in harm's way trying to protect me. I prayed we wouldn't get hit by a stray bullet.

I could've sworn I heard someone yell, "Police, let's go!" followed by a loud thud.

An eerie silence then cloaked the room, my breathing the only thing giving away our hiding place. I dared not move knowing there was still someone out to get me, and I had a chilling feeling he was the one moving towards us. "Ms. Pantophlet, didn't I tell you to stay clear of trouble?" a male voice broke the silence. Something about the way it was said seemed familiar.

I looked up and found a man with his face concealed, wearing black, baggy pants and a long-sleeved shirt with K.W.P.D. on it. He was all geared up, and I was relieved to know he was one of the good guys. He instructed one of his men to help get the paramedic for Curtis.

He then beckoned us to stand. I could breathe again, glad that it was all over. I accepted the hand extended out to help me to my feet. That's when I saw Danny coming up from behind the couch. "No!" I yelled, ripping the gun from Trevor. I then attempted to squeeze off a shot at Danny, my efforts foiled by the man in the mask who knocked my hand down, sending the bullet into Trevor's leg. I watched in horror as Trevor went down. "Lady, I'm on your side!" Danny shouted in annoyance with his hands up in front of him while the gun was being stripped from me.

"You shot me," Trevor groaned, pressure building in the vein popping in the middle of his forehead. He was trying his best not to cry, I assumed, watching him struggling with controlling his breathing, wincing in pain.

"Not on purpose," I quickly replied, bending to assess the damage. I went to touch it, making him flinch and move his leg from me.

"Don't worry. We will just write this part off as a domestic dispute," the masked man tastelessly joked, causing Danny to crack up.


If tonight had taught me anything, it would be not to handle a loaded gun. I walked out of there observing that two men were wounded and one, Mr. Unknown, was dead. Jerome had gotten out of there by the skin of his teeth but would soon be paid a visit by the taskforce. At the station, I was informed of the investigation they had launched over three years ago with Danny working undercover.

They had hoped he would have gotten close enough to Curtis, who would have eventually led Danny to his boss, Mr. Exius Azard. I started snooping when things started to rattle and they were having breakthroughs. I connected that to my father's involvement to the man they were trying to catch.

My pictures at the boathouse of Danny being shot were indeed deleted because, according to them, they couldn't have a reporter printing images of what was going on, compromising the case. There was too much at risk. Danny had to continue playing the part just in case the big boss man had stuff he wanted to spill himself. He was trying to secure me as a witness when all hell broke loose. The Kingdom's Special Forces had been tracking Curtis for months knowing he wasn't the only suspect in a murder that happened years ago. Curtis had only helped with covering it up. Seems like the two had buried a body of a man Mr. Azard had killed in cold blood. They just needed to flush him out of hiding. The detectives giving me the story didn't hold back from directly blaming me for continually putting myself, his team, and the investigation in jeopardy with my obsession to expose Curtis. He stressed how they'd already had enough information on Curtis to lock him away but had released him so that he'd lead them to his superior. They never expected to actually catch their guy tonight.

One of the good things coming out of this was that Curtis would be heading to jail. And as for my father, he had disappeared again.


I had just finished up in the police station and stood outside at the base of the stairway, waiting for my friends to come and get me. "So, is it always going to be a dangerous adventure with you?" Trevor asked, coming towards me. My arms folded, he grasped me by my elbows. My gaze went to the floor. We stood in brief silence.

"Trevor, maybe we shouldn't," I said, not yet looking at him. "I mean, things were so crazy tonight. I think I need time to digest everything."
He licked his lips and looked away.

"If that's what you think is best…" He released me. "I do. But believe me, I will call when I'm done." "Then take all the time you need," he said after a few moments, wiping under his nose before turning and walking away. My timing was wrong, I knew that, but I also didn't want the events of tonight clouding our judgment and making it the reason why he stuck around.

# Chapter 16
# Not Quite Picture Perfect

I woke up in the hospital slightly groggy from the procedure. I looked around, seeing a bag of clear fluid hanging with a tube leading downward. I followed it and saw that it led straight into my arm. The drip line injected into me allowed the rehydration of my body. I had finally gone through with it after the pain started getting worse. I'd seen my doctor, complaining of intense pain which led to me being prepped for surgery. My pre-op doctor had informed me that I would be going under the knife immediately because of an added complication.

Now I laid flat on my back, a little lighter with a couple of fibroids and one cyst cut from my womb and one ovary removed. The good news, I was already pregnant. I managed a smile while moving a very heavy hand onto my abdomen. Aniah would be thrilled hearing she was going to be a big sister. The father, I hadn't told yet, and to be honest, I wasn't planning on telling him.

I'd also made my friends swear not to. After all we'd been through, I thought a little break from me would go a long way, and I needed quality time alone with my daughter. Unaware of my situation at the time, I'd ignored his calls and grew used to not hearing from him after a month had passed. I figured he'd gotten the hint and decided to move on. I didn't want surprising him with news of being a father to make him feel obligated to stick around; plus, he had his business to take care of. All of that led up to me being here at Loterie Farm with Aniah and a few friends, where they'd set up a huge screen for an outdoor movie premiere.

In celebration of her officially being adopted by me, we opted for this setting instead of the usual. According to her, sitting outside in chairs just wouldn't cut it. "Aniah, where are the fruits I packed, and why are there so many sweets in here?" I asked, taking out a handful of them. "Ma, I told you, kids don't just want candy, they *need* candy. I gotta go to the bathroom," she stressed, then ran out. I gestured to Mariska to follow her, which she did, vanishing behind the netted barrier protecting us from mosquitos—that and a couple of cans of lit citronella candles.

"You are so gonna have your hands full with her. Good!" Kayla said while laughing. "Hey, she wanted this, let her take what she gets," Mich added. "You guys are so supportive," I said, frowning before going into a light chuckle, knowing I wouldn't have had it any other way.

"Shh, remember that friend I asked if I could bring? She's here. Let me go get her," Mich said after checking her phone and texting back. She then left. "So, have you thought of any baby names yet?" I laughed thinking how overjoyed Kayla was hearing I was pregnant, but it was still too soon to be picking names. "I need to know if it's a boy or girl first before I do that. I'm just happy everything is going well."

"It's so awesome for you." I saw her hesitate to say something.

"What is it?"

She looked at me, her gaze soft. She took a

breath before asking if I was still not going to tell Trevor.

"Honestly, I'm tired of that question. I just want to move on and do things unattached. I don't want to have to account to anyone," I explained further. "It feels right that way." "Okay, I get you," she said, and the chatter of Aniah's return to the cabana placed a definite stop to the conversation.

"And here is our own," she said, pulling Trevor by the hand past the screen. He stopped in front of the entrance, not budging any further. I gasped, wondering where she'd found him. She was just to go to the toilet and back. He stood there, still, as if he dared not enter the lioness' den. "Come, come, go inside," Mich said, coming up behind him. Veda was with her.

"This is gonna get resolved right now. The both of you have been walking around all grumpy, too proud to admit that you miss each other. You ain't fooling nobody," Veda stated while stomping into the cabana. She then shoved him into the seat next to me.

"Veda, what is this? I thought I told you to stay out of my business," Trevor said. "You're both too damn stubborn. Just take a chance on each other," she pleaded.
We didn't budge.

"God, he's so infuriating!" Kayla defended me, making me grin.

"Yes, but she, she's just too used to being independent. She doesn't remember what it is to rely on someone." Veda stepped towards me. "You're scared and guarded. We get that, but you don't need to be scared with him. It's okay to let him lead, sweetie." "And him, he needs to get out of his own way. He should know she isn't gonna submit if he's only trying by calling and then not calling," Kayla stated.

"Bria, you could try being softer. That would work," Mich said, making me flinch.

"Mich, I really don't want to be coached on how to get a man." "Clearly, you don't. You shot him, but the good news is that he's still here," she said boldly, embarrassing me.

"That's enough," I said, going to my feet. "All of you, leave now!" "Sit down," Aniah said, stunning me, making me look at her. This child better not had thought she would be getting away with disrespecting me in public. "We are all going to leave," she said, taking Mich's hand and gesturing to Kayla to follow. "But the two of you will stay and make up. No arguing!"

"Both of you are a mess," Mich said on exit.

They all left, leaving us there, neither of us uttering a word. I figured the show would be starting soon and they would all be back again, crowding the space—Aniah no doubt planting herself between us. So, I decided to wait it out.

He gave a faint chuckle, making me look over at him. "What's so funny?" I asked yet pretended not to care, folding my arms for effect. My gaze on him, I observed that he wasn't as closed off in his posture as I was. He was stretched out in a relaxed position, enjoying the comfort of the cushions we had brought to decorate the place with. In fact, he seemed to be getting a bit too cozy, as if he'd helped rent the thing.

"Aniah sure told you," he said teasingly,

making me crack a smile. I looked away so he didn't see it. "How is it that such a small, little thing like her could get adults to do her bidding?" he added, causing me to watch him as I pondered the question. "I don't know," I said, accepting that I couldn't stay mad while talking about her.

"She's so much like you, maybe even worse," he said, making me smile again.

"I feel for the boy who falls for her, or even worse, the one who catches her eye. She's surely going to bully him." "Stop!" I laughed out loud, knowing it to be true. "You know I adopted her." "Really?" he said, amazed.

"Yes." "Man, that's awesome! Congratulations to the both of you."

I smiled thinking how great it was indeed. I then sobered, wondering if I should drop the bomb on him.

"Yeah, thanks," I simply said, deciding not to.

"I'm still mad at you though," he said before looking away. "Why?" He turned and gazed at me. "I've been waiting for you to call."

"What, no, you said *you* were going to call." I tried remembering a conversation that never took place. "Bria. I've been calling. You just never picked up, and our last conversation, you said—"

"The both of you are wrong," Kayla bellowed. "Now shut up and make up already!" Mich commanded. "Yeah, shut up!" Aniah added before being scolded by Veda to not speak that way to her mother. I heard her apologize and thought how I would definitely live by the "It takes a village to raise a child" proverb.

Abruptly, I rose to my feet. "Trevor."

286

"Yes."

I turned to face him and found him standing so close it made me gasp. He must have thought I was about to leave. My eyes fell to the floor. "I don't know what to say. It's been so long."

"Then say nothing."

He stepped closer to me, taking my hand, his eyes on the action. He then rested it on his shoulder and started to sway. I followed his lead. "Remember on the hill when I pulled you close and did this exact same thing?" "Of course I remember." I closed my eyes, recalling how even though I felt embarrassed being out there where the world could see me trying to dance, I felt so aligned with him.

"I never expressed how nervous I was doing that or how right it felt being on that hill with you, even though you stepped on my feet a couple of times and scratched my good shoes." I laughed and tried to pull away, but he wouldn't let me.

"I told you I love you that night."

I stopped swaying, knowing the mood had changed. He allowed me to pull away, and I stood staring into his sober eyes. "I've been waiting for you to say it back," he said, seemingly needing to catch his breath. A mischievous smile crept across my face.

"You need me to say it back?"

He shook and then dipped his head, coming to me. He took hold of me by grasping me by the waist. He then drew me into him. His nose grazed against mine, and the warmth of his following words being spoken on my lips sealed it for me. "Yeah, I need you to. More than you think," he said, coming in to kiss me.

The kiss was slow and sensuous. I gave into it knowing I'd been yearning to taste him again. Why had I fooled myself that I could do without it when nothing could top it? Not even the creamy goodness of rum raisin ice cream, which I loved so much. I enjoyed the light buzz it gave me and the shameful lethargic feeling that came with it. My eyes closed, and I leaned into him, wanting and encouraging him to take what was his. To take all of me.

I was mildly disappointed when he broke the connection, but quickly reminded myself of where I was and whom I'd come here with. I didn't want to run the risk of being inappropriate in front of Aniah. "What if I hold off and make you work for it, how about that?" I teased. He pulled away, his face wearing a confused look.

"I've been working for it ever since I met you. I've been punched, fired, and shot. I think I've proven myself enough." That made me step out of his embrace. "You're the one who's been coming around me." "Yeah, and my life was always in danger when I did. It probably is now also," he said, looking around. "Is everyone gonna keep on me for shooting you?" He shrugged and pulled me back into his arms.

"Just know that I fear for my life, yet I wouldn't have it any other way. I want to be with you. It would be just the three of us." I wondered how he would feel about my response to that. I held my breath and corrected him. "You mean the four of us."

He slightly released me, pulling away just enough to read my face. "I'm pregnant," I clarified, completely terrified of his reaction. I saw him clench his jaw before releasing a sigh of acceptance. "Were you even planning on telling me?"

"I was thinking about it." My brows went up in surrender. "You're lucky Aniah warned about arguing."

His look fell to the side and returned with a smile that transformed into a scowl. "No more snooping around. I don't want to have to take my child to see his mother in prison," he said sternly.

With a sly grin, and before seizing another kiss, I wrapped my arms around his neck and said, "That would never happen." I pecked his lips. "Because I'll be acquitted every time." I couldn't help smiling at his wary expression. "Don't you know my baby's daddy is the best criminal defense lawyer on the island?" His brow shot up, totally unamused by my joke. He took a deep breath and sighed. "So, you're planning on getting into trouble?"

That made me smile and lean into him. *He should already know the answer to that.* Catching his lower lip between my teeth, I hushed any further objections with a kiss.

His embrace tightened, and I felt like I could stay there forever.

"Okay, so you guys are back on track," Veda said, barging into the cabana with the others trailing behind her. Trevor's hold only loosened when Aniah took his hand and mine and then led us to the lounging chairs. She sat right between us.

"Those mosquitos out there are crazy," Mich stated, dropping on the seat. Trevor leaned over Aniah, his breath tickling my ear.

"I can't wait to get you alone tonight, and I'm so sleeping over." I looked into eyes filled with pure mischief. I shook my head in disagreement. "Why not?" His brows dipped.

"Well, although she has her own bed," I said, trying my best to whisper, "Aniah seems to find mine more appealing. There is no space for you," I said, trying to hold back a smile. I was then shushed by our company. "Well, we are getting a bigger bed or a bigger apartment. Plus, she has aunts to babysit," Trevor remarked, loud enough so everyone could hear. Again, we were shushed. I started laughing by his determination to find a solution. I must admit, I was yearning to feel him between my legs again.

"Don't worry, I know she's here," a male voice announced, interrupting my laughter and forcing all attention to the doorway. Everyone sat up, waiting to see who was intruding on our privacy. Questions started when the dark, tall, chiseled bald man with small yet intense eyes wearing a suit and tie stood blocking us from seeing the projector screen.

"What now?" Veda asked.
I sat there under a cold sweat, praying for the best. I wanted to disappear between the few pillows. This was not going to happen. *Please, God, not here.*

The man exhaled audibly as his eyes rested on me. "Bria, tell him it's okay," the man said, referring to the usher. My throat dried, making it hard to swallow. I mustered a nod, signaling to the usher that it was. He then left.

"Who's this?" Trevor asked, which went unanswered. He then started moving forward, ready to throw the intruder out. "Why, Bria? Why would you have me served while in a meeting with some very important people? You know how embarrassing that was?" My heart skipped a few beats when he

290

pulled out the envelope I had tried on several occasions to have handed to him.

"Dennis, now is not the time for this," I said, my voice evidently shaking. I sprang to my feet and tried to show him out. Trevor now stood, tensed. "But it seems to be the perfect time," he said, sizing Trevor up while refusing to be led out of the cabana. "What's going on, Bria? Who's this boy?" Trevor asked between clenched teeth.

Dennis chuckled.

"'Boy'? Bria, you better collect this fool," Dennis said, stirring Trevor. Hands resting on both their chests, I stood in the middle of the two. The air was thinning and threatened to render me unconscious. "Bria," Dennis said calmly, gaining my full attention. "Should I, or—you know what, let me." "No, please, not here." My words were but a faint sound.

"I'm her husband," Dennis announced, needing not to repeat it. "Oh, shit," Mich muttered before following everyone else into silence. A grin raced across Dennis' face, and I could only imagine what was going on with Trevor. I dared not look at him. "Bria, is it true? Are you married?" Trevor asked, confirming that I'd heard Dennis correctly— that he'd gone ahead and outed me by revealing the one thing I'd secretly thought to conceal from ever being known. I bowed my head and closed my eyes, allowing the silence to engulf me. The questions echoed in my head.

My secret was exposed. The one not even my closest friends knew, but that was the least of my troubles. After all the truths I had uncovered about others, here I was being confronted with just the one I dared not make mention of and give power to flourish. I'd neglected handling things myself, trying to ignore and separate that reality from the one that positively fueled my passions. The energy that being married to this man exhumed brought the worst out of me. And it had me so unbalanced at times that it was hard to find my center.

How would I explain this? How would I explain the man who once held my heart to the one I felt would actually be my perfect fit? Karma, that bitch, like so many, had misjudged me and had allowed the universe to deal with me in its own cynical way. And to think, I thought I could relax and enjoy the unconditional love Trevor had already shown me. Dealing with this would devour my focus until resolved, and I knew it would be hell before Dennis allowed me the peace I felt I was due. Him being difficult was the one thing I could always bet on.

# Author's Notes

**HEY, GUYS, I HOPE YOU GOT JUST AS MUCH OUT OF READING THIS ONE AS I DID WRITING IT!**

For those of you who read my second book, *Chronicles of My Deception: Kayla's Truth*, I'm sure by the end of this you will understand that I'm turning it into a trilogy, with *Bria's Focus Captured* being the second book.

Although it took a while (You can blame that on my writer's block after the hurricane), I actually found this book a bit easier to write.

As you can tell, I take time to point out issues we women seem to overlook, and just in case I was too subtle, I'm stressing on our health and well-being. Nothing is more beneficial to being a woman and those around her than when she knows her worth and stays true to herself. Don't be afraid to stop and find your balance. Take care of yourself. For the male readers, I'm sure there is a woman in your life that you can empower. I'll reiterate hoping the surprise elements were gratifying enough.

At the end of this book, you will find bonus material about the character of Mich. I hope to end the Secrecy trilogy with her story. I've already committed myself to that and have given you a sneak peek of what to expect. I think it's
going to be very intense seeing how dramatic she is. I had fun, guys, and truly hope that you enjoyed the

story and are looking forward to the closing chapter. Thanks again for your support!

—LaToya Lake

*LaToya Lake*

# Being the Other Woman
*** *Without Consent*

Adding agitation to the feeling of being swallowed up by the world, I sat waiting at a congested bar for the rest of my coworkers to find themselves at this little farewell get-together that was to take place here. One of my colleagues was heading back to Suriname to live out her pension years, and so in honor of her years of service, my boss felt the occasion warranted celebrating and had reserved a table for the nurses under her supervision. Normally, I would be fashionably late, but because of him, I couldn't get out of the house fast enough.

I'd left it in a state my mother would not be thrilled about. I just couldn't be bothered tonight to clean up before departing, and I wasn't really up for another clash with my mother about me needing to find my own place because of our differences in opinion when it came to my lifestyle.

I'd wanted to discuss the way he had handled things a couple nights ago and had voiced my displeasure on him not calling to apologize, but things didn't go the way I thought they would. I was still in disbelief, having him basically dismiss me, then insult me by dropping a stack of money on my bed, acting like I was his personal prostitute and the money was to shut me up. This was the final straw that set things off. It was a shame I'd missed his head when I threw the lamp. I was still mad as hell at him and now hoped to drown my troubles in some alcohol.

I needed a drink after all that had happened, and since this would all be on my boss' tab, I figured why not. My coworkers were due for an appearance at any minute, so while I waited, I took claim to a seat at the bar and allowed myself to be mildly amused by a man who'd bought me a martini in exchange for my attention. I didn't feel like entertaining this guy, but I had time on my hands that I didn't want to spend replaying tonight's clash.

I frowned and spun around on the bar stool, then took a sip from my straw, playing with it with my tongue. My gaze skipped through the room, landing on faces of people unknown to me. And as if I'd conjured him up, he strolled in with his woman. My eyes narrowed with hatred for her. I was pissed at him even more so, now seeing his so-called night out with the boys was more of a date night.

He dared walking by me, not acknowledging my presence. My eyes followed them over to their table, and I observed her in a floral-patterned dress while he wore a casual shirt with short cargo pants, acting like he was the owner of the establishment. He didn't even match with his date or the setting.

"Whatever."
I released a completely exaggerated laugh, seemingly surprising the man trying to engage me in a conversation. I was so annoyed at this point and decided against staying any longer.

I got to my feet and—
"Hey, you're actually on time and... not at all overdressed," Julie said while taking me in. Overdressed, maybe not, but I never looked like a

boring housewife either. My eyes went to the corner where lover man sat with Ms. Thing.

I wore red pumps, giving myself the height I usually needed to not be considered short. My legs weren't long, but they were toned as hell. I chose to show off this fact with tight, white shorts that stopped just below my ass cheeks. A loosely fitted, thin-strap top that forced me to exclude wearing a bra was icing on the cake. My perky breasts made women who needed to strap up jealous. Hair brushed into a mohawk with dangling golden earrings and red lipstick brought the look together.

My body was perfect, and until that day came when it started to sag, I would make no apologies for showing it off. "Come, let's take a seat," she said, taking me by the arm and leading me over to our reserved table. The first hour of the night was spent with me trying not to glare as I watched him enjoy himself. He was holding her hand and stroking it, playing with the glittering band on her finger. He obviously couldn't care less about how seeing him with her would make me feel. Why did I get involved with somebody else's man? It's not like I didn't have options. I had to simply get over this asshole and forget about him. "And Michelle, her hairstylist probably got more mouth from her today than we are getting right now, which is new," my boss said.

It was something else how it was seen as acceptable for her to talk to me the way she did, but when I spoke my mind, it was perceived as disrespectful. "Yeah, what's wrong, Michelle? We did say we were going to get back to this discussion. You still don't have an opinion?"

An opinion I had. I'd just rather not voice it but, "What, talking about gay love? No woman has ever touched me inappropriately." I sneered in disgust, making those at the table freeze, totally shocked by my directness. I was annoyed and didn't care to hide it.

"Why you so mad?" Brenda dared asking.

I shrugged and headed back into my own world. That was sure to stop them from inquiring about my sexual preference. If they only knew what a man with a thick dick did for me, they would know how silly they were for even trying to connect my name with that of another woman.

They could judge me for being homophobic, but they would never understand what that dark chocolate, sexy piece of man did to my body. At some point after being with him intimately, I realized I didn't care who I was sharing him with because when he was with me, he was all mine. I just loved how he knocked against my walls and the way he felt between my legs. Oh my, he was a perfect fit! Playing his favorite game of pretending not to know who he was and having made-up names added to his allure. My heart leapt when I looked up and found him staring in my direction from across the room. He had indeed seen me, and I could bet I knew what he was thinking about. I bit into my bottom lip and ran a finger along the rim of my water glass. Crazy how he was here with her, yet I felt him yearning to connect with me.

I wished there were some way of reminding him of what he was going to be missing out on. There would be no more manic sex in his future; I had planned to punish him by denying him what he once begged for. I crossed my legs and started to squeeze, hoping to still the sexual itch building between them.

My mind just wouldn't stop thinking of his hard rod rubbing against the plumpness of my clit, my center ready to give him a hero's welcome back. I had to still my thoughts of him if I was to make it through this night without running home to play with myself. I exhaled and tried to focus in on the surrounding conversation.

"Because I don't want the mess that comes with dating. You think I want to wake up with a mind full of thoughts of a man? No, I got shit I need to get done and bills to pay. I can't have the thought of a man's genitals having me refuse to work or eat," Kristie said. The ladies started to laugh, and I threw myself into it with them. Joel seemed to be fidgeting, uncomfortable in his seat. But I assumed he just needed one more drink before he stood up for the male species. No matter how feminine he was.

"Just read the book *Men Are From Mars, Women Are From Venus,* and you'll understand exactly why I said what I did."

If I understood correctly—and honestly, I was half-assing it—the conversation had wandered into how differently men and women saw relationships. Really, why were we still trying to figure them out? And reading? Why would such knowledge be found in a book? Women today were so silly thinking all that there was to know on the topic would be readily available to us. Who would have given the information? Not a man for sure.

Because that would cause a power shift, and I myself would enslave a few. My lips curved on one side of my face. I then neatly took a mozzarella

299

stick from the tray set in front of us as appetizers. I bit into it, completely disregarding my pledge to stay away from dairy products for a month.

Yep, that would be catastrophic for them.

And all those gurus on the internet advising us on how to get one, claiming to have a sure way of making him ours were hilarious. I'd had stomach cramps from killing myself with laughter while scrolling through my Facebook page, finding it full with inspirational feministic quotes from my friends. Unlike them, I had better things to do with my time, and I was sure not going to be posting about my happiness or sadly lying about it like some I knew. Why waste energy?

In her best Jamaican accent, Kristie said, "He said, 'Baby, you're so beautiful, but I'm after your heart, and if I can't have that, I don't want any part of you.' And all I could think about was who else he had tried that line on. What a dumbass." She sighed, then took a drink while the others weighed in on her revelation.

I shook my head at the table of man-bashers, then diverted my gaze elsewhere. My eyes centered on Mrs. Antoine Cornet.

Just look at her prissy ass. She wasn't capable of fulfilling his fantasies. Not like I was. And her little show of pretending to be the perfect housekeeper and mother to his children, looking the part to the outside world, was fooling everyone but me.

God, she didn't even take care of herself or his basic needs, yet here he was showering her with feigned affection, while in my arms, he was constantly complaining. To know that he was getting his pleasure on the outside would kill her, assuming she didn't already know. Probably why he kept up the charade of being satisfied by her. Such a weakling. The last thing such a man needed in his life was a doormat... or was that what he wanted? What was certain was that he didn't need a lady in bed. He needed someone tempting who would be willing to quench his thirst at night and not have him jack off alone in the shower. Someone who desired his release. His reason for staying, I understood, was his caring heart. He just couldn't up and leave the mother of his children. She would undoubtedly become suicidal after putting so many years into the relationship. Him walking away without batting an eye would crush her, sending her over the edge. She would surely retaliate by discrediting or destroying what he had built by defaming his name. That was sure to be her game plan if she ever found us out.

I took a sip of martini and briefly stared into my glass. The thing was, I wasn't getting what I truly wanted, and that was time with him. I was left seeking company in material things and getting sick of it.

"Please, don't give men excuses for cheating. There is no 'poor them' scenario that will work tonight," my coworker retorted directly at Joel. He had finally said something, and I had missed it. Must have been a good one to get such a response. I smiled behind my hand.

Hmm, the reason why some men cheated, I would have to say, was because of boredom and lack of sex, but I doubted Joel would be so blunt. I happened to know this to be true about my own lover. I knew he didn't desire her just by the many nights he'd called so I could take him to ecstasy simply with words, allowing his thoughts of me to run free.

I couldn't help staring at her ignorant, fat, can't even dirty talk ass. "Like they are masters in bed. The man couldn't find my g- spot even if he had a Google map, had asked Siri, and was using a GPS." That made me choke a bit on my own saliva. "I think sex is so overrated. Relationships should be more than just the physical," Julie interjected, her eyes rolling. "Let me guess, you're not getting any," I said, a bit rude.

"It's not that I don't get it," she stressed with attitude, briefly glaring at me. "It's more of what is returned. You know once I had an ungrateful bastard take the cookie out, lick it, then put it back in the damn jar because he didn't like the taste of it," Julie spat out like there was nothing to admitting that in a group. The Amaretto she was having had clearly gone to her head and had broken something in her shame box.

We all laughed at her analogy properly because it was somewhat relatable. Why did men go after us, pulling out all the stops up until we slept with them, then U-turned it? Ignoring the hell out of us after getting the cookie? Such jackasses! No one was going to play me like that though. Antoine wouldn't dare.

The aroma of liquor filled my senses, making me follow its stream path. I was stunned and almost stumbled onto the lips of a strange man in the process of whispering into my ear. He said something extremely tempting, then like a schoolboy with a crush, passed a note on a napkin with a number on it before leaving me with my mouth agape. The girls cooed while I caught myself and swallowed hard. Completely into the audacious move, I playfully fanned myself with the tissue.

"Why can't I get something like that to happen to me?" Julie said, reaching for the note. I yanked my hand away and tsked at her.

"Like everyone, you have to work for your own," I taunted. Sharing was not one of my strong suits. I smiled and shook my head at her. I guess she wasn't just the coworker that slacked off and expected everyone to carry her load of the work. Crazy that it counted here as well.

My phone, which rested in front of me on the table, started to ring. I saw the number and peered up in search of him, finding him no longer at his table. I purposely hesitated before picking up, shifting my seat back and turning to my side to avoid someone eavesdropping on my conversation.

He had the nerve to be questioning me about the man who had just dropped me his number. I scanned the room again in search of him and found him standing behind a pillar. He was angry about my encounter—plain jealous and scolding me on allowing another man to approach me, as if it was all my fault.

I refused to argue something that was out of my control and hung up. A smile settled on my face thinking how I had set him off by simply doing nothing. My phone rang again, and this time, I didn't answer. I looked up and found his hot glare on me. He was pissed, and I was enjoying it. I reentered the group, feigning interest just for the hell of it. I had gotten under his skin, causing him to

react even though he was with her, and that said a lot.
"Everyone is having sex except me. Like Beatrice from the pediatric ward. She's like ancient, yet just the other day, she was asking me for advice on birth control. Can you believe the nerve, and at her age?" Jasmine said, squinting in disgust while taking another sip of her drink.

Honestly, I was about over the conversation and the evening and decided I would be leaving shortly. All this talk about sex was for some reason getting to me, making me think on why I would never be giving him any again. And it was a shame because I enjoyed it with him. I couldn't wait to have him taste me whenever and wherever because that was crazy hot to me. And how he demanded easy access and I was simply his to command, my god, such a turn on. But that was over now.

I wiped at my face, completely agitated. May his balls be forever blue with her. "Ha," was the sound that drew all eyes at the table to me. "Are you okay? What's that under your eye?" Marita asked. Quite sure of what she was referring to, I didn't bother to answer. I decided now was a good time to hit the restroom before saying my goodbyes. "Ladies, a little unsolicited off-topic advice. A man unwilling to throw a vibrator into his repertoire is just plain selfish," I said, quite sure I was leaving them with something to talk about.

With my bag in hand, I strutted past where he was sitting, allowing him a peek of my flawless, creamy skin down to the small of my back. I was sure his eyes fell to my buttocks as well. The door creaked as I entered the women's restroom, my nose being knocked with a heavy odor. *Someone*

304

*clearly dumped their meal in here*, I thought and continued straight to the mirror. I rested my bag on the basin counter and took a moment to view myself. I saw that I indeed had something up with my face. Actually, I'd overlooked a spot. I pulled out my foundation and started to dab at the darkened bruise. *He has such a bad temper, and I really shouldn't have provoked him*, I thought, remembering how he'd smacked me because of me egging him on.

It was silly that I'd made him react that way. That I'd caused him to become extremely upset and violent again. I should have known better. He was into rough sex, but this didn't lead to that.

Finished, I headed into a stall to relieve my bladder, taking a moment longer to think.

I should've been a bit more observant because if Bria or Kayla would've seen that, I wouldn't have heard the end of it. These last few months were already crazy with them. I didn't want to fall into the cycle. *Our group is surely cursed*, I thought while flushing and laughing to myself.

My smile was replaced by surprise on exit, finding Antoine waiting for me. He was boiling.
Without a word, I headed over to the faucet to wash my hands. "So, you're gonna pretend you didn't hang up on me?"

"Look, I ain't going into this here. Set a date like you normally do, and I'll see if I can make it. I'm done with this," I said, pulling the paper towel out of the dispenser, grabbing my bag, and attempting to make my dramatic exit.

Without warning, his hand was at my

305

throat. I tried with no avail to hide my fright. He then took me into his clutches, spun me around, and locked my hands at my back. Through the mirror mounted on the wall, I watched the man fighting with rage while still holding my neck. He applied a bit of pressure, and for the first time, I thought of how he could break me if he wanted to. He harshly jerked my head to the side,
holding me by the jaw. I moaned in pain when he dove into my neck, sucking hard at it.

"You fucking pig, let me go!" My voice trembled. "Pig? I thought this was what you liked."

A hand quickly undid my pants and roughly found itself within my panties and between my vaginal walls. "What are you doing?" My words were being obstructed by fear and the fact that he was now squeezing my throat.

"You like playing with me," he said, his breath hot against my neck, his teeth grazing the flesh. My eyes closed. He had clearly had too much to drink and was acting out his frustration with me while under the influence. I started to struggle against him, hoping to free myself from his grip. He released my hands but that was only for the time it took him to undo his pants. With a jingle, they dropped to the floor. He then went for mine. I tried denying him by releasing my weight a few times, but he succeeded in getting my shorts down my thighs. He then pressed me against the marbled surface.

"No!" I cried out a few times, praying someone would hear me. I reached back in search of his eyes, hoping that pain would cause him to release me. That only aggravated him further.

"Behave your fucking self!" he snarled into

my ear, then forced me to bend forward, pressing my temple onto the marble with a palm. My hands sprawled across the surface, bracing me for what was to come. I felt his forced entry and screeched in pain, the tears building with the sting of what was happening.

He was ramming viciously against me, thrusting like a maniac. All I could do was tense. Him partially cutting the oxygen to my brain incited a headache. My hands were now trying to stop me from being constantly banged against the wall. In horror, I took his repeated and unapologetic thrusts into me. His grunts of pleasure mixed with my whimpers. If I would only pass out and not be conscious during this ordeal. I just wanted to leave my body behind because I knew this would haunt me forever, and I wasn't sure I was strong enough to survive the aftermath of it all.

I would need to somehow fool myself that this hadn't truly taken place if I wanted to be normal again. I would need to forget, and that would take me lying like I never had before in order to convince myself. His final few thrusts came sporadically as he released into me. My breathing shallow and jerking, I laid there waiting for him to finish and retract.

"Aww," he moaned, repulsing me.

He shoved at me, then hunched over. "Don't fuck with me, and make sure nothing comes out of there," he commanded, referring to the possibility of an unwanted pregnancy. He rezipped his pants, straightened his shirt, and then exited the women's powder room. Trembling out of control, I fought for composure. I was disgusted and so angry, more at myself for being such a coward and not fighting hard enough, even at his weakest point.

Completely sore and wanting nothing else but to run out of this place, I went through my knees and brought my shorts up. I took the comb from my bag and dared to look at myself in the mirror. My mascara mixed with my tears, creating a huge black spot on my face. Uncontrollably, I started sniffling while scooping the water running from the faucet and using a bit of hand soap to wash the mess from my face. Doing so had fully revealed the blemish I had previously tried to conceal.

"Oh, my god," I sniveled, my hand over my mouth. This was pure insanity. The stall door directly behind me swung open, startling me. An older lady stepped out.

We stood there staring at each other. I felt angry again knowing that someone was in here and didn't make so much as a peep, which could've scared my assailant off. I grabbed my bag and broke for the door. I didn't bother with goodbyes and found myself outside flagging down a bus.

I was relieved getting home and finding my mother sound asleep. I headed for the toilet to relieve the pressure in my bladder. I tensed as the burn of his forced entry found it necessary to remind me of what I'd gone through.

I stepped into the bathroom, hoping that the water falling from the showerhead would cleanse my body and wash my mind. I could just drown now, and that would take care of everything. I'm not sure how long I was in there for, but I had somehow mustered the strength and was now sweeping up the mess I had left behind. Among the things resting in pieces in the garbage, I would need to replace the lamp I had thrown at Antoine's head, which had missed him by a mile. I stood gazing into the garbage bin, staring at all I had swept up and dumped into it. My dignity was surely to be found amidst the contents.

I felt hate building along with another urge to use the bathroom and suffer through yet another burning episode. Someday, that smug bastard would get what he deserved, then he would experience what it's like to be taken against his will. I wrapped my arms around myself as a single tear streamed down my face.

# ABOUT THE AUTHOR

LATOYA LAKE WAS BORN ON THE ISLAND OF ST. MAARTEN AND HAS LIVED IN THE NETHERLANDS FOR A CHAPTER OF HER LIFE. A PHARMACIST ASSISTANT BY PROFESSION, SHE ENJOYS SINGING AND THE FREEDOM OF CREATIVE WRITING, AND SHE ALSO FINDS TIME TO FEED HER MOST RECENT CREATIVE OUTLET. SHE HOPES TO DEVELOP AND BROADEN HER KNOWLEDGE IN THIS FIELD AND WOULD LOVE THE OPPORTUNITY TO DEPICT HER IMAGINATIVE THINKING ONSCREEN.

This is her third book; the first one being *It's Like Déjà Vu With You* and the second being the first in her Secrecy trilogy: *Chronicles of My Deception: Kayla's Truth*. She hopes to conclude the trilogy in the near future.

Lake shares her heart with the love of her life and her daughter, who inspires her to challenge herself by trying new things.

Feel free to send questions or follow her on **www.facebook.com/ArtofLarae** or **email her at Laraebooks@gmail.com.**

310

www.ingramcontent.com/pod-product-compliance
Lightning Source LLC
Chambersburg PA
CBHW051331020726
47501CB00007B/2035